STEELE FACTOR

AN AMANDA STEELE MYSTERY

E M RICHMOND

Leanne Warr (t/a EMR Books)
Palmerston North
New Zealand

First edition. Published by Leanne Warr. 2020
www.elldubak.wixsite.com/leannewarrwriter

ISBN: 978-0-473-51419-8

Steele Factor

AMANDA STEELE IS BACK IN A NEW MYSTERY.

"Unlike <u>some</u> people, I can actually sing. I mean, what exactly did you call that rendition of Hotel California? Sounded more like my neighbour's tomcat trying to serenade the ladies. Which is all good, by the way, if you're a cat in heat."

Amanda Steele and Jim Andersen have a mutual antagonism going on but even he is stunned to learn his sometime 'frienemy's' talent in singing has resulted in her being asked to go undercover once again, this time as a contestant in a national, televised talent show.

The producers of the show are desperate to learn who is behind a number of accidents before the show has even begun and turn to Amanda's bosses for help.

Just as Amanda gets through her audition, there is another incident and they presume it's just another accident. Until the victim ends up dead.

This time, it's murder.

Amanda now must work with Jim to identify the culprit while at the same time dealing with difficulties in her personal life.

This is the second in the Amanda Steele: Private Investigator series.

Chapter One

The days had begun to shorten, and the weather had turned colder. Amanda Steele was not one to complain about the cold but for her, late Autumn was always the worst time of year. Not quite winter, it could go from cold one day to too warm the next. On top of that, it was never quite settled so it could be raining in the morning and by the afternoon it would look as if there had never been any rain at all. Or it was the other extreme where it would rain heavily, causing the streets to flood.

Catching the train and walking to work was always a risky proposition on those days. Amanda never knew what to put on in the morning. If she wore a coat on the way to work, she likely wouldn't need it on her way home.

Today was one of those days. It had been pouring with rain when she'd got up and she'd chosen to wear a heavy coat but by the time the train had got to the central station she was too warm.

She sighed as she unlocked the main door to the office of Moody and Knight Private Investigators before stripping off her coat. Her boss – one of them at least – was already in as the heating had been switched on and his coat was on the rack. As she walked past the open door to Bob Moody's office, on her way to make the coffee, she called out a "Good morning." She didn't hear a reply and didn't expect one from the usually dour senior partner of the small investigations firm.

Moody had been almost grudging in his congratulations when she had given him her complete report on the outcome of the case at Fraley High two months earlier. He'd also made it clear that despite her success, her job as their Girl Friday wasn't likely to change. She could live with that, she supposed but was hoping her boss would eventually let her tackle another case.

She knew she had more or less gotten in over her head with the case, coming very close to becoming one of the group's victims herself. However, Amanda had found herself with a surprising ally.

Jim Andersen was a detective and worked in the West Side police CIB unit with her father. He had met with Bob Moody and told him exactly what had gone down and Amanda's own part in uncovering the truth.

While she was grateful to the detective for setting her boss straight on a few things, that didn't mean they were best friends. He still annoyed her and from the things he'd told her in the past few weeks, she annoyed him just as much.

So, it was a surprise when he turned up at the office late that afternoon with a gift in hand.

"Your dad told me it was your birthday," he said, handing her the wrapped present.

"Uh, thanks," she said, a little taken aback by the gesture.

He stood there as if waiting for something. Amanda looked over the gift. It had been beautifully wrapped in plain teal blue paper. A white ribbon had been tied around it. The bow wasn't quite as neatly done as the rest of the gift, which suggested Jim had done it himself.

"My stepmother always used to tell me when you're giving a gift to a girl, make an effort with the wrapping," Jim told her with a grin.

"Oh. She taught you well."

"Lesleigh would like you, I think. You'd have a lot in common."

"You mean charming and gorgeous?" she asked, batting her eyelashes at him, unable to resist flirting with him.

"No. A pain in my arse," he retorted. "I mean, let's face it. When they were handing out charm, you had to get a rain check."

She was almost taken aback by the veiled insult. They hadn't known each other long but from the very beginning, it had been a game of one-upmanship. Or who could come up with the best insult. He'd obviously been thinking about it.

"Been holding on to that one for a while, haven't you?" she said.

"Maybe," he replied with a smirk.

She decided to unwrap the gift and found a small velvet box. When she opened the lid, she saw to her surprise and delight that it was a gold-plated charm bracelet. A small charm with her initials had been added to it. She held it up to examine it in the light. It was pretty.

"Thank you," she said. "I love it."

"You seem surprised," he observed.

"Well, I … I mean, it's just really thoughtful. And it's beautiful. I mean it. Thank you."

She stood up and moved around the desk to kiss him on the cheek. He looked just as surprised at the gesture. Amanda felt her face becoming warm and looked away coyly. She went back to her chair.

Jim sat on the desk. "So, what do you have planned for your birthday?" he asked.

"Oh, Matt and I are meeting friends for dinner at a karaoke bar," she told him.

He looked at her, raising his eyebrows. "Matt? As in Matt Donaldson?"

Donaldson had been the principal at Fraley High. After the case had been solved, he had asked her out and she'd been seeing him on and off for about a month. The man was quite a few years older than her, being closer to her father's age than her own, but she had never really cared about the age difference. They had a good time together and that was what was important.

"Do you know any other Matts?" she said with a shrug.

Jim frowned. "He's a little, uh, old for you, isn't he?"

Gee, that was tactful, she thought.

"Thirty-eight isn't old!" she said in protest, wondering why she felt the need to justify her social life to someone who was barely even a friend.

"You're only twenty. That's eighteen years."

"Yeah, thanks. I can do the maths, you know."

Before Jim could respond, her phone rang. She

picked up the call, glad for the interruption. It was almost time for her to pack up for the day and she didn't want to spend the next few minutes arguing.

"Hi," a deep voice said when she answered. It was Matt. "What time do you want me to pick you up?"

She glanced at her watch. It was an antique gold-plated one with a small face. A birthday gift from her father. He had told her it had been her mother's.

"About half an hour," she said, glancing up at Jim. He was trying to pretend he wasn't listening in to the conversation. She shot him a sly look. "I have to take care of a little pest problem first."

Matt sounded a little puzzled at the reference when he replied, but Jim got it straight away, looking as if he was about to have a fit of some kind. She ended the call, suppressing a giggle at the detective's expression.

"Pest problem?" he exploded, huffing. "I suppose you've been holding on to that one for a while."

She laughed in his face. "Nope! Just thought of it actually," she said. Really, the man needed to be quicker than that.

He stared at her, the disbelief obvious on his face. She giggled harder. "What can I say? Can't help it if you're a little slow on the uptake."

She could bet that he was very tempted to either throttle her or spank her. She loved the fact that she had managed to get the better of him once again.

Then again, he had been nice enough to get her a birthday gift, which he didn't have to do. She knew what her father would say. "Be nice, Amanda."

She raised her hands. "Okay, okay, that was a little mean. I'm sorry."

He glared at her. "You just wait, missy. I'll think of a decent comeback. Then you will be really sorry."

She couldn't help herself. "Well, I won't hold my breath waiting," she replied.

"You always have to have the last word, don't you?" he retorted almost through clenched teeth.

"Yes," she said simply before shrugging. "What can I say? I just love winding you up."

He grumbled and turned to walk out of the office. "See if I go out of my way to be nice to you again," he muttered as he left.

"You wish!" she returned, unable to resist the final shot. She heard him give what sounded like a strangled scream.

Less than a minute later her boss, or one of them, came in, handing her some documents. Jerry Knight smiled at her.

"Was that detective Andersen I saw just leaving?" he asked.

She nodded. "Yeah. He came to give me a birthday present."

The older man's eyes widened. "Oh, crap! That was today?"

She giggled at his words. The word 'crap' sounded odd coming from him. Jerry was an ex-cop, like his partner, but a little more soft-spoken and a lot more easy-going.

Unlike Moody, her other boss had been happy with the way she had resolved the case at the high school. He'd begun to encourage her to consider enrolling in a course in private investigations, despite knowing that most investigators tended to be former police officers. He knew of her unsuccessful attempt to join the police herself and was more than willing to help her gain a little more experience in the field.

"Well, anyway, happy birthday. What are your plans?"

"I'm going out tonight with a friend," she said, unwilling to categorise Matt as a boyfriend. They'd been going out only a few weeks and had never really gone any further than a light peck on the cheek. Matt was nice, but she wasn't sure if there was any future in their relationship.

"Oh, that's good."

"If you're not doing anything, maybe you'd like to drop by. It's at Danny's Bar and Grill."

Jerry frowned. "Isn't that a karaoke bar? Hmm, thank you for the offer, Amanda, but I'm afraid I have to decline. I'm not much of a singer."

"I think the same could be said about eighty per cent of the people who go to those bars," she returned with a smile. "It's all good fun. No worries, I understand."

She glanced at her watch. "I should go change my clothes. My friend is picking me up in about twenty minutes."

"Well, I won't keep you then. Enjoy yourself tonight, but don't drink too much."

She snickered and held up her hands in mock surrender. She had had to mention in her report the night she had got drunk but only for the reason that the man who had helped her get that way had been one of those responsible for the problems at the school.

"Don't worry. I learnt my lesson."

After he left, she went to the bathroom to change into a pair of black jeans and a light-coloured top. She chose to put on a little more make-up, enhancing her eyes with eyeliner and a bit of eyeshadow.

She didn't often wear much make-up at work but did wear more when she went out. Her suede jacket completed the outfit. Part of the fringe on the sleeve of the jacket had been torn off in a struggle and she'd never got around to repairing it. There was also a stain on the front which she assumed was alcohol from when she'd got completely trashed. The stain had set, and the dry cleaner hadn't been able to get it out. Still, it was her favourite jacket and she wasn't going to throw it out because of some stain.

Matt arrived on time and handed her an envelope. She opened it to find a birthday card and a gift card from the local department store. It was one that she rarely shopped in, but she decided he had no way of knowing that.

"Hope that's okay," he said. "I wasn't sure what you'd like."

She chose not to comment. They'd been dating for a while and he still didn't know her tastes, yet Jim, who she barely tolerated at times, had bought her a lovely charm bracelet.

As he led her out to his car, he paused. "Are you sure you want to go to Danny's?" he asked. "I thought you would have preferred a nice dinner in a nice restaurant."

She shook her head. "This is what I want. To spend time with friends and have some fun. Besides, the food's not that bad at Danny's."

The bar and grill served simple fare, but she liked it that way. Some of her friends didn't like to eat fancy food and she wanted them to have a good time. Just because it was her birthday, it didn't mean she should be the only one having fun.

Matt was quiet as he drove to the bar. It was on the corner of a main thoroughfare in the central city and a reasonably busy area for both road traffic and pedestrian traffic. It took a little while for him to find a car park and he grew increasingly frustrated as he drove up and down the side streets until he found one. As he manoeuvred the car next to the kerb, he briefly held up the traffic and drivers in the cars behind him beeped their horns impatiently.

"Keep your shirt on," Amanda muttered. She grabbed her bag and pulled out her compact, quickly re-checking her hair and make-up. She normally wore her blonde hair either clipped back or in a messy bun at work but had chosen to wear it down for the evening.

"You look great," Matt told her. She smiled at him and nodded, reaching for the door handle. He put a hand on her arm. "Listen, I, uh, I wanted to talk to you."

"Can it wait?" she asked. "They'll be expecting us."

He frowned at her. "I don't get you, sometimes," he said.

"What do you mean?"

"There are times when you can be so closed-off. I mean, I get it. I've known your dad a long time and I know he's been fairly protective of you."

"Where are you going with this?" she asked. For a grown and seemingly confident man, he appeared a little unsure of himself.

"I don't think we should see each other anymore."

"Why?" she asked.

"Well, the fact that I'm much older than you."

"I never really cared about that. And if you're

worried about what my dad thinks, he doesn't mind."

"I mind. Besides, there are some things I would like that I just don't think you're ready for."

"You mean sex," she said bluntly.

He coughed. "You are direct, aren't you?"

"Sorry," she replied with a shrug. "Look, Matt, I like you. And, well, I wish I could say that I'm disappointed, but I think we both knew where this was going to end up. I'm only twenty and … you know what? You're right. I'm not ready for that kind of relationship." She shrugged again. "Maybe someday, sure. With the right guy."

"That isn't me," he said, sounding put-out.

"Now who's being direct," she returned. "Matt, please don't end this on a sour note. I mean, I think we could have built a really good friendship. We still can. In the meantime, I would like to have a fun night with my friends." She shot him a look to say that he was included in that group.

Amanda didn't have a lot of close friends. She had always believed that friends were the kind of people who would be there for her in a heartbeat if she should ever need them. Of the many people she knew, she could count those types of friends on one hand.

Tonight wasn't just about that small circle of friends. While she hadn't wanted to invite her flatmate, Penny Cameron, she had known that the older woman would have found out about it anyway. Penny was the type of girl who thought she was God's gift to any man and woe betide any other girl who tried to come between her and the man she was interested in.

Amanda had been disgusted when Penny had turned the charm on Jim Andersen the night the detective had come to the house to talk to her about the case. Her father had asked his colleague to liaise with her on the investigation and make sure she didn't get herself into trouble. Not that that stopped her, she thought with a grin as she walked with Matt up the hill to the bar.

When Jim and Penny had first met, Amanda had thought he was like every other guy around her flatmate. He'd flirted with the pretty brunette briefly, giving her compliments, but after a while, Amanda got the impression that his compliments had been worded in such a way to discourage the woman from staying while they discussed the case.

He'd visited the house a couple of times in the past two months, giving her an update on further arrests they'd made, and each time had shown no interest in Penny whatsoever. That hadn't stopped her flatmate from trying. Jim was a good-looking man, Amanda thought begrudgingly. It just galled that the other woman thought she had the
right to flirt with him right in front of her.

Speak of the devil, she groaned quietly to herself as she walked in the door. There he was, talking to her father, a glass of beer in hand. He was easy to spot in the crowd with his short, dark locks and tall, athletic frame.

Matt walked away to get them drinks while Amanda went to greet her father.

"Happy birthday, sweetheart," he said, giving her a hug and a kiss on the cheek. He'd already phoned her that morning to wish her a happy birthday and given her her present the night before.

"Thanks, Daddy." She turned her head and glowered at Jim. "What are you doing here?"

"I invited him," her father told her. "Be nice."

She dearly wanted to blow a raspberry but decided that was far too immature. As Matt handed her a drink – an orange flavoured vodka cruiser – a woman about a year or two older than her approached Jim. She had pretty, elfin features which suited her short dark hair and wore steel-rimmed glasses which nicely framed her face. She was a little shorter than Amanda, with a petite figure, contrasting with Amanda's own athletic one.

"Oh, Amanda, this is Gaby. Gabrielle Rutledge, this is Amanda Steele."

Gaby smiled. "I don't think we've met before, but I've heard all about you. I work at the West Side station with the I.T. Department."

"Otherwise known as the Geek Squad," Jim amended with a grin. Gaby shot him a look that Amanda took to be saying she was offended by the nickname, then laughed. It seemed to be an old joke between them.

As Amanda looked around, she saw Penny in the far corner, glaring daggers at Gabrielle. She rolled her eyes, then excused herself to talk to her flatmate.

"Grow up!" she hissed.

"Who is she?" Penny asked, sounding almost accusing.

"She works at the police station," Amanda told her. "And you have absolutely no reason to be jealous. You know Jim's not interested in you."

"Hmph," the brunette muttered snippily before turning away. Amanda watched her sidle up to a man who was obviously the flavour of the month from the way Penny had draped herself all over him. He had gingery-blond hair and pale, freckled skin. He was nowhere near as good-looking as Jim, who had wavy brown hair and amazing blue eyes that appeared to bore into whoever he was talking to. And I did not just think that, she thought.

Her father touched her shoulder. "Going to open your presents?" he asked, nodding to a table near the bar.

"Mm, maybe later," she said, sipping her drink.

Pete Steele frowned as he looked over at the man who had brought her.

"Matt seems a little quiet. Everything okay with you two?"

She bit her lip. "Uh, we sort of broke up."

Her father sighed. "I did wonder. Is it the age thing? Because you know I wasn't worried about that."

"No. Well, maybe. I think he just wanted more than I was ready to give." She sighed. "Dad, how will I know when I've found the right guy?"

He squeezed her arm gently. "Honey, if I knew the answer to that question, I could make squillions off the internet selling the secret."

"Ha ha, no really."

He looked at her. "Well, let me ask you this. How do you know Matt's not 'the one'?"

She shrugged. If she was honest with herself, she wasn't that broken up over ending things with the school principal. It was just the way it had happened that bothered her. Did she really come across as closed-off and distant?

"I guess I just knew. I mean, you know how I told you that stuff about me and that guy." He nodded. "I didn't want that with Matt either," she said.

She'd long ago decided that she wasn't going to be like some of her friends who had already slept with a lot of guys. It wasn't that she thought it was wrong. They had the right to do whatever they wanted, within reason. Sex was something that, in her eyes, was an act of intimacy and to her, it didn't feel right to share something that intimate with someone she might not see again.

"I don't know," she said with a sigh. "I just wish I could see into the future or something."

"Sometimes you just have to open your eyes. Either that or it's just timing."

"Or maybe I just have to kiss a lot of frogs before I figure out what I want," she suggested.

He wrinkled his nose. "Like I need that picture."

"Figuratively speaking, Dad. I mean, how many girls did you go out with before Mum?"

"Ooh, don't even go there, kiddo! Even when I did meet your mum, I didn't know straight away."

"Yeah, I remember you telling me." She sighed again, telling him she worried that when the right guy came along she would miss him. Her father had an aunt who had spent her life alone because she had missed opportunities to meet someone and fall in love. Amanda had always felt sorry for her great aunt, who had seemed so sad and lonely.

"Sweetheart, you're only twenty. We're not living in the Dark Ages where girls as young as twelve are married off to the first guy that accepts them. You do have time."

She snorted. "Yeah, thanks, Dad," she said with not a little bit of sarcasm.

She decided to circulate for a little bit, greeting all

of those who had come to the party. It was another half hour before they could order the food and almost an hour after that when the deejay announced the start of festivities.

He stood on a raised platform, microphone in hand. The bar staff had distributed a list of the songs available on the karaoke machine and each person who had decided to participate was allowed to choose their songs.

"Okay, so let's kick things off," he said. "Where's the birthday girl?"

Amanda grinned and stood up as the man handed the microphone over to her. She had known she would be first on the list and had chosen a song that would fit. It was clear from the enthusiasm of everyone else in the room as the music began that they loved her choice. A song by one of her favourite artists, titled: *Get This Party Started*. While it wasn't really a song that suited her range, it was still a good way to get things going and had a great beat that had everyone tapping their feet.

When her turn ended, Amanda's best friend Kerry Marshall got up. The redhead wasn't bad, per se, but she wasn't great either. When her friend finished her song, a man Amanda vaguely knew through her father's work got up. As soon as he opened his mouth, Amanda knew it was going to be horrible. He had no idea how to sing in tune and it sounded worse than a former neighbour's dog which had howled at all hours.

Jim got up after some others had their turns, obviously having been pushed into it by his date. Gaby exchanged a look with Amanda and shot her what could only be an evil grin. Amanda laughed at the other woman's brass. She might have terrible taste in dates, but she certainly knew how to have fun with them.

Right from the get-go, Amanda could tell Jim had absolutely no talent at all in music. If she had thought the man who had sung after Kerry had been bad, Jim was worse. She smirked to herself, thinking of the fun she would have teasing him about it later.

Chapter Two

Jim had taken up his boss' invitation if only to get back at Amanda for her earlier teasing. Of course, he would have vehemently denied it if someone had asked. The truth was, he got as much of a kick out of annoying her as much as she did with him.

He still remembered the first time she'd insulted him. Pete had asked him to help with the case if only to keep his daughter out of trouble. Amanda had not been happy at the thought of working with him, calling him a troglodyte.

Jim could take a lot of insults. After all, he'd been a cop for a few years now and he was used to some pretty strong words from those he'd arrested. Being called a troglodyte, especially from a slip of a girl who was clearly spoiled, had taken the cake.

Pete would have said it was because he liked her. When Amanda wasn't acting like a spoiled brat, or arrogant, she was actually a highly intelligent young woman. He would never admit it, but he did find her attractive. Not that he was interested in dating her, he told himself.

He couldn't help but notice that Matt Donaldson, the man who had contracted the private investigators to check out the school, didn't look happy as they sat down to dinner. He watched as Amanda exchanged a look with the older man and said something he couldn't hear. Matt shrugged but sat down at the same table.

Jim escorted his date to their own table, seating himself next to his boss. He wanted to ask Pete what was going on with Amanda's date but decided it wasn't his place to do so.

He could see why Amanda had chosen to celebrate her birthday at
this bar. Karaoke was a good way to get everyone participating and they could all share a few laughs. Amanda, being the birthday girl, was first and she did sing a pretty good version of the song which kicked things off. He might not be able to sing well himself, but he knew a good voice when he heard it.

There were a few others who got up to sing after Amanda, including a trio of two girls and a guy, but they couldn't sing in tune to save themselves.

Gaby nudged him and handed him the list of songs. He shook his head, not really interested in participating but happened to glance Amanda's way. She shot him a knowing smirk. He could tell from the look on her face she was calling him a chicken. He might be a lot of things, he thought, but he was no chicken. Gaby continued to prod him, and he gave in, choosing a song for himself.

He got up when it was his turn and began to sing the introductory bars to a famous song by the Eagles, one of his all-time favourites. His inner voice groaned at how bad it was and he was relieved when there were no more lyrics. He handed the microphone back to the deejay as the last part of the song began playing. A glance at Amanda's table told him she was going to be teasing him endlessly about his lack of singing prowess.

Gaby laughed at him when he returned to their table. "Well, I'll give you points for even attempting it, but seriously, the Eagles? No one and I mean no one should try to sing their stuff without at least some skill."

He shrugged. "I didn't think it was that complicated."

She snorted. "Yeah, don't give up your day job, mate!" she replied.

He wrinkled his nose at her. "Rightbackatcha."

"Well, who says I'm going to get up there," she said with a chuckle. He stared at her.

"So why did you make me get up there?"

"Because I'm evil," she told him. He rolled his eyes. "So I could make fun of you at work tomorrow. Why else?"

"Gee thanks."

"Serves you right for saying I work for the Geek Squad."

"Well, that's what everybody calls it. Even your own department boss," he said, watching as Amanda got up to take her turn again. She launched into her own version of a popular song. She sang it so well that everyone watching appeared entranced.

Jim was taken aback by her singing. The first song she'd done didn't even measure up to the skill it took to not only stay in tune but to take an already well-established song and sing it another way. Especially that well. Amanda sang as if she had been born to it.

He realised she must have had some training as she was better than anyone else in the bar by a long shot. If she had ever decided to give up her dreams of joining the police, he thought, she would have a great future as a singer.

He glanced around the room and saw that most of the people there were just as surprised. A few knew about her talent, judging from the smiles on their faces.

As the song finished, the room was dead silent for a few moments before they broke out into wild applause. Some people got up from their seats to talk to her even as the deejay called for the next person to come up. Not even sure why, he got up and stopped her before she could get back to her seat. She was blushing prettily, clearly not used to all the compliments.

"That was amazing," he told her honestly. "Really. You have a beautiful voice."

He was vaguely aware of his boss watching but didn't pay much attention. Amanda stared at him, clearly taken aback by his compliment. He couldn't resist the snappy comeback. Every time they traded insults, she had to have the last word.

"Lost for words?" he quipped. "That's gotta be a first!"

She scowled, obviously not liking being mocked.

"Well, unlike <u>some</u> people, I can actually sing. I mean, what exactly did you call that rendition of Hotel California? Sounded more like my neighbour's tomcat trying to serenade the ladies."

He blinked, not quite sure how to take that. Was that supposed to be an insult of some kind?

She smirked. "Which is all good, by the way," she

continued. "If you're a cat in heat."

He huffed, the sound coming out more like a growl. "Why, you little …"

She walked off, still smirking. He felt a sharp smack on the back of his head and looked around. Pete had smacked him. He rubbed his head and shot his boss a wounded look.

"Should have quit while you were ahead," Amanda's father said with a grin.

He returned to his table to find his date staring at him. "So, it's like that, is it?"

He frowned at her. "What are you talking about?"

"You and Amanda."

He stared at her, confused. "Me and Amanda what?"

"You have feelings for her."

He snorted. "Please, I can barely stand the gir … woman. I only met her two months ago and she's been a pain in my arse ever since."

"Yeah, right," she said with an answering snort of her own. "That's why you went up to compliment her on her voice and then snarked at her."

"Then you're reading it wrong. So, I paid the kid a compliment. I was being honest, that's all."

"Uh-huh."

"Hey, come on. We've been going out a few weeks now. Don't I pay you compliments?"

She sighed and bit her lip. "Okay, fine. Deny it all you want but I saw a little spark between you two."

"There's no spark," he insisted. "Not even an ember."

Gaby smirked. "As the man said: 'methinks thou doth protest too much'."

He shot her a glare, then ignored her, listening as

more guests decided to get up and have a go at the karaoke. None of them even measured up to Amanda's skill. He overheard someone talking to the young blonde.

"You should really give it a try. I mean, with that kind of prize money, it's worth a shot."

Amanda was frowning at the speaker, a man around her age. He had clearly had a bad case of acne in his teens as his face showed some scarring.

Jim strained to hear the conversation amid the noise from the bar.

"I don't know. You know, I don't think those talent shows are all that good."

"Yeah, last year I went to this show and they had this guy on who was nowhere near as good a singer as you. I mean, I'm no Elvis …" She snorted at that last bit. "But I know real talent when I hear it. Plus, you're way better looking than some of the girls that try out for these things."

She snorted again. "Is it a talent contest or a beauty contest?"

"Okay, fine. But you can't tell me that they base the win just on talent. Looks do come into it."

"Oh, really?" she asked, cocking an eyebrow sceptically.

He nodded. "My last year at high school, we decided to do a talent show. The girl who should have won – she was really talented, but she wasn't going to win any beauty contest." Jim continued to listen as the man explained that the audience had to vote for their choice.

Amanda shrugged. She glanced in Jim's direction and frowned. He realised she'd caught him listening in. He shrugged in reply and looked away, turning to talk to Gaby, pretending he didn't care what the pair had been talking about, but he was intrigued all the same.

At the end of the night, he saw Matt Donaldson talking to Amanda. He didn't look happy. Neither did Amanda.

"Wait!" she said, catching the other man's arm but he shook his head and moved away. Jim watched as he walked out the door.

"Great," Amanda said, sighing. He sidled up to her.

"Everything okay?"

"No," she replied, shaking her head. "Matt was my ride here, but he's got the pip. We broke up if you must know."

"I'm sorry," he said, refraining from giving her the 'I told you so' speech. She didn't appear to be too cut-up about it, but she clearly didn't need a lecture.

She shrugged. "It's not like we were, you know, engaged or anything. Anyway, I guess I'm gonna have to get a taxi. Dad left an hour ago and Penny's gone home with Mr Flavour-of-the-month." She scowled. "You know, I deliberately didn't drive because I wanted to have a few drinks. I mean, okay, it's not like I've been chugging down the wine or anything, but …"

"You wanted to be sensible about it," he said, admiring her for using her common sense. Unlike some, he thought.

When he'd just started out in the police he'd had to deal with a lot of drunken drivers. The first accident he'd ever attended had been caused by a guy who had insisted he'd only had a few drinks and had been perfectly fine to drive. He'd killed a mother and a young child. Jim had never really got over that.

He still remembered combing the city looking for Amanda the night she had got drunk. She had been upset over something that had happened in the case and he'd gone after her, only to find her almost falling-down drunk. She had clearly learnt her lesson from that night.

"Look, why don't we give you a ride home?" he suggested kindly, but she looked reluctant.

"I don't want you to go out of your way," she said.

He shook his head. "It's okay. Gaby lives near your place anyway. I'll drop you off and then take her home."

She looked at him. There was no hint of teasing in her eyes. She was tired and possibly a little tipsy, but she was clearly grateful for the offer.

"Thank you."

Gaby nodded knowingly when he told her what he was going to do. His girlfriend appeared to have taken a liking to Amanda as they had talked a few times during the evening. She told him she understood. It was nearly midnight on a Friday night in the central city and taxis were always busy.

Amanda grabbed her things. She'd been given a few birthday gifts and had unwrapped them all. Most of them had been either gift cards or little gifts that could fit in one bag, so she didn't need any help with them. The bar staff had already got rid of the wrapping.

She was quiet in the back of the car as Jim drove to the house she shared with Penny. He wondered if there was something on her mind, but chose not to ask her about it. For all her protestations that she was fine after breaking up with Matt, he expected her to feel a little depressed about it. He still chose not to comment even though he'd thought the man was completely wrong for her. Amanda was a vibrant young woman. Matt was practically her complete opposite and they had very little in common. The one thing they did have was the case that had brought them together.

He left the car idling in the driveway as Amanda got out. She paused at his door.

"Thanks for the ride," she said quietly.

"Sure you're okay?" he asked.

"I'm fine. Birthdays just make me a little … contemplative, I guess."

He understood that, since he often felt the same way, but wondered if there was more to it than that. While they still bickered more often than not, she had been quieter since solving the drug case. The fact that a simple investigation had turned into a homicide had probably had a lot to do with it. She had gained a certain maturity in the past two months. No longer the naïve girl who saw the world through rose-coloured glasses.

"We had fun tonight," Gaby told her with a smile. "I've got plenty of ammunition against Jim now."

Amanda grinned back. "Good. Gotta keep that head from swelling. The man's ego's big enough already."

"Hey!" he said. "I'm right here!"

She laughed. "Yeah, I know. Why do you think I do it?"

He growled and narrowed his eyes at her. "You're trouble, Amanda Steele."

She snorted. "And you're just figuring this out

now? Where have you been?"

He waited until the lights went on inside the house before turning the car around and driving off.

"She was awfully quiet for a while there," Gaby observed. "I'm guessing that's a little unusual for her."

"Yeah. She broke up with her boyfriend tonight. Although I think it was the other way around, from what I saw."

His girlfriend did not look impressed. "On her birthday? That really sucks. What kind of jerk would do that?"

"I don't know. I mean, I know the guy and he seems decent but yeah, it's a little rude." He was tempted to give the man a piece of his mind but didn't think it would help the situation.

"She seems nice, though."

"Except for the fact that she drives me nuts," he returned.

"Aww, you just hate being teased, don't you?" she said.

"I refuse to dignify that with an answer," he told her.

"Poor baby," she drawled, laughing at his put-upon expression.

He drove her home and walked with her to the door, kissing her goodnight. They'd only been out on dates a few times and he had been taught by his parents to respect women.

"Do you want to come in?" she asked, clearly hinting.

"Do you want me to?" he replied.

"Well, I wouldn't ask if I didn't."

He had no answer for that. He let her take him by

the hand and pull him inside the house.

Jim took his girlfriend out to breakfast the next morning before returning to the house he shared with Craig and Susan to shower and dress. It was his weekend on duty at the station.

He bumped into Stu Dawson in the West Side station car park. He was obviously also on duty that day.

"Hey, how was the karaoke?" the man asked. Dawson had been a little miffed that Amanda hadn't invited him to the party. Not that she'd invited Jim either. Amanda had little time for the senior constable who tended to leer at her every time she was in the police bar. She usually came most Friday nights to spend time with her father.

"It was fine," he said.

"Just fine?" Dawson asked with a smirk.

Jim wasn't about to give the man details, ignoring the uniformed officer as he took out his security access card, passing it over the reader until he heard a beep.

He headed upstairs to check the case roster for the day. It had been quiet around West Side for a change. Other than the homicide and the assault cases he'd been working on, there had only been a couple of armed robbery attempts. Both of those had clearly been done by amateurs as they had left with nothing.

He decided to read the papers online to see if there was anything interesting. They'd had a few run-ins with the editor of the local rag, but they hadn't come to anything serious. The man must have had an axe to grind with them, he thought.

There was a story in a bigger publication about a nationwide search for talent to audition for an upcoming television show.

Jim recalled the conversation he'd overheard between Amanda and the young man the night before. This must have been what he was talking about. The prize money was $100,000.

Jim agreed with Amanda. He'd seen a few different talent shows on television and there had been times when he had wondered how someone had managed to get through as there had always been something lacking. Of course, since they were heavily edited, he doubted they showed the full story.

Like any reality show, he understood their version of reality and the truth were worlds apart.

He shrugged and closed the news sites, turning to the case files on his desk.

Chapter Three

"So, I hear you were the hit of the party on Friday."

Amanda paused mid-chew. She'd just bitten into a teriyaki chicken sub from the local sandwich restaurant. The sauce was oozing from the sandwich, dripping down onto the wax paper. She quickly swallowed the bite and wiped her mouth with a paper napkin.

"Uh, how did you hear about that, boss?" she asked.

Mr Knight grinned at her. "I bumped into your dad when I was playing golf with a client on Saturday. We chatted over a couple of beers at the Nineteenth Hole."

Dad and his golf, she thought. He certainly wasn't any great shakes at it and probably only went so he could socialise with his mates at the clubhouse.

The older man sat down beside her. "Your dad's very proud of you, you know."

"Yeah, I know," she said, not bothering to add that he was probably biased. "He's my dad."

"He told me you had some singing training when

you were younger."

She wrinkled her nose. "A little, I guess. We had this teacher at primary school who really loved music. Mostly old pop stuff – you know, from before I was born. She set some of us up in a choir and a couple of us had lessons. We won a few competitions too."

She thought about those competitions as she ate her sandwich. The teacher, Helen Bennett, had been very keen to ensure that their choir won against a rival school. Amanda had later heard that the teacher leading the choir at the rival school was a former friend of her own teacher. She had never asked the teacher why they were no longer friends but there was definitely a sense of bitter rivalry between them.

She had enjoyed singing in the choir. It had been around the same time her mother had left them and she had sought solace in the activity. Her best friend had convinced her to join, telling her she sang better than most of the girls already in the choir. She'd even gone on to join the youth choir for a year or two before studying for high school exams had forced her to quit. If she'd stayed, the choir leader had told her she would have become a soloist the next term.

"Did you ever think about doing it professionally?" her boss asked as he put a container in the microwave. There were several beeps as he pressed buttons. He muttered something, sounding frustrated. There were more beeps before the oven began heating whatever it was.

She shrugged. "Honestly? Not really. I mean, I enjoy it, but I don't think I'd enjoy the pressure."

He turned and looked at her. "Being a cop is way more stressful," he told her with a wry grin.

"You'd know," she returned, recalling that he'd retired because of his own disillusionment with the system. He shot her a look which she couldn't quite interpret.

The microwave beeped to let him know it was done and he opened it, hissing as he pulled out the now hot contents. Amanda shook her head and sighed as she watched him grab a paper towel to pick up the container. He carried it back over to the couch and sat down then got up again to get a fork from the drawer.

"My advice? Don't let an old cynic like me or Bob deter you from doing what you want to do. If you want to be a cop, then you shouldn't let anything stand in your way."

She watched him as he dug the fork in the container. His wife had given him leftovers from dinner the night before and he crinkled his nose at it. She couldn't blame him. It appeared to be a casserole of some description but looked very unappetising. The gravy, if it could be called that, looked more grey than brown. The vegetables were mushy, and the meat appeared to have been burnt.

"YMCA, huh?" she said. He frowned at her, obviously puzzled at the term. She chuckled. "That's what my dad calls it. Yesterday's Meal Cooked Again."

Jerry laughed. "I've never heard that before. I'll have to tell my wife that." He made a face. "Then again, she's likely to throw it at me if I complain." He shook his head, grinning. "She's not the greatest cook. The woman can't follow a recipe to save her life."

Amanda, who had begun cooking all the meals for

herself and her father from the age of thirteen and cooked her own meals in the flat, couldn't understand how someone could mess up following a recipe. To her, it was something so basic that she hadn't really given it a lot of thought.

"When Mum left, Dad got someone in to look after the house and cook the meals. At least until I was old enough to look after myself. She taught me to cook. Nothing fancy, but I liked it."

Jerry sighed, dropping his fork. "Maybe you should give my wife a few lessons. Then again, I think she might be a lost cause."

"Oh, don't say that," Amanda said in protest.

"Trust me, we've been married for nearly forty years. I know a lost cause when I see one." He smirked. "I'm gonna go across the road and get myself a decent sandwich. Just pretend you know nothing if she calls."

"Deal," she said, laughing at her boss.

She finished her lunch and went back into the small office to get back to work. As was her usual routine, she checked the local papers online. Her bosses sometimes spotted something which could potentially bring them business.

Working as a private investigator in a big city wasn't as adventurous as it looked on television crime dramas or in crime novels. Usually, it was mundane stuff. A major part of their income was from investigating cheating spouses. Occasionally a local business would call in an investigator when they suspected a staff member was stealing from them but those were rare instances.

Amanda would sometimes have to send generic emails or letters to various companies advertising their services. After more than eight months in the job, she was now trusted to just send out the emails rather than have her boss look over a draft.

She sighed as she skimmed over the articles in the city's main metropolitan newspaper. There was nothing too exciting happening and there didn't appear to be anything that could bring work their way.

There was a brief article of note from the entertainment section. Amanda remembered one of the young men from the party on Friday telling her about auditions for a national talent quest. She hadn't been particularly interested in signing up for it.

The article mentioned an accident at one of the auditions where someone had been taken to hospital. The accident had obviously been serious as the contestant had subsequently dropped out of the competition.

Amanda printed out the article and put it aside. It was probably nothing, but it couldn't hurt to get a little background, she thought.

Mr Moody came in as she was checking the email inbox.

"Anything interesting?" he asked.

She shook her head. "Not really. Usual enquiries about cheating spouses. I did see this," she added, handing him the printout of the news article, "but I don't think there's anything in it."

He glanced at it but didn't comment. He looked up at her.

"I need you to call Roy Hanley. He's delinquent in his payment."

"Already taken care of, boss," she said. "Called him this morning. I told him he had until Friday to pay and if he didn't settle his account it would be going to small claims." The man had been belligerent, but she had been firm with him, even ignoring any threat of legal action on his part. Hanley had hired Moody to investigate an insurance claim which had turned out to be fraudulent, then tried to refuse to pay his account.

Jerry had told her not to be afraid to be assertive with clients like Hanley. As long as she remained professional, she could say whatever she pleased to them. If they swore at her, she could note it in the paperwork they'd send to small claims.

Amanda had seen the problem of dealing with such clients as good
experience for when she became a police officer.

He smirked at her. "That's very efficient, Amanda. You're doing very well."

She took the praise as meant. Her boss rarely praised her work or said anything that could be construed as positive so when he did it meant he was pleased.

The rest of her day she sent out emails and followed up on some other correspondence. Mondays she normally expected more mail as the office was closed on weekends.

When she left work, she was surprised to see Jim standing outside waiting for her.

"Thought I'd give you a ride home," he said.

She remembered telling him that she sometimes took the train rather than pay for expensive parking in the inner city.

"How do you know I didn't drive?" she asked.

"Please," he said with a snort. "Credit me with a little intelligence!"

"Isn't that some kind of oxymoron?" she quipped. "Police. Intelligence."

"You're thinking of military intelligence," he said, obviously trying to counter her teasing.

"Well, you were in the army, weren't you?" she replied with a smirk. He shook his head and huffed at her.

"You …"

"Me what?" she asked.

"Don't make me regret doing you this favour," he said. He opened the passenger door of the car for her. "Get in the car."

She mock-saluted him. "Sir! Yes, sir!"

She adjusted her seat and snapped her seat belt in place as he got in and started the car.

"I figured this would be out of your way," she said.

"I had some stuff to do in the city, so I was close by."

"Oh."

"I wanted to talk to you anyway."

"About what?"

He studied her for a moment. "You seemed a little down on Friday. After you and Matt broke up."

She shrugged. "I'm okay."

"You sure? You can talk to me, you know. We're friends."

She raised an eyebrow. "Oh, we're friends now? Hmm, that's news to me."

"Cut the wisecracks, Amanda."

She bit her lip, touching the chain on her wrist, reminded of the gift he'd given her. "Okay. Sorry. I mean, it was nice of you to offer me a ride."

They didn't always bicker. She'd met him a few

times at the police bar and they'd ended up talking about their shared love of books, even if they didn't quite share the same taste in genres. Jim had told her he enjoyed reading science fiction and fantasy, like Tolkien or Pratchett. She'd been surprised at that, thinking he would prefer crime fiction or thrillers.

"Why would I want to read crime fiction when I deal with it every day?" he'd countered. She had to admit he had made a good point.

Amanda had been forced to admit she sometimes read authors like Danielle Steel, and not just because of the similarity in name. She also liked the legal thrillers like those by Grisham. She'd argued about those with Jim who had said they were a little unrealistic. At least in science fiction, he didn't have to suspend disbelief because he knew those worlds had been created and didn't have much basis in fact.

Amanda had a few friends who thought reading was a waste of time and energy. Most of them were involved in various sports activities, which was fine by her, but she knew there was more to life than sports.

She watched as Jim negotiated the heavy traffic and headed toward the motorway.

"Mr Knight's been talking to me about doing a course in investigations," she said.

"Really? That sounds like a good idea."

"You think so? I still want to join the police."

He glanced at her. "Why is being a cop so important to you?"

She had to consider that for a few moments. She'd wanted to be a police officer because her father was one. At least, initially. As she had matured, she had realised that reason wasn't enough.

"I want to make a difference," she said. "I mean, I know police work isn't all about car chases and hunting down bad guys."

"Then why?"

On her application, she'd written that she wanted to do something to help the community. To be there for those who couldn't help themselves. She told Jim this.

"I get that, but you could be a social worker, in that case."

"I guess," she conceded. "I mean, you might as well suggest that I could be a reporter or something. Not that I'm any great shakes as a writer."

She sighed. "Growing up, my dad was my role model, you know? I mean, there were days when he'd get a bit down and sometimes, he'd come home and just shut himself in his bedroom and cry. I knew those times it was bad. Like there'd been a violent death or something. I know stuff like that is pretty hard to deal with. Especially when it's something that could have been prevented. It's those kinds of people I want to help. If I could stop one old lady from being attacked and badly hurt, or worse, then it's worth it."

"That's actually pretty good reasoning," Jim said. "Are you going to apply again?"

"Maybe in a year or two. They said I needed to get some life experience, so I think what I'm doing now will help."

"That's sensible."

"Why did you become a cop?"

"Same as you, I suppose. Because of my dad. I mean, Dad gets cynical sometimes. My step-mum,

Lesleigh, has to pretty much pull him off his soapbox whenever he starts complaining about the system. I joined the army first, thinking I'd like that as a career, but I didn't really relish the thought of peacekeeping overseas. I wanted to stick close to my family."

"Your step-mum sounds great."

"Yeah, Mum's a really great person. I mean, who would take on a single dad with a kid?" He laughed. "I was such a brat in the beginning. I saw her as kind of replacing my real mum and I did a lot of things that drove Mum crazy. She sat me down and told me that no matter what, it was okay for me to miss my real mother. It wasn't until she had my little sister that I really began to appreciate her."

"You have a little sister?"

"Yeah. Lydia. She's fourteen now. Driving our parents nuts." Amanda could see the smile on his face, and it told her he was very fond of his little sister.

"Don't we all at that age?"

"Touché."

The traffic was light, and the commute didn't seem to take as long as it normally would. Amanda watched as Jim took the exit from the motorway and turned off into her street. He stopped at the bottom of the cul-de-sac.

"Thanks for the ride," she said, reaching for the door handle.

Jim put a hand on her arm. "I know you said you're fine, but if you do need to talk …"

She smiled at him. "I know. I appreciate it. Thanks."

She got out of the car and waited until he drove away before walking down the drive to her flat.

Chapter Four

Jim reported for duty as normal on Wednesday, having taken both Monday and Tuesday off. He had spent those two days running various errands in town and catching up on his chores.

He was still living with Craig and Susan Brophy. The couple had got married a month earlier and had decided to take a month-long honeymoon in Europe since it was spring there. Which meant the house was quiet, for another few days at least.

He liked his flatmates but there were times when he wished they wouldn't party so much. It wasn't that he disliked parties, but he just wasn't in the mood to do it every weekend. He was on duty one weekend out of every four and it could get annoying when they had people over late into the night when he was trying to sleep. Especially when he had to be on duty early in the morning.

He knew he had to find himself another place – one he could either buy or afford to rent on his own, but it was easier said than done. Most of the properties were out of his price range. Those that weren't were either run down or tiny one-bedroom units. He wasn't that desperate.

"Morning Andersen."

Jim looked up and smiled at his colleague. Detective Constable Chris Chapman was new, having only just qualified to the Criminal Investigation Branch a few weeks earlier. He'd recently moved from one of the smaller regional centres and was taking his time getting to know all his colleagues.

He was about a year younger than Jim with dark blond hair. A couple of centimetres taller, his form appeared to lean toward skinny rather than Jim's own lithe frame.

Jim tried to be friendly with the other man even if he did appear to be a little stand-offish and would speak rather abruptly at times. He supposed it was because the detective was new to the area and it was natural for him to be a little reserved. Jim himself had often found it difficult to get to know his new colleagues but he hoped he hadn't been as abrupt as the other man.

His stepmother often told him when he'd been little and first getting to know her, he'd tended towards shyness. As he'd related to Amanda, he'd been a little jealous of any time his father had spent with his then-girlfriend, who had done her best to include him on anything.

He would often chuckle when he thought of the things he'd got up to as a child. Not that he was bad, although there had been a couple of incidents where his father had threatened to spank him. Lesleigh had taken it all in stride. It was one of the things he loved most about his stepmother.

"Morning Chapman. Anything new on the agenda?"

"You might have to ask the boss that," he said. He paused and studied Jim. "I hear the weekend was kind of quiet."

"For once," Jim returned with a smirk. There had been a few weekends lately where a spate of attacks had been reported in the West Side city centre. Fortunately, the weekend Jim had been rostered on, there had been nothing of note.

Chris sat on the corner of his desk. He quickly looked around the office, before glancing over at Pete's office.

"So, uh, I hear you know the boss' daughter," he said quietly.

Jim was immediately suspicious. He knew of a few other officers who had asked about Amanda. Usually, it meant they were hoping he would put in a good word for them. He snorted to himself. He would rather be flung into a nest of vipers than talk up his colleagues to a girl like Amanda. Besides, he thought. She was perfectly capable of getting her own dates.

"The answer's no," he said.

Chapman looked at him in surprise. "I was only asking …"

"I know what you were asking. If you want to know about the girl,
ask Pete for her number. Don't make me the middle guy."

"I just figured you could put in a good word for me. I mean, I've seen her photo. She's cute."

"Look, Amanda might be a pain in the arse sometimes, but if you want to ask a girl like her out, then just ask her. She'll probably be at the bar on Friday. She usually comes up to spend some time with her father."

The other detective looked horrified at the thought of trying to talk to Amanda in the presence of her father. Jim glanced up and saw the very man approaching the desk. He was about to hiss a warning to the younger man, but Chapman spoke before Jim could do so.

"I can't just … I mean, the boss would probably kill me!"

"Well, that remains to be seen, doesn't it?" Pete said.

The detective constable's eyes widened, and he just about fell off the desk in his haste to stand and face their boss.

"Uh, boss, I was …"

"Obviously not doing your job. I asked you to check the emails and print out anything of note for the staff meeting. Which," he added, glancing at his wristwatch, "is in five minutes."

Chapman swallowed and hastily moved to comply.

"Uh, yes, sir. Emails. Right away."

Jim smirked as the younger man scurried away. Pete winked at him before he went back into his office. Jim didn't know if his boss had heard the entire conversation, but he'd obviously heard enough.

A few minutes later, the detectives assembled in the room which stood as the detective sergeant's office. It wasn't a huge room by any means; barely enough to fit a desk and a couple of cabinets.

A couch sat against the wall to the side of the

desk, one end right up against the outer wall of the office. It was an old couch and rather uncomfortable to sit on as the springs had gone. Jim had once gone to sit down only for his butt to be poked by a loose spring. He'd asked his boss why he didn't get it replaced but it came down to the usual problem. Money.

He made sure to sit on one of the chairs. They were almost as uncomfortable as the couch, being a hard plastic with metal legs, but they were better than nothing.

He sat next to Kirsten Taylor, who had been a detective for five years. She was now a Detective Senior Constable, the rank just above Jim's. The attractive brunette had told Jim the first day they'd met that she was a career officer who wasn't interested in having a family. Her attitude toward him had been puzzling until he'd learnt that from the moment she'd joined the police, every male officer had treated her as if she was only there to meet a husband.

It seemed the old double standard still applied, he'd thought at the time. Kirsten had worked hard to prove herself as a highly intelligent and extremely capable officer, notwithstanding the little matter of her gender.

The only person who had never treated her that way was Pete, whose only requirement when taking on new detectives was that they worked hard and did their jobs to the best of their ability.

Amanda might say that her father was overprotective, but Pete had never discouraged his daughter from pursuing her dream of becoming a police officer. He was the one who had suggested the job working for the private investigators but only so she could gain the life experience she needed to reapply.

Jim knew from some of the women he had worked with in his five or so years in the police that they were just as capable as men at their jobs. Once Amanda had matured a little and had a bit of life experience behind her, he was sure she would make an excellent police officer. If she decided to continue pursuing that dream.

"Andersen, you with us?"

He looked up, realising Pete had been speaking to the assembled detectives.

"Uh, sorry, boss. I was miles away."

"Yeah, I noticed," Detective Sergeant Steele said dryly. "Moving on. I read your report on the weekend activities. No more attacks?"

He shook his head. "No. We're still investigating the earlier attacks. While the weekend was quiet, we're not hedging our bets."

Pete nodded. "Beatty's still going to have a team patrolling the city centre this weekend. It may be that whoever's behind the attacks knows we've added patrols in the area."

That didn't mean anything, Jim thought, listening as his boss discussed the investigation.

Kirsten finally spoke. "So, that new show is holding auditions in town."

"What new show?" Chapman asked.

The detective shrugged. "I forget what it's called. I think I've seen something like it on telly before. Some kind of talent quest."

Jim nodded. "I read about something like that in the paper the other day. What about it?"

"I just heard some of the guys from Central have been asked to keep an eye out. Dunno if they're expecting trouble or what."

Pete nodded. "You know the drill. Eyes and ears. What affects Central affects everyone."

The meeting ended shortly afterwards. As they all got up to leave, Pete spoke.

"Andersen, hang back a minute."

Jim sent his boss a questioning look but sat back down, waiting for whatever it was the older man had to say.

"Amanda said you picked her up from work on Monday."

"It wasn't really … I was in town. Figured I'd save her the commute."

The older man studied him for a moment. Jim wondered what his boss was thinking.

"She seemed a little upset when I left on Friday."

"Yeah. You know she and Matt broke up." Was it technically a break-up if they had only been seeing each other as friends? His boss nodded.

"Amanda told me, but I thought it was mutual."

"I guess so," he replied. "The jerk decided to take off without her, so I dropped her off home."

Annoyance flashed over the other man's face for a moment and Jim gathered he wasn't pleased that Matt had chosen to leave without at least ensuring Amanda had a way of getting home. He smiled at Jim.

"Thanks for looking out for her."

He shrugged. "She's a good kid."

Pete grinned at him sardonically. "You're hardly an old man yourself, you know."

"Yeah, boss, I know."

Work was routine over the next couple of days. Jim didn't mind as it gave him a chance to catch up on paperwork. He still had to follow up on the case at the high school, since it was yet to go to trial. The court was backed up and it would likely be months before anything moved forward there.

By Friday evening, he was more than ready for a good drink. He joined his colleagues in the bar, noting Amanda was already there with her father, drinking her usual vodka and orange fizz. She wasn't a big fan of beer, she'd told him. After her experience with the whiskey, she stayed well away from the hard stuff and stuck to light mixes. While they were mostly sugar, she figured it was better than drinking something that could get her plastered too quickly.

He saw the younger detective eyeing the girl and sauntered up to him, beer in hand.

"Stop staring and go ask her, for crying out loud!"

Chapman looked at him with what he could only describe as a 'deer-in-the-headlights' look.

"Oh no, I couldn't. I mean she's ... look at her."

Jim turned to look at the blonde. "What about her?"

"Well, I mean, she's ... God, she's more than cute!" The man was red-faced as he struggled with obvious embarrassment. While Jim did think she was an attractive girl, he had dated a few women and was well past the blushing stage. Chapman clearly wasn't.

"Pete isn't going to kill you for asking his daughter out! She's a big girl."

Gaby came in and joined him. They'd had dinner at her place a couple of days ago and had planned to go see a movie after work.

"Who are you two gawking at?" she asked.

"Chapman's trying to get up the courage to ask Amanda out."

"She's a nice girl," Gaby assured their colleague. "And I don't think the sarge has murdered anyone yet who wanted to date his daughter." She laughed at the terrified look on the other man's face. "That was a joke."

"Well it isn't very funny," Chris returned, gulping down his beer.

Jim grinned at his girlfriend. "Dutch courage," he said.

The other man shot him a withering glare before stalking off. Gaby laughed quietly.

He couldn't help remembering the events of two months earlier and mentioned it to his girlfriend.

"Think I should tell him about the time she took out that guy?" he asked her.

"Which one?"

"You know, the one involved in the drug scam at the school. She took that guy down even with a concussion."

He'd told her about that. Amanda had been hit from behind while she'd been talking to the man who had turned out to be the ringleader. She'd been taken to the man's house where he'd planned on raping her. His accomplice had been a student at the school. Both had planned to film the attack, not only to ruin Amanda's life but in an attempt to thumb their noses at police. She had fought back, even while suffering a mild head injury.

As obnoxious as she could be sometimes, it had proved to Jim that she could take care of herself.

He continued to chat to Gaby even as he watched

Chris talking to Amanda. From the way the pair were smiling, it looked like the rookie detective had been worried over nothing.

He finished his beer and turned to his girlfriend. "Wanna go? We should be able to catch the 6.30 showing."

"Sure. I just need to get my stuff from downstairs."

"I'll meet you in the car park then."

As they lined up at the theatre to purchase their tickets, he spotted Chapman ahead of them with Amanda. He nudged his girlfriend. Gaby looked then frowned at him.

"Don't even think about it!" she warned.

"Think about what?"

"Starting something with them. She doesn't need it right now."

He frowned at her. "What do you mean? I wasn't going to do anything obnoxious. Not unless she starts it, anyway."

"That's exactly what I mean. This little competition you two have got going might be funny to you guys, but it's just really annoying to the rest of us. And it gives the wrong impression."

"I'm not interested in Amanda!" he said in protest. "We're just friends!" She shot him a look and he raised his hands in mock surrender. "Fine! I'll shut up and say nothing."

He had no idea whether the girl had heard them, but she turned her head to look at him. She sent him a smirk before turning her attention back to her date.

Chapter Five

Amanda was early as she walked to work a few days later. She was normally supposed to start half an hour before her bosses but she'd caught an earlier train so she could stop at the local supermarket and pick up something for lunch.

Despite the winter chill in the air, she enjoyed her walk from the train station. The atmosphere was crisp, reminding her of the frosty mornings when she walked to school. Unlike many of her high school peers, she had refused to let her father drive her. She was very aware of the dangers out there, but she had never encountered any problems.

She'd always loved seeing the grass berms covered in frost. Snow was a rare occurrence in the city. Ice on the grass was the closest she would ever get to it. She could still remember as a child running out into the yard in her gumboots, loving the sound of the grass crunching under her feet. There would always be marks in the ice from her footprints and she would dance around, giggling, generally making a mess, until her father came out to pick her up, tossing her over his shoulder and carrying her back inside.

She'd once read a story set in the mid-west of North America where the character talked about making snow angels. It wasn't possible to do the same in the frost, but Amanda used to think about trying it.

One year she had gone on a ski trip with her class. She hadn't enjoyed the skiing, but she'd persuaded a friend to go out the back of the lodge and play in the snow. She realised now why her father had told her making a snow angel was not the best idea. She'd been so cold her lips had turned blue.

The office was about twenty minutes' walk from the train station. Luckily it hadn't rained that morning, so the footpath was reasonably dry. Her breath came out in a mist as she walked up the hill toward the office. The central city was rather hilly since it was built on extinct volcanoes. At least, she hoped they were extinct.

She passed two uniformed police officers chatting to one of the homeless people sheltering in a shop doorway. She'd read a story in the local paper that the council was considering banning all homeless people from the city centre. She wondered where they were supposed to go in that case, since the shelters were usually full up this time of year.

She had talked to a reporter friend who had done a story on the homeless in West Side. Her friend had told her that in the winter the people who slept under bridges and what-not out west would usually migrate to the central city as they thought it was warmer.

One of the officers smiled at her as she walked by.

She recognised him as Gary McConnell. The senior constable had transferred from West Side to the central station about a month after the high school case.

Gary had asked her out once, but she had been barely sixteen at the time and had still been in high school, whereas Gary had been five years older. At the time, she had been more focused on school than dating.

He hadn't taken offence at the rejection. She'd talked with him on and off and knew he'd been one of the officers working on the case at the school. He knew how well she could handle herself.

She had seen Kerry and Gary talking together when she'd gone for drinks at the police bar, acting very friendly. She suspected they were dating but her best friend was yet to confirm it.

Amanda had always been careful about dating her father's colleagues. Not that either of them saw anything wrong with it, but most of the officers had known her since she was at least eight years old and the thought of going out with any of them was a little weird.

At least Chris Chapman was new enough that he didn't know her history. When he'd got over his initial reticence, he had turned out to be rather sweet. She had sensed he was a little reserved when he'd spoken to her and probably a little intimidated by the fact that her father was his boss, but they'd had a good time.

She was looking forward to going out with him again on Friday.

She unlocked the office door and went into the break room to switch on the hot water unit. Moody always preferred the unit to be switched off overnight. It was connected to the plumbing, so it filled up automatically when the water level became too low.

She unloaded the dishwasher and set out cups for her bosses. Mr Moody usually preferred black tea, which at times could be annoying as it stained the inside of his cup. He had supplied the office with a set of cups but preferred to use a novelty mug with a Superman shield. Amanda had had a quiet chuckle when she had spotted the mug. Her boss might be a serious kind of man, but it was good to know he had a quirky side.

Mr Knight, on the other hand, had brought in his own mug which had a series of jokes on it. He preferred coffee. The stronger the blend, the better, he'd told her.

Having set up the kitchen, she went to her little office and logged on to the computer to begin her morning routine. As she checked the email, a reminder came up on the calendar.

That's funny, she thought. I don't remember putting an appointment in the calendar for this morning.

She opened the calendar and read the details of the appointment. All it said was there would be a meeting in the conference room at 9.30 am. It was clear she was expected to be there as well.

Meetings in the conference room usually meant an important client that required the presence of both detectives. What wasn't usual was the expectation that she would be there as well. She wondered whether it meant that they were considering changing the scope of her duties.

She continued with her morning routine, checking all the emails and forwarding anything important to her bosses. By the time she was done with that, it was five minutes before the meeting.

She grabbed a notepad and went to the conference room, knocking on the door. A voice called out for her to enter. Mr Knight smiled at her as she came in.

"Ah, good, good. Thank you, Amanda. I'm just waiting for Bob. The client will be here shortly, I imagine."

She sent her boss a questioning look. "What is this about, boss?"

"We'll tell you in good time. Help yourself to a coffee," he said, gesturing to the espresso coffeemaker sitting on a silver tray on the credenza.

It was becoming obvious the client was an important one, possibly worth a good retainer at least. They only brought out the coffeemaker for meetings like this.

The door opened again as she went to help herself to an espresso. She turned and smiled at her boss, then at the man and woman standing in the doorway.

Mr Moody smiled back at her. "Amanda. Good."

"Can I make anyone a coffee?" she asked.

The woman, a willowy blonde in her early forties, nodded. "Thank you. That would be lovely. Cream, two sugars."

"Black for me, please," the man said. He didn't appear to be much older than Amanda, but she recognised him as a singer who had made a name for himself in a children's talent show as a teenager. He had brown skin and close-cropped dark hair typical of someone with Maori ancestry, and a kind, handsome face.

Without being asked, she also made a tea for Mr Moody, who took his cup with a smile of thanks. She could tell that he was pleased with her initiative.

Mr Knight had clearly already made himself a coffee but held up his cup.

"How about a top-up?" he asked.

She mock-glared at him. "How many cups have you had already?" she asked.

He made a face. "This would be my third."

She shook her head. "That's it. I'm cutting you off. You know you shouldn't have too much coffee!" she scolded. He had been diagnosed with high blood pressure and was told to cut back on the caffeine.

"Boy, you're strict," the woman commented.

"Yes, she is," Mr Knight replied with a grin. "I wouldn't get on this young lady's bad side if I were you. She has proven she knows very well how to take care of herself."

"Ooh sounds like you would have quite a story to tell," the other client replied.

"Nothing that bears repeating," Amanda told him with a look at her boss. "He's exaggerating."

"Not from what Bob's told me about you," the woman said. She turned pink and put a hand to her mouth. "Oh, lord, sorry. We should introduce ourselves. I'm Sarah Kennedy and this is Tama Rawhiti."

Amanda placed their cups in front of them and shook their hands in turn. "I think I saw you perform once," she told Tama. "You were on that tv show years ago, weren't you?"

Tama's grin was a little sheepish but he was obviously pleased.

"Yup, Young Talent. You remember it?"

"Well, I was only a kid but yeah, I did see some of it."

Her other boss cleared his throat and indicated for them to sit down. Amanda put down her own cup and glanced expectantly at Mr Moody.

"Right. Sarah, why don't you tell us why you're here," he said.

"Thank you, Mr Moody. As I'm sure you know, we are holding auditions for a new show called Star Quest. I'm one of the producers and Tama here is one of the judges."

"I saw that in the paper," Amanda replied. Tama nodded.

"I'm sure you've seen those British and American shows," he said. "This is our own home-grown version."

She nodded her understanding. No doubt they would follow a similar format.

"Anyway, we have literally hundreds of people auditioning initially," Sarah continued, explaining that most people signed up online, but offices had been set up in other centres to allow people to fill in their applications on site. "We hold them all over the country and then we bring the successful ones up here to compete."

Tama took up the rest of the explanation. "We thought about having a variety of acts, but it turned out ninety per cent of the applications were for singers, so we restricted it to that. At the end of the competition, the winner gets the prize money, of course, a recording contract and they get to work with someone who has some expertise in the industry."

"How will they choose the winner?" Amanda asked.

"Each show will have a panel of judges, until the finale," Sarah explained. She added that the shows would all be recorded except for the last one, which would be live. There would be five finalists chosen who would be asked to perform three songs each in a two-hour format. The television audience would then be allowed to send in their votes for their favourite.

"That sounds reasonable," Mr Knight replied approvingly

"So, what brings you to us?" Mr Moody prompted, although from his expression it was obvious he knew what it was all about.

"I'm sure you've read of a few accidents at some of the auditions," Sarah told her. "We're concerned someone may be trying to sabotage the show."

Amanda frowned at Sarah, remembering the article she had printed out for her boss a week or so earlier. "So, it sounds to me like you don't think these accidents were accidents."

"And you'd be right," Tama confirmed. "We don't have proof, unfortunately."

"That's where you come in. We need someone to investigate this."

Mr Moody set aside his cup. "I'm sure you realise that there is no easy way to do so without arousing suspicion."

The two partners exchanged a look, their expressions thoughtful. Then they turned to look at Amanda.

"What are you thinking, boss?" she asked.

"You did very well with your first investigation," Mr Moody told her, surprising her with the compliment. "This would be a good opportunity, I think."

Her other boss looked at him. "Are you thinking perhaps she work on the crew?"

Sarah and Tama looked at each other.

"That certainly sounds like a good idea," Tama responded. "It would attract less attention. And it would give her access to everything backstage."

Mr Knight shook his head. "No. I think she would require some technical skills in order to fit in with the crew." He glanced apologetically at her. "I'm sure you understand, Amanda."

She nodded. Mr Moody studied his partner.

"You have something else in mind?"

"Yes. I think Amanda should audition."

She stared at her boss. "Wait. What?"

"Well, you can sing, and extremely well, from what I've heard." He turned back to the producer. "If you suddenly replace a crew member, it may also look suspicious. Since you're still holding auditions, it would make more sense."

Tama looked at her. "You sing?"

Amanda felt herself blushing. Jim might have accused her of acting like a spoilt when she'd worked with him on the other case, but she didn't really set out to be the centre of attention.

When her friend had suggested she try out at the karaoke night, she hadn't given it much thought. She wasn't really looking for life in the limelight.

"Uh, a little. I used to sing in a choir until I was about fifteen."

Sarah turned to her partner. "It does sound logical."

"It means we'd have to tell the other judges to let

her through."

"Is that really necessary?" Mr Knight asked. "If what her father tells me is true, I don't see a problem with her making it through without that."

Tama grinned. "Okay. We're holding more auditions this Saturday. I can get you the forms and bring them over tomorrow. Maybe give you a little bit of coaching," he added.

When the pair left, she sat back, feeling more than a little overwhelmed. She had a new case and both her bosses were one hundred per cent behind her. Still, there was a big difference between singing karaoke and actually singing for a competition.

Moody had surprised her with his praise. He'd always been a man of few words, but he was clearly trusting her to do a good job.

She just hoped her nerves didn't get the better of her. Amanda wasn't usually given to feelings of anxiety, but this was different. There was a lot riding on her success at getting through even just the first stage.

Chapter Six

The week had been mostly routine stuff and the CIB had been quiet for once, but Jim was glad when Friday came around. As bad as things could get sometimes, he liked it when he was busy as it made the week go by a little faster.

He entered the bar, unsurprised to find Amanda already there with her father and Chris Chapman. The rookie detective was drinking orange juice by the look of it. He'd been rostered on for his first weekend duty and probably wanted a clear head.

Jim glanced at Amanda, noticing she was quieter than usual. Normally, she would be chatting animatedly to her father or to one of the officers who had known her since she was a toddler, but not tonight.

He turned to get himself a drink from the bar.

"Hey Margie, can I get a beer, please?"

"Sure thing, hon. Usual?"

"Yes, please," he replied, handing over the money.

Margie was a motherly kind of woman. She had

been working at the police station for years; longer even than Pete. She knew everything about the station and everyone. She was also the type of woman who refused to take crap from anybody.

Jim had had a few run-ins with her when he'd first started at the station. She had a certain way of doing things and woe betide anyone who tried to tell her how to do her job. Fortunately, he had figured out a way to get on her good side and had earned himself brownie points.

Amanda appeared at his side and waited quietly until Margie had handed over his beer.

"Can I have a Coke please, Margie?" she asked in a quiet voice.

The older woman shot Jim a puzzled look before turning to grab a bottle of the soda out of the fridge.

"Here you go, honey."

Amanda turned away with her drink without even offering some kind of snarky comment. Something was definitely up, he thought.

He began walking over to a table when Pete beckoned to him to join them. With a shrug, he did so, sitting on one of the stools.

"Amanda was just telling us she was assigned another case."

He looked at the blonde. "That's great," he said with a smile. In spite of how close she had come to getting herself seriously hurt in the last case, he was genuinely happy for her. It would be good practice for when she became a cop.

"Thanks," she said. "I, um, have to be up early tomorrow, hence the Coke."

He shrugged. "Did I look worried that you weren't drinking?"

"Well, we both know how you like to monitor my drinking habits," she returned, reminding him of the first day they'd met. He'd commented that she looked too young to drink alcohol.

Yet her comment lacked its usual snark. Jim didn't retort, sipping his beer, hoping the girl would give him some clue as to what was going on.

Pete went to chat with another colleague about something and Chris began talking to Amanda about their date, asking her where she would like to go for dinner. She opted for something casual since she wasn't dressed up. The younger detective frowned at her, questioning her choice. Irritation showed on the blonde's face.

Jim decided to take the younger man aside.

"Hey, what's the problem here?" Jim asked. His colleague glared at him.

"There's no problem."

"Then why are you giving her a hard time?"

"Why do you need to know? It's none of your business!"

"Amanda's a friend and I don't like the way you're talking to her."

"The way she talks about you, I think friend is pushing it."

He rolled his eyes. "Yeah, fine. Whatever! Just have a little more respect."

Chapman made a sound like a low growl and went back to the table. He spoke to Amanda, shooting him a dark look, then walked off.

Jim returned to the table to find his friend looking a little upset.

"Are you okay? You're really quiet tonight."

She bit her lip and sighed. "Guess I'm not going

out tonight," she said.

"Well, maybe it's a good thing if you have to be up early. I don't have a date with Gaby either. She's working late. Why don't I go pick up some pizza or something and we can go back to your place? You look like you could use a friendly ear."

"Well, maybe not friend, exactly. I wouldn't use that term to describe us."

He smirked. "What would you call us?"

"Frienemies?"

"Really? Is that how you see us?" He had to laugh. Amanda broke out in a wide grin, lighting up her pretty face.

"Pizza sounds good," she said. "I like Hawaiian."

He cocked an eyebrow. It was his favourite pizza too. "You do? Most people I know hate Hawaiian!"

She shrugged. "Guess I'm not most people."

They finished their drinks and Amanda went to say goodbye to her father. Jim called in an order for the pizza, arranging to pick it up.

He arrived at her place about twenty minutes later. Amanda's car was in the driveway, but not Penny's. He guessed her flatmate was out for the evening.

He didn't really like Penny Cameron. When Amanda had officially introduced him to the older woman, she had immediately tried flirting with him. He'd bought food, planning to talk over the case he and Amanda had been working on, but Penny had acted as if her flatmate hadn't existed, practically inviting herself to dinner with them.

Jim had tried to be kind, complimenting her and convincing the woman to go out on the date she'd already set up for the evening while subtly hinting her presence wasn't wanted.

Penny struck him as the kind of woman who felt the world revolved around her. On the few occasions he'd visited Amanda at her home, the other woman had been all over him. The last time she'd done so, he'd made it clear to her he wasn't at all interested. Not that it seemed to have gotten through to her.

How his friend tolerated the woman's behaviour he had no idea.

The door was open when he got out of the car. Amanda had obviously seen him pull up. He entered the house and put the pizza box down on the coffee table.

"Amanda?"

"Hey. I'll be out in just a sec." He heard water running and guessed she was in the bathroom.

A few moments later she came out, grabbing paper napkins on her way through the kitchen. No sooner had she sat down on the couch when she got up again.

"I should get something to drink," she said.

He put out a hand to stop her. "Don't worry about it. I think we'll survive if we don't have a drink in our hands."

"Sorry."

He opened the pizza and waited for her to grab a slice before picking up his own.

"Don't be sorry. Just tell me what's going on. You looked a bit down."

She sighed. "Yeah, I, uh, I'm a little anxious about tomorrow."

"Why? What is this case you're working on?"

She screwed up her nose. "Don't laugh," she said. "You know that Star Quest show?"

"I've heard about it. Some of the guys at Central have been assigned to crowd control. Why?"

"Well, they think someone's trying to sabotage it. So, they hired us to look into it."

"That's nothing to be worried about."

"Um, Mr Knight suggested I audition."

Jim choked on a mouthful of pizza. "As what? A comedian? You'd bomb on the first try."

"Ha ha, very funny. No, as a singer."

He remembered the karaoke night and the guy who'd suggested she try out for the show. She was a good singer. No, she was better than good.

"Well, if you want my two cents, you don't need to be anxious about auditioning. You're good."

"Thanks, but I wasn't looking for endorsement. I just … I would have preferred working as one of the crew, but Mr Knight thinks it would have looked a bit suspect if I suddenly turned up. He said I have no technical skills. Not that he's wrong about that. It's just … I guess it would make me stick out more."

"That makes sense to me," he said. "But I get the feeling that's not the only thing that's going on."

She sighed and grabbed another slice of pizza. "This is really great pizza."

"Avoiding the subject."

She sent him a long look before sitting back, a resigned look on her face.

"Okay, well, Tama – he's one of the judges, came over on Wednesday to coach me for the audition tomorrow. Anyway, Penny was here, and she began flirting up a storm. You know, the way she did with you."

He made a face. "God, that woman's as bold as brass! What did Tama say?"

"What could he say? I was so embarrassed! After he left, I had a go at her. I mean, it was work! Yet she thought it was a perfect opportunity for her to get her hooks into someone else, even though she's dating Matt now."

He stared at her. "Matt? As in the guy who dumped … sorry, split up with you on your birthday?"

"Yeah. Apparently, they got to talking that night."

Damn, the woman had some nerve, Jim thought. He'd heard enough about Amanda's flatmate to know that Penny was always butting in where she wasn't wanted. She clearly thought she was better than Amanda and was always trying to steal men away from her friends.

"God, what a bitch!"

"Anyway, she started hurling all sorts of accusations at me, saying that Matt broke up with me because I wouldn't sleep with him."

"Wait! What?" He'd thought Matt was a decent kind of guy, certainly not the type to dump someone for such a trivial reason.

"Yeah. Then she called me a freak because I told her I'm not like her and I don't want to sleep with anyone!"

He almost choked again on his pizza. Did that mean she was … that she hadn't …

"Anyone? Like, never?"

She sent him an odd look. "Does that make me a freak?"

He blinked. "No, God no! Far from it! If anything, I admire you. It's a very mature thing to do."

"It's not like I'm saying never. It's just, when it happens, I want to be sure, you know?" She looked a little uncertain. "Is that wrong?"

He shook his head. "No. I mean, don't get me wrong. I've had a few girlfriends and I've slept with them, but … and this is not a sexist thing in any way. It's just … different. Sex is very much a personal choice."

She nodded. "I get that. There was this guy in high school. We were going out for a while and I really thought I … you know, I really thought he cared about me. One night we were making out and he started, you know, feeling me up and stuff and I told him I wasn't ready for that. I mean, I was seventeen! Well, he got kind of annoyed and practically accused me of being a tease so I told him if that was his attitude then we shouldn't see each other anymore. The next day, he's already dating another girl!"

What an asshole, Jim thought. Here was a great girl, who … okay, sometimes she could be a pain in the arse, but she was smart, funny, pretty as hell and her ex-boyfriend had the nerve to get angry with her because she wasn't ready for sex?

"If you ask me, you got the better end of the deal."

"I guess," she said glumly. She looked at him. "So, you don't think it's stupid?"

"No, I don't. I think it's sensible. I wish others – men and women – were as mature as you."

"How old were you when you …"

"I was nineteen. It was a girl at police college. We'd been going out a few weeks by that point. I wish I could say it was great, but it wasn't and I kind of regretted it the day after. We broke up not long after that."

The night had been a disaster. Neither one of them

had had much confidence when it came to sex. He'd ended up hurting her when things hadn't gone quite according to plan and it had gone from bad to worse. It was little wonder he hadn't seen her since.

Amanda nodded sympathetically. "I'm sorry."

He shrugged. "Meh! Sometimes you do things that look like a good idea at the time that end up disasters, but I count it as a learning experience."

He looked kindly at her. "All I can tell you is, don't listen to Penny. The woman goes through men like they're going out of style. I think you have the right idea. I do think you should consider moving out though. If she's making you this unhappy, I mean."

"Yeah, I can't afford anywhere else. I did hear about a bedsit in the central city but it's an old house and just about falling down."

Jim groaned in agreement, telling her his own troubles with finding a decent place to rent for a good price. Real estate prices had boomed in the past few years and it appeared landlords were taking advantage of the demand for housing by charging well above market rents, even for tiny apartments. Jim liked his space. He didn't want to live in a shoebox, or an apartment too small to swing a cat. Not that he wanted a cat.

Once the pizza was gone, they sat and relaxed, chatting about different subjects. He couldn't help smiling as he drove home later. When Amanda wasn't being sarcastic, she was actually great to talk to. She had a good general knowledge – enough for a good debate on just about anything.

He'd been out with young women who he seemed to have a lot in common with when he first met them, but he'd often found that after a while they had nothing to talk about.

He'd learnt from his parents a long time ago that relationships were more than about love and romance. If a couple couldn't talk to each other then what was the point?

Maybe he and Amanda weren't exactly at the point that they could categorise their relationship as a friendship, but it was a good start.

Chapter Seven

A crowd was already lined up when Amanda turned up to the audition, which didn't help her nerves. It wasn't the actual audition that had her so nervous. It was the fact that there was a lot riding on her initial success.

Tama had assured her she was more than good when he'd coached her the other evening. Since his own time on Young Talent, he'd taken on the role of coaching young singers, choosing to forgo a professional singing career.

As a teenager, he'd once dreamed of becoming a famous performer, but he'd slowly realised that no matter how talented he was, he would never achieve the heights of other performers, especially those in the UK or America. There simply wasn't the money to support talent from a little country at the bottom of the world. Most especially because New Zealand didn't have a big enough profile on the international scene.

There were always exceptions to the rule, of course, but in those cases, the artists had worked hard for years, or spent time building their profile in other countries.

Not only that, but the world was highly competitive, Tama had told her. Talent was never enough. Performers needed to be ruthless, at times. They needed to be strong enough to cope with the stresses of constant pressure to be better than anyone else.

That was why, he added, many people who entered these talent quests ended up cracking under the pressure.

She wondered if that had anything to do with the accidents. She'd been doing a little research and had talked with her reporter friend who had done a little digging herself and learnt that the so-called accidents hadn't been isolated incidents. They'd been happening at other casting calls around the country.

It was looking more than likely it was a member of the crew, which meant she would need to find out who out of the more than 50 people working at each audition had worked in other centres at the same time the accidents had occurred.

She had her work cut out for her.

She lined up at the back of the queue and waited, watching as a security guard went down the line, checking those with entry forms to see if they had been filled out correctly. Those who had entered online had a confirmation slip. There were a few who had not brought either and they were swiftly ejected from the line-up.

"You bring your form?" the guard asked her.

She nodded and quietly handed it over. He checked it and wrote a number on the top of the form before handing it back. He spoke gruffly, barely looking at her. "When they call your number, give the form to the floor manager. He'll tell you what to do."

"Thank you," she said politely. He ignored her and moved on.

She studied him, familiarising herself with his appearance. He was brown-skinned, probably Polynesian descent. His body was fairly muscular with bulky upper arms which had stretched the thin material of the black t-shirt he wore. His head was bald but with a slight shadow making it obvious it was shaved rather than naturally bald.

She took note of the nametag, pulling out her phone and keying it into the notes app. She pretended to be looking something up so as not to draw attention to herself. At least half the people in line also had phones out and were either sending texts or checking the 'net.

"Hi," a voice said.

She turned and looked at the source. A young man about her age grinned at her. He looked a little sleepy-eyed as if he was barely awake, his dark hair tousled as if he hadn't had time to comb it.

"Hi," she returned, careful to keep her tone neutral but friendly.

"So, what are you here for?"

"Auditioning," she said, indicating her form, as if it wasn't obvious. She quickly looked him over, wondering if he was there for another reason as he didn't appear to have his own form. "What about you?"

"Oh, I'm just here to provide moral support." He practically leered at her. "You needing some moral support?"

"No," she said quickly, her instincts telling her this guy could be trouble.

"I don't see anyone with you."

She bit her lip, studying the young man. He seemed to be awfully nosy for a guy who was just here to provide moral support to someone.

"Is that really your concern?" she asked, adopting a frosty manner.

"No need to get testy, Princess."

She narrowed her eyes at the man. If there was one thing she loathed, it was being called 'Princess'. Jim had called her that in one of their arguments. For her father's sake, she had chosen to ignore the taunt, but she wasn't about to take it from someone who had no idea who she was.

"I'm not getting testy. You don't even know me."

He snorted. "I know your type. Think you're better than everyone else. I mean, look at you. Sure as hell you have to be good at singing 'cause with your looks, you wouldn't get by on your brains."

She resented the implication that because of her looks she was some kind of a brainless bimbo. As much as she wanted to put this idiot in his place, she knew it wouldn't help her find out who was behind the accidents.

For all she knew, he could be involved. It seemed odd that he would approach her. Then again, while she hadn't seen him approach anyone else, it didn't mean he hadn't.

The guard who had spoken to her earlier must have seen what was happening as he came back down the line and grabbed the young man's arm.

"Hey, I've talked to you before about accosting contestants. Now beat it."

"I wasn't doing anything!" the youth protested loudly. "I was just talking to her."

"I've had complaints down the line. I catch you one more time and I'll have the cops arrest you. Got it?"

He nodded and turned away. The guard returned to his job checking slips. The young man turned back to her.

"I'd drop out if I were you," he advised. "My sis is gonna win this one. She's the one with the real talent."

"Go away!" she hissed.

She took out her phone again and ignored him, waiting until he had stalked off further down the line. He obviously wasn't done making a jerk of himself as he began talking to another girl. Amanda took the opportunity to get a photo of him and sent it to Jim, asking him to check into the guy's background.

She spent the rest of the time in line watching other hopefuls. The mood among those ahead of her wasn't exactly positive. She managed to hear snatches of conversation in which some of those still waiting to audition were deriding others, or the competition itself.

It occurred to her to wonder what those people who were making fun of the competition were actually doing there in that case. Then again, she supposed it was rather like someone watching a disaster in action. As much as they knew they should look away, they couldn't.

Since she had no actual interest in winning, it gave her a good opportunity to observe human behaviour. In her final year of high school, she had done a class on the topic. Her teacher had told the students that the worst of human behaviour could often be seen in highly competitive situations.

She knew that as much as the reality shows wanted to portray it otherwise, those who missed out on the top spots in talent quests were more likely to hold a grudge against those judged to be 'better' than them.

As far as Amanda was concerned, the smiles as they congratulated the winners were just an act put on for the cameras and once the spotlight was off them, they would let their real feelings out.

"Hello."

She looked around. A girl probably aged a year or two younger than her stood beside her. She had long, curly dark hair and wide, blue eyes.

"I'm so nervous. Aren't you nervous?" the girl said.

Amanda nodded. "Yeah. I am."

"You don't look it."

"Trust me, I am."

The girl laughed shakily. Her face was so pale it looked almost green. She was wearing a green hooded sweatshirt, so that probably accounted for it, Amanda thought.

"I'm so scared I think I might throw up when I get in there." She spoke rapidly, her words almost jumbling together. It was a sure sign of anxiety.

"I know what you mean," she replied, although her nervousness was obviously nowhere near the same as this other girl's.

"Oh, I'm Julie," the girl said.

"I'm Amanda," she replied.

Julie looked around, studying the other contestants.

"Geez, they all look so confident."

"Not all of them," Amanda assured her, having heard a few of them talking."

"I started singing when I was little. My mum says I was just about born with a microphone in my hand." She laughed again. "I guess she'd know. What about your mum?"

Amanda shrugged. "My mum left when I was a kid. It's just me and my dad."

Julie looked mortified, opening her mouth in an audible gasp.

"Oh, I'm so sorry. I just put my foot right in it, didn't I?"

Amanda didn't mind and sent a reassuring smile to the girl.

"It's all right. It was a long time ago."

Julie nodded. She chatted quietly as they continued to wait, clearly trying to ease her nerves. She appeared to be a nice if somewhat sheltered girl. Then again, Amanda had learnt the hard way the last time she had been undercover that appearances could be deceiving.

The line moved up and she saw they were close to the entrance to the convention hall. She had no idea how many people were waiting inside, but things appeared to be moving fairly quickly.

"Can I ask you something?" Julie asked.

"You just did," Amanda replied with a grin.

The girl giggled. "You're funny. No, I … are you from around here?"

"Yeah, I grew up out West Side."

"Did you go to Lynn Street High?" Julie asked.

She nodded. She had decided she didn't need a cover story this time and had stuck with the truth on her entry.

"I thought you looked familiar. I was a couple of years behind you at school. You were in the choir."

"For a while, yeah. Then I got busy with exams and stuff. You know how it is."

Julie nodded. "Yeah, I do. You're a good singer. How come you decided to audition?"

She shrugged. "Somebody heard me sing and thought I should give it a go. What about you?"

Julie sighed. "I always wanted to be a professional singer, but my dad ... he didn't even want me trying out for this. He said I'd be wasting my time."

"Maybe he just wants to protect you," Amanda told her gently, not sure if she believed it herself. Her father had always been encouraging.

The other girl shrugged. "I don't know. He's kind of ..."

"What?"

"Well, mean. Oh, not mean, exactly. I mean, he doesn't ... he's not like that. He just says stuff that kind of hurts."

"Julie, you don't have to listen to your dad. Sometimes people say things that do hurt but you have to tell yourself that you're better than that."

She felt sorry for the girl. She had been friends with another girl when she'd first started high school. Her friend had always acted a little secretive until one day Amanda had seen the girl arguing with her father. The man had then grabbed her arm and pulled her hard enough to unbalance her.

She had reported what she'd seen to her father and later learnt the girl's father had been arrested several times for domestic abuse and the mother had run away each time, only to return to him when he'd found the children.

She could still remember the look of devastation on her father's face when he'd come home late one night. Amanda's friend hadn't been at school and no one knew where she was.

Her dad had sat her down and told her that her friend was dead. The girl's father had tracked them down once again. He'd managed to get a shotgun and killed her mother before shooting the two children and turning the gun on himself. Only the couple's son had survived.

It was one of the few times she'd ever seen her father cry.

Amanda had been horrified at what had happened. She had gone to school the next day barely able to function, so lost in grief for her friend. She could remember telling her father that she was glad the girl's father was dead.

She'd had a long talk with her dad over those feelings. He'd eventually made her realise that being angry at the man was okay, but it wasn't healthy to hold onto that anger. It wouldn't bring her friend back.

He'd told her that he often heard of incidents of domestic violence in his job. While their family life was not picture perfect, she knew she was luckier than most kids her age.

Maybe Julie's situation wasn't as bad as those her father had talked about, but clearly she wasn't getting much encouragement at home.

"I'm sorry your dad's so negative but you know, it's not really his opinion that matters. Not in this competition."

The toughest part was that no matter how good a singer Julie was, if she didn't believe in herself and wasn't strong enough to handle the stress of the competition, it wouldn't make any difference.

"Thanks," Julie said, smiling brightly. "I feel better."

She calculated they'd been waiting about two hours when her number was finally called. They'd managed to get all the way into the main hall where the auditions were going on in the staging area.

She approached the floor manager, giving him her form. She was directed through a set of double doors. Four people sat at a trestle table at the far end. The room was lit with about four sets of overhead lights. Three cameras were set up around the room, clearly angled to get different shots of both the contestant and the judges. The floor manager had instructed her to ignore the cameras.

Gaffer tape was placed in the centre of the room in the shape of an 'X'. She guessed she was supposed to stand on the mark.

It was hot under the lights. Despite the cold outside, Amanda began to feel very warm. She'd chosen to wear just a simple pair of jeans and a woollen jumper with a t-shirt underneath but the heat from the lights had her sweating.

She saw Tama sitting at the end of the table. He smiled encouragingly. She smiled back, her nervousness returning.

There were two women in the judging panel. Amanda recognised the blonde from a show in the UK. She was a well-known actress and singer from the UK who, Amanda had been told, had been brought out by the producers to help with the competition.

"Hi there. What's your name?"

"Amanda," she said, fighting the urge to fidget.

"And you're how old?" the man sitting on the other side of the two women asked.

"Twenty."

Tama pretended to look at his tablet. She guessed her information had been scanned and sent to the device.

"You're a local girl?" he asked as if he didn't know.

"Yes."

"What kind of music do you like?" she was asked.

"Um, it depends. Some stuff from the 60s and 70s. Mostly pop or classic rock. Some of the modern stuff is okay, but my dad's a big fan of classic rock so I kind of grew up on that."

"What kind of classic rock?" the blonde asked.

"Steppenwolf, Pink Floyd." She named some other rock bands she'd grown up listening to. The judges looked suitably impressed.

"That's quite a list," the second woman said. There were nameplates in front of each judge, and she saw the second female judge was a singer who had been popular long before Amanda was born.

"So, what are you going to sing for us?"

"*Dream A Little Dream of Me*," she responded. It was the song she had practised with Tama and she felt confident she could do a good job.

The judges relaxed as she took a few deep breaths, then launched into the song. She sang clearly, remembering Tama's coaching, letting herself drift a little. It was a song she'd remembered her mother singing to her when she was very little. Before things had got bad between her parents. When her mother would say goodnight, she would often say: 'dream a little dream of me'.

As the final notes faded, the judges were quiet. The actress was smiling.

"Just beautiful," she said.

"What I like is you took a very well-known song but gave it a little something extra," Tama said. "What were you thinking about when you were singing?"

"My mum," she said. "She used to sing it to me when I was little. She left when I was a kid, but it always reminds me of her."

"So, sort of a bittersweet memory," the other woman pointed out. "You certainly brought that out in your singing. You're very talented, Amanda."

She looked at the others. "I think we should put it to a vote."

There were nods from the other three. Tama was first to respond. "Yes, from me."

The actress also nodded. "A definite yes."

The second man nodded. "Yes." It was curious that he hadn't commented on her audition but from what she remembered from the bio she'd been given, he rarely gave comments.

The second woman, who appeared to be the leader of the group, smiled. "That's four yeses," she said. "Congratulations. You're through to the next round."

"Thank you."

Amanda was guided to another room where a production assistant gave her the details for the next round. She lingered, reading through the paper

As she did so, the sound of Julie's voice could be heard as she sang.

She wondered if it was the girl's nervousness as, while technically brilliant, there wasn't much heart to the singing. The judges were understanding, at least, as they also voted for her to go through to the next round.

Julie was still pale but smiling as she came through the doors.

"I got through!" she said.

Amanda smiled. "Me too."

"I know. I heard you. I love that song." She threw her arms around Amanda's neck and hugged her. "Thank you for helping me out there. I was so nervous, but you made me feel so much better."

They turned to leave but a clattering sound had Amanda looking around. She glanced at Julie. Together they ran out to the main entrance, ignoring the production assistant who tried to call them back.

The floor manager was lying on the floor just outside the double doors. The judges had also come out to see what the noise was.

Julie gasped. "Look!" she said.

What appeared to be a heavy wall divider had fallen on top of the man. There was a pool of blood quickly spreading on the floor beneath his head. He'd clearly hit his head hard when he fell.

One of the judges bent down to check the man. A man who looked like an assistant came over with a cell phone in hand.

"I called an ambulance," he said. "Is he …?"

The woman nodded. "He's conscious, but it doesn't look good."

Amanda could tell they were trying to keep it

quiet as the judge and the assistant spoke.

"That's the fifth one," the assistant told the woman, who nodded.

"I know."

They both looked up and frowned, obviously having seen her watching. Amanda bit her lip and turned away, guiding Julie away from the scene.

Chapter Eight

Jim usually spent his free weekends out on his bike, cycling the trails and the back roads of West Side. The area was hilly, with winding roads leading out to the west coast. They were narrow, making it risky at times when local drivers decided to hug the side of the road instead of leaving him some clearance.

When he wasn't out cycling, he liked to drive out to the beach to surf. He was still learning the sport since he'd only taken it up when he'd moved to West Side. He'd grown up in a small town in the lower part of the North Island and apart from going out fishing with his dad, he'd never really spent much time in the water.

He'd had to be a fairly good swimmer when he'd joined the police, but he'd spent most of his time at the town's only pool instead of out in the ocean.

This particular Sunday, he had decided to skip both the cycle ride and the surfing. While it wasn't a cloudy day, it was a little windy and too cold to be in the water.

He went out to get some groceries. He normally

shared shopping duties with his flatmates but there were some things he preferred to buy for himself. Craig and Susan tended to drink more than he did, although he had noticed that since he'd been living with them, they had been more careful not to drink to excess. He had chosen not to lecture them on drinking and driving but they took more care anyway.

It was obvious that for some, living with a cop had its downsides.

He walked around the town centre and checked out the local real estate office for the property listings but didn't see anything within his price range. He'd managed to put a bit of money away for the past few years, hoping to use it as a deposit on a house, but even with his savings, he doubted he would be able to get a mortgage. Or at least enough to afford the kind of house he wanted.

As he turned to cross the road to head to the supermarket, he saw a group of youths loitering, yelling out something he couldn't hear to a woman walking past. The woman was a few years older than him and a little overweight. She was clearly trying to ignore whatever the youths were saying but Jim could see from the expression on her face that it bothered her.

Two of the group had decided to stand in her way, again yelling something which appeared to upset her. She tried to get past, but they would not let up.

He decided to talk to the youths and see if he could distract them but figured he should at least have some back-up on hand. He pulled his phone out of his pocket and dialled.

"Yeah, Dawson, it's Andersen. You got some guys near the mall?"

"Yeah, a couple of them are patrolling the mall. What's up?"

"A group of teenage boys. They're hassling a woman. Figured I should speak to them."

"Isn't this your weekend off?" Stu asked.

"Yeah, but you know how it is."

"Yeah. I'll send the guys over." The senior constable told him to tread carefully and hung up.

Jim approached the youths. The five boys smirked at him. They appeared to be trying to look 'gangsta', wearing denim jackets with patches and bandannas on their heads.

With the group's attention focused on him, the woman was able to move away. She shot him a look of gratitude

"Hey guys, how's it goin'?" he asked, keeping his tone casual.

"Yeah, bro. All good."

"You guys wouldn't be hassling that lady, now would you?"

"Nah, we're just having a bit of fun, bro."

"What're you doin', bro?" another asked.

"Just hanging," he said.

"You got money for smokes, mate?" a fourth asked him.

He shook his head. He'd got a whiff of stale cigarette smoke and something else. Two of the youths looked as if they had been smoking whatever it was. Their eyelids drooped a little and were slightly red-rimmed. He couldn't be sure without testing them but wondered if they'd been smoking P.

"Wish I did but I'm flat broke," he lied, relieved to

spot two uniformed officers heading toward the youths.

"Aw, sucks to be you!"

The two officers, both from West Side station, nodded at him as they reached the group. They obviously knew him but didn't let on to the boys.

"You boys shouldn't be loitering," Constable Kevin Doherty said.

The protests were loud and vehement.

"Man, we're not doing nothing!"

"We have reports you've been harassing pedestrians," Doherty told them. "Either move along and find something useful to do or you'll have to come with us to the station."

"You can't make us!"

"Yes, we can."

It looked as if it was about to be a stand-off, but the group got up and walked off, still protesting loudly about their rights. Jim watched them go, turning to the officers.

"Thanks," he said.

"No problem," the woman replied. She was pretty with olive skin and dark hair. She had a slight accent when she spoke. "They're pretty well-known. Gang wanna-bes." She frowned. "Andersen, right? You transferred from Wellington about four months ago."

He nodded. "Yeah. You are?"

"Ana Subramani. I was based at Central, but I started at West Side a couple weeks ago."

"Oh. Right. You know those guys from Central?"

She nodded. "Yeah. They hang around the city centres and then move on. They mostly seem pretty harmless."

"I don't know. I think one or two of them might

have been smoking meth. I caught a whiff of something, but I don't think it was weed."

Ana nodded her agreement. "But you know how it is."

The bosses at police headquarters had sent word down the line that they were to be more cautious when making accusations just on a hunch or circumstantial evidence. Jim didn't like it, but since it was the official word, he had little choice.

The order had come after a complaint had been made to the Police Complaints division. A youth had been suspected of smoking drugs and the parents had objected to the way their son had been questioned. The fact that the police handling the case were proved right later hadn't changed the outcome.

Jim carried on into the mall and got the things he needed at the supermarket. He always liked to get in and out as quickly as possible. Gaby had kidded him about that, saying it was such a typical male thing to do.

He should give her a call, he thought. See if she was doing anything that afternoon. Then he remembered she was on duty that weekend.

As he turned to leave the mall, he heard his name being called. He turned around and Amanda caught his arm.

"I was calling you," she said. "I saw you in the supermarket."

"Sorry. Guess I was miles away."

He noticed a glint of gold as something on her wrist caught the beam of sunlight coming in through a gap in the roof of the carpark. He was pleased to note that she was wearing the charm bracelet he'd given her for her birthday.

"So, what's up?" he asked.

"Did you get my text yesterday?" she said.

He frowned at her. "What text?"

She huffed in reply. "I texted you when I was at the audition. There was some guy hanging around, bothering some of the girls there. He started hassling me and I thought it was a little weird, so I sent you a pic. Don't you have your phone on you?"

He felt for the phone in his pocket, trying to remember if he'd received any messages the day before. As he looked at his phone, he realised she had sent him a message and he hadn't even looked at it. It happened. He got several messages each day and he had overlooked a few before.

"Oh, shit! Sorry. I didn't even look at it."

She scowled. "Well, some help you are! Did you know there was another accident yesterday?"

"Another one? How many does that make it?"

"I heard someone say it was the fifth one. I think there have been others in other centres. Can you look into some of the crew? See if there's some kind of correlation?"

He frowned again at her. "What am I? Your own personal search engine?"

"Well, it's not like I can hack into police records, now is it?" she replied with a smirk.

"I'm sure you would if you knew how," he retorted.

Her eyes widened in apparent innocence. She slapped a hand against her chest.

"Would I do such a thing?" she asked.

"I wouldn't put it past you," he replied. "Anyway, how did it go?"

"It went all right," she said. "There was a girl

there who was way more nervous than I was. She seemed nice though. She was there when the accident happened. The floor manager."

"What happened?" he asked.

"I think it was a set divider or something. I don't really know what they call those things. One of the heavy ones. It fell on him. It looked like he cracked his skull on the floor when he fell. I texted Tama but I haven't heard back from him yet."

Jim looked at her. "Tama would be …?"

"One of the judges. He came with the producer to talk to the agency." She frowned. "I told you that on Friday! Did you forget already?"

He shrugged and apologised. "Guess I did." He held up his bag. "I should get this stuff in the car," he said. "Walk with me."

Amanda followed him, telling him about the audition. He was impressed. While he assumed the judges had been told to let her through anyway, he was certain she would do well, if she could get over her nerves.

The young woman hadn't struck him as the nervy type, but he guessed that after what had happened the last time she had got so involved in a case, she was worried about doing a good job.

"So, what are your thoughts?" he asked as he put his stuff in the boot.

"It's too early to draw any conclusions," she said.

He nodded, accessing the text message she'd sent the day before. He groaned quietly to himself as he recognised the kid in the photo.

"What is it?" Amanda asked.

He showed her the photo. "I just saw this kid not half an hour ago. Damn it!"

He quietly berated himself for having missed the text. Had he known earlier, he might have been able to question the youth further.

"You think it's something?" she asked. "I mean, he was just hassling a few people. Girls, mostly, from what I heard."

"Yeah, that's what he was doing earlier. Hassling women. I'll check up on him. Thanks. That was good spotting."

Amanda looked quietly pleased. Jim frowned as a sound came from her bag. It reminded him a little of the background music to a Tom and Jerry cartoon chase scene.

She dug in her bag and pulled out her cell phone, turning away from him to answer it.

"Amanda Steele. Hi, Tama." There was a brief pause as she listened. "What? My God! Thanks for letting me know."

She looked upset when she finally turned back to face him.

"The guy who got hurt yesterday. He's dead."

Chapter Nine

Amanda drove home, wondering how the new development was going to affect the case. From what Jim had told her, the accident was going to have to be thoroughly investigated. If not by the police, then by the local investigators at the occupational health and safety agency

It didn't bode well.

Penny was home when she got in the door, watching something on television. She was still in her pyjamas.

"Plan on getting dressed sometime soon?" Amanda asked. "It's after eleven."

The brunette scowled at her. "It's Sunday. I don't have to do anything."

Amanda sighed. It was always the same. Penny was the lazy one in the flat, refusing to do dishes on weekends. Not that she did them during the week either. Housework was a dirty word to the twenty-four-year-old.

She flopped down on the couch, pushing aside the empty packets of potato chips and chocolate her flatmate had tossed carelessly.

"You keep eating that stuff, you'll get fat."

Penny snorted. "You can talk."

"At least I exercise," she said.

"Well, bully for you. Oh, your ex-boyfriend said to say 'hi'," she added with a smirk. Amanda was annoyed. The other woman constantly tried to rub it in that she was now dating Matt.

"Do you think I care that you're going out with him? All I can say is, he must be nuts to even consider someone like you."

"You're jealous."

She bristled at the woman's accusation. Not that she was right. It was more the fact that Penny seemed to think she was a far better choice because she was willing to sleep with someone. Amanda had long decided that sex was something she would consider only if the relationship was serious. She didn't believe in one-night stands herself.

"No, actually, I'm not. Because as far as I'm concerned, if a guy chooses to break up with me because I won't sleep with him, then he's not worth crying over."

Penny shrugged, looking as if she didn't believe a word Amanda was saying. She turned back to whatever she was watching on the television. Amanda could see it was a soap. It ran on weekdays, but they also ran all the episodes from the week on a Sunday morning. She snorted. She had better things to do than watch melodrama.

She went into the kitchen to put away her small bag of groceries, only to find that Penny had not only not done her dishes, but she'd also used those Amanda had washed that morning and left to air dry. Sighing, she began filling the sink with water to wash them again, grimacing at the food scraps still on the plates.

"Bathroom needs cleaning," Penny called out.

"What am I? Your servant?" Amanda shouted back. "Go clean it yourself!"

"Eww, no! There's hair in the shower drain."

"Yeah, and it's dark hair, so that means it's yours!"

"Whatever!"

Amanda rolled her eyes and continued washing. Just as she pulled the plug to let the water out, Penny came in with more dirty plates.

"Here you go," she said cheerfully.

"Forget it. I just finished washing the mountain of dishes you left. What the hell do you do with them all? Leave them in your room?"

"God, you're such a grouch!" Penny replied with a scowl.

"I wouldn't be if you actually did your bit around here instead of leaving me to do it all!" she retorted.

Ignoring her flatmate's complaints, Amanda went to her room to tidy up and vacuum the floor. She had just finished when Penny barged in.

"Your 'friend' is here to see you," she said with a smirk.

Frowning, Amanda stared at her. Penny just shot her a bitchy look and walked out. She finished putting things away and went out, in time to hear her flatmate gushing to the visitor about how she had been busy cleaning.

From the answering snort and the low rumble of the man's voice, Amanda could tell the visitor didn't believe her at all.

She returned to the living room. Penny was shooting flirtatious looks at Jim, who appeared to be oblivious. He'd told her a few weeks earlier that he didn't like her flatmate but in the interests of keeping the peace he pretended not to notice the other woman's behaviour.

"Hey," she said as if she hadn't already run into him that day. "What's up?"

"I was at a loose end and thought you might want to come for a drive." He shot a hard look at Penny, who didn't seem to notice.

"Yeah, let me just grab my keys," she said, jumping at the chance. She knew he was just giving an excuse so Penny wouldn't be too nosy. He knew she tried not to discuss her work with the other woman.

"What about the cleaning?" her flatmate asked.

"I've done my bit. It's your turn to clean the bathroom."

"But ... I don't ..."

"You know what they say about clutter, don't you?" Jim told the brunette.

"No, what do they say?"

"That it's a sign of a cluttered mind."

Yeah, right, Amanda thought. That airhead has a cluttered mind?

Ignoring the other woman's protests, she grabbed her jacket and keys from her room and left the house. Jim held the passenger door open for her.

They were quiet for a few minutes as he pulled out of the driveway and drove out of the street before turning onto the highway.

"God, how can you stand that woman?" he asked finally.

She bit her lip. Penny had her moments. When she wasn't being self-centred, she could be a good friend.

The trouble was those moments were rare.

"You know what she is, don't you?"

"No. What?"

"A narcissist."

She frowned. "I don't see that."

"Don't you? My mum would say she exhibits classic symptoms of narcissism. She thinks the world revolves around her and is more interested in getting what she wants than in getting along with others."

"Is your mum a psychologist or something?" Amanda asked, thinking Jim had to have got the idea from somewhere.

"Yeah, actually. She teaches it at Massey." Massey was a university in a city further down the island, although it also had campuses in Auckland and in Wellington. It had started off as an agricultural college but had expanded and now offered several different disciplines, including psychology.

She sighed. If she recalled the definition correctly, a narcissist was often arrogant and took advantage of others. They also tended to be more demanding. Penny was certainly all of that.

"How did you end up living with her, anyway?" Jim asked.

"Well, I went to school with her brother. Lucas. He's at uni now. Canterbury. Studying law, I think. Anyway, Dad kind of kicked me out of home and I was looking for a place to live. Lucas suggested I take over his room. Penny was okay back then. A little self-centred, I guess, but we got along okay in the beginning."

He was staring at her. "Wait a second. Back up a bit. Your dad kicked you out?"

"Well, it wasn't really like that. He just thought

that I should find a place of my own. I mean, I'd always been sort of independent since Mum left. Dad's a big believer in letting me find my own way. You know, cutting the apron strings, so to speak. Not that he ever wears one, except when he's barbecuing."

Jim snorted with laughter. "Yeah, somehow I can't imagine your dad wearing an apron saying, 'Kiss the Cook'."

She laughed. "Yeah. One year for Father's Day I got him this joke apron. It had this picture of a naked woman's body on it. No face or anything. It wasn't rude. He thought it was hilarious."

"Ha! Sounds like Pete!" She watched as he drove along the motorway, headed for the city. "You and your dad seem really close," he said.

"Yeah, we are. I mean, don't get me wrong. Dad and I have had our share of fights. He used to be kind of over-protective. It's not his fault. I guess it was hard for him, being both Mum and Dad."

Jim nodded. "I hear that."

She studied him for a few moments. "Can I ask you something?"

He turned his head to grin at her. "You just did."

"Oh, you're funny!"

"I try. What's your question?"

"How old were you when your real mum died?"

She winced at the phrasing. The way he talked about his stepmother, she was as much his real mum as if she'd given birth to him. He obviously loved her a great deal as he always adopted a fond expression when he mentioned her.

"Sorry, that was badly phrased. I meant …"

"I know what you meant," he said quietly. "I was

only a few months old when she died."

"How did she …" She hesitated. "That was way too personal. I'm sorry."

"It's okay. It was breast cancer. She was only twenty-three."

Amanda sighed. As much as she and Jim could at times be at odds with each other, she felt bad that he'd lost his birth mother at such a young age.

"God, so young! I'm sorry. I guess you never really got a chance to get to know her."

"No, but it's okay. Anticipating any other questions, Dad met Lesleigh when I was six. I was a little shit to her at first, but she won me over."

She remembered him saying something about that earlier. She sat back, returning to watching the road, trying to figure out where Jim was taking her.

She got her answer a short time later when he turned into the main entry for the hospital and took a ticket for the parking building.

"What are we doing here?" she asked.

"I wanted you to meet someone." He turned into a car park. "I called him after I met you at the supermarket. Uh, how squeamish are you?"

She looked at him suspiciously. "Why? Where exactly are we going?"

"You'll see. Come on."

She followed him into the hospital, frowning as he took the lift down to the basement and led her along a maze of corridors.

"You're taking me to the morgue?" she asked.

"Well, Pathology, actually. Yes," he added, before she could ask. "It is where they do the autopsies."

"This guy …"

"Is a friend of mine. We went to school together."

He stopped at a door and was about to knock when it opened. A man who appeared to be the same age as Jim came out. Amanda saw he was of Asian descent and very good-looking. He was wearing a white lab coat that had an ink stain on one of the pockets.

"Hey, Jim. I figured you'd be here about now. I was just going to get a coffee at the café. Join me?"

"Sure. Billy, this is my friend Amanda. Amanda Steele, Billy Chang."

Amanda put her hand forward to shake the man's hand but hesitated. He winked at her.

"Don't worry. I haven't had my hand in a body all day today."

"Oh, that's comforting," she replied snarkily. "You know if I hadn't known already that you and Jim went to the same school together, I would have guessed it anyway since you two seem to share the same sense of humour."

Billy laughed and looked at Jim. "Well, can't say you didn't warn me about her."

Jim wrapped an arm around her shoulders. "Amanda's an acquired taste," he replied.

She shoved him, only half-teasing. "So are your jokes," she retorted.

"Man, everyone's a critic!"

Chapter Ten

Jim noticed that Billy and Amanda seemed to hit it off straight away. They were chatting amiably as they sat at the table in the café, having already ordered their coffees.

"So, Jim tells me you work for a private investigator," Billy was saying.

She nodded. "Yeah. I've been working for them for about eight months now. It's okay work. Nothing too demanding, I guess."

"You wanted to be a cop? Like your dad?"

Amanda shot Jim a look. "Gee, Jim's been doing a lot of talking about me, I see."

Billy laughed. "Yeah, he's a regular gossip. Seriously, he hasn't told me that much. Just that your dad is his boss and that you want to be a cop one day."

One of the café workers came over with their coffees and deposited them on the table. Amanda took hers.

"One day, I guess. I mean, I like what I'm doing now. Did Jim also tell you I'm helping on a case?"

"He mentioned it."

What am I? Chopped liver? Jim thought, feeling a little left out as the pair continued talking. Amanda began telling Billy about the case she'd worked on and Billy responded by telling her what he was doing in the morgue.

"I like it. I'm thinking of specialising in it when I'm finished my residency. I mean, I know it's not as exciting as it looks on tv, but it's nice to be able to help families get some sort of closure."

Jim decided to interject. "Are you assisting on the autopsy of the man who fell at the Star Quest auditions?"

Billy shot him a look. Jim had already mentioned the case when he'd called his friend. The autopsy probably hadn't even been started, so a resident wouldn't have been assigned to assist yet, the other man had told him. Jim had wanted to introduce Amanda to his friend thinking he might be able to help her a little.

He knew what Gaby would say. He was just doing the kid a favour. It wasn't as if he had any actual romantic feelings toward her.

Amanda looked at Billy. "Uh … that's the case I'm working on now," she said quietly. "I was there when it happened." She sighed. "I didn't see him fall if that's what you're going to ask."

"No, it's okay. Jim just loves playing white knight."

Amanda snorted. "Yeah, sure. He probably just figures that he's cutting out the middleman, so I won't pester him for information."

It was Jim's turn to snort. "Yeah, right. You really think I would do that so you'd annoy Billy instead?

Give me some credit. I just thought it would be useful for the two of you to meet."

"Yeah, you keep telling yourself that, dude," Billy replied.

Amanda cocked an eyebrow. "'Dude'?" she said. "You either spend half your time surfing or you watch way too much tv."

Billy laughed. "Don't look at me. He's the surfer," he said, pointing with his thumb at Jim.

The girl shot him an amused look. She didn't have to say a word. Her expression said it all.

"Okay, you two need to stop making fun of me," he retorted.

"Oh, but you're so easy to make fun of," Amanda replied.

He narrowed his eyes and glared at her. His friend laughed at his reaction.

"Too easy," Billy returned. He turned back to Amanda. "Anyway, I'm not too sure who's been assigned to the autopsy, but I can find out and give you a call if we find anything unusual."

She beamed at him. "Thanks. Let me give you my number."

Eventually, the conversation turned to other things. Billy had been dating a girl for a while but had recently broken up with her.

"I hear you're dating a girl from the Geek Squad," the other man said.

Jim shot his friend a look. He thought the term had only been used around work.

"Gaby," he said. "And she's hardly a geek."

"Actually, she's really nice," Amanda said. "I've met her. Although I don't know what she's doing with this loser." Billy snorted with laughter.

Jim bristled and glared at them both. He was surprised Amanda was so complimentary about Gaby, but then again, she was only ever sarcastic with him.

Billy had to get back to work so Jim left him to it, driving Amanda back home.

"Thanks," she said. "For introducing me."

"You're welcome," he replied. "I thought Billy would be a good contact for you to have. He assisted on the case you had before. You know, that girl Lori?"

"Yeah."

Lori had died of a drug overdose, but Billy had uncovered information that told police she had been murdered.

"So, I start rehearsals tomorrow," she said. "I think there are about fifty of us. Then they whittle it down to five finalists."

"Is this thing televised?" he asked.

"Yeah. Well, it will be. I think they're recording the first few shows and airing them later. The final show's going to be live," she explained.

"You might want to talk to Tama and see if you can find out what insurance they have on the production. If these accidents keep happening…"

"They might decide to cancel it." She nodded. "Thanks. I'll check it out."

Jim made a note to see if there was any footage or surveillance of the conference hall. He'd have to go through channels, but he was sure once Pete knew the score, he'd make sure they got what they needed.

He drove Amanda back to her place. Penny's car was gone which meant she'd taken off somewhere. They'd been gone maybe two hours at the most and he doubted the woman would have done any cleaning.

He stopped the car in the driveway, putting it in 'park' before turning to look at Amanda.

"What are you going to do about Penny?" he asked.

She shrugged. "I don't know. It's not like I can afford to live anywhere else."

"It's obvious she's causing a lot of friction between you two. Look, Amanda, maybe we're not friends," he said, remembering she'd referred to them as 'frienemies' in a previous conversation, "but I can't help noticing you've been a little down. And I'm fairly sure it's got something to do with her."

She sighed. "It has everything to do with her. I mean, her dating Matt and rubbing it in my face. I told her I don't care, but …"

"You do."

"I mean, what kind of person does that? So, she gives him something I won't."

"You really need to find a new place to live," he said.

"Yeah, I get that," she replied. "I want to get a place closer to work, but the closer you are, the more expensive it is. I don't earn much."

"How would you feel about living with a cop?" he asked. He was sure he'd heard somewhere on the grapevine that one of the officers in central was looking for someone to share their place.

She looked at him, cocking an eyebrow. "You mean, you?"

He choked back a laugh. "God no! We'd drive each other crazy in the space of five minutes. No. I thought someone in town might be looking."

Amanda looked out the window at the building. She was clearly not happy living there. Her flatmate seemed to think she could just do whatever she wanted and treat others like they were beneath her. The few times Jim had visited the place, he'd never seen any kind of decoration which gave any hint of someone other than Penny living there. It was as if Amanda didn't exist. Or she was only there to be a servant.

"Okay," she said. "Maybe I'll talk to my dad in the meantime." She opened the door and smiled at him. "Thanks."

Pete called a meeting early the next morning. The detective sergeant quickly dealt with the normal weekend report and handed out assignments.

"Anyone got anything else?" he asked.

Jim took the opportunity. "There was an accident at the Star Quest auditions on Saturday," he said.

"I thought Central was looking after that," Kirsten said.

"They are, but the floor manager was hurt. He died Saturday night."

"And you would know this how?" the woman asked.

"Yeah, I haven't even looked at the emails yet," Chapman interjected.

Jim shot him a withering look. It was always the rookie's job to check communications before the meeting. Greg Mitchum, who was Pete's second in command, began to chastise the new team member. The detective appeared annoyed at being told off and was muttering something, which started Kirsten murmuring something else.

Pete raised a hand. "All right, simmer down,

people. Andersen, what else do you have on this?"

"Not much, just that a divider fell on him. My contact in the morgue isn't handling the case but he will find out who is and get back to me. I'm guessing the cause of death is going to be blunt-force trauma."

"That show's been plagued with accidents since they announced auditions," his boss remarked. He looked at Chapman. "Follow up with the producers and get a list of the accidents at other centres, then see if anyone's been looking into them."

"Sure, boss," he said.

Jim hung back after the meeting. Pete looked at him expectantly. He obviously knew enough about his daughter's involvement, but she must not have told him about the accident.

"Amanda was there when it happened," he told him.

Her father immediately looked worried, but Jim shook his head.

"She's fine. A little upset, but that's understandable. She didn't see what happened. I was going to see if I could get any footage."

Pete nodded. He stroked his chin. "Those dividers are quite heavy," he observed. "They wouldn't fall by themselves."

"No, I guess they wouldn't," Jim replied. "But then I've never been on a movie set."

His boss frowned. "They film that show out here somewhere."

"What show?" he asked. Pete frowned.

"Maybe more than one. I'll make a couple of calls."

"You want me to go talk to them?"

"We don't know if there's anything to investigate

other than a sudden death," Pete reminded him. "But contact the producers and see if they'll hand over the footage. I'm sure Nixon will already have had the guys check out the conference hall so follow that up with them."

"Will do, boss. I guess it goes without saying you want me to keep an eye on Amanda?"

Pete grinned. "Think you two can get along without resorting to childish name-calling?"

"Hey, she started it," he replied, chuckling. Well, she had called him a cave-dweller.

"Out!" his boss ordered.

Chapter Eleven

The convention hall was already busy when Amanda got to rehearsals late that afternoon. The first show was going to be in three weeks and all the talent would need to work with coaches before they could perform.

As she made her way through the crowd to report to the woman who would be her singing coach, she saw a uniformed police officer and what she assumed was a detective talking to a man she recognised as a former talent show host. She'd read in the packet Tama had given her that the man, now a radio host, was one of the producers.

The man's claim to fame for years had been a baby-face. He'd acted in a couple of local shows before getting a job hosting a talent show – a precursor to the one Tama had been in. Aged in his late fifties, he had moved up to management for one of the local production companies.

The hall where the accident had happened had been taped off and a security guard stood in front, keeping people from entering the area.

She heard her name being called and turned and looked at the woman.

"I'm Debbie," the woman said, smiling at her. She was probably in her forties, although it was hard for Amanda to tell. Her hair was dyed a blue-grey, a colour which had been extremely popular among celebrities for a while.

She could smell the faint acrid odour of cigarette smoke on the older woman. Debbie also had a husky voice characteristic of someone who smoked regularly, and her skin had that aged look she'd seen with other smokers.

"Any trouble getting here?" she asked kindly.

"No. I work in an office not far from here. I live out west, but I usually commute on the train. Parking's a nightmare."

The other woman nodded. "Yeah, I hear you." She gestured toward a room off the convention hall.

"We'd normally meet in my studio, but unfortunately, it was booked by my business partner, so we'll have to make do. I read in your application you don't play an instrument."

"Not really. I started learning piano when I was a kid but after my mum left my dad couldn't take me to lessons, so I stopped."

Debbie showed her to a darkened room. As she switched on the lights, Amanda saw a large piano in the centre. It dwarfed the rest of the room.

"This was used as storage," Debbie explained, "but with so many people needing to rehearse for the first show, they did the best with what they had. The acoustics are pretty good though."

Amanda nodded. Knowing she needed to get started on her investigation, she wondered how she was supposed to approach this.

Debbie studied her for a moment.

"I can see we need to break the ice a little, so before we get started, I think we should spend a little time getting to know each other. Don't you?"

"Sounds like a good idea."

They sat on the piano bench. Debbie smiled at her as Amanda sat on the end, leaving a little space between them.

"I don't bite," she said.

"Oh, it's okay. I'm just a big believer in personal space."

"Why don't I start then?" the other woman suggested. "I moved here from the Netherlands when I was five. I began singing in school, tried to make it as a pop singer, didn't make it, then got into musical theatre. Let's see, married, two kids, divorced. Both kids in high school now."

"Wow!" Amanda said, amazed at the way she'd condensed forty years of her life into less than a minute. "Okay. Mum left when I was eight, Dad's a cop. Only child. I work in an office downtown. Um, I started singing not long after Mum left. Got into the school choir and the teacher I guess took a shine to me, so she began teaching me some of the technical stuff. That's it."

"Why did you decide to join Star Quest?" Debbie asked.

Tama had coached her carefully on what to say. One of the things Amanda had learnt was the best way to lie believably was to use just enough of the truth without giving it all away.

"Well, this guy I know heard me singing karaoke and he suggested I audition. I mean, I'm not really expecting too much. Most people don't even make it through the first round."

The older woman nodded. "You seem to have a good grasp of the realities of shows like this. You're right. Most people don't make it through the first round, but I think you'll go a little further than that. I heard your audition and you are a good singer. Never doubt that." She sighed. "A lot of people come to auditions with stars in their eyes hoping to make it big."

"I guess the competition can get pretty fierce," Amanda said.

"I've been to a few of these things. You want to see fierce, try auditioning for a part in a musical," she added with a grimace. "We're talking cat-fights. And that wasn't even for *Superstar*."

"You were in *Jesus Christ, Superstar*?" Amanda asked, referring to a world-famous musical which had been performed many times over. By many different casts. "I always wanted to see that."

Debbie nodded. "Oh yes, I was understudy to Rochelle Conley. I took over when she had to leave the show. For personal reasons," she added.

Amanda smiled at the other woman, storing the information away. Rochelle Conley was a well-known singer who had become famous after she had won an international music competition with her band. While her career had stalled after she had semi-retired to have a family, she had made a comeback with famous roles in musicals. Then about twenty years ago she had stopped performing.

"What about the man in the accident the other day?" Amanda asked.

Debbie patted her knee. "I wouldn't worry about that. I'm sure that was just an accident." She got up. "Let's get to work. What song were you planning on singing in the first show?"

"Um, I don't know. What about something from R.E.M.?"

Debbie looked dubious. "I'm not sure that's wise. You're soprano?"

"I think I'm more mezzo-soprano. I don't quite have the range."

The woman sat down at the piano and began playing scales. "Let's start with something simple. Why don't you sing *Amazing Grace*?"

She listened as the introductory bars played and tried to recall the lessons her teacher had taught her about breathing, beginning to sing the first verse in a key slightly lower than the one Debbie was playing.

She stopped as the woman frowned and cleared her throat.

"Sorry. Wrong key," she said.

"That's all right. Just take a few deep breaths. You're probably a bit nervous."

"Yeah, a little," she admitted, although not for the reason the other woman was thinking.

Debbie turned on the seat. "Let's try a few exercises first. Roll your shoulders," she said, demonstrating first one way, then the other. "Relax your neck. Try gently rolling it around." Amanda did so. "Good. Now take a few deep breaths, letting them out slowly."

The singing coach showed her a few more exercises, finishing by getting Amanda to place her hands on either side of her cheeks and massaging her jaw.

When they tried the song again, she was more relaxed and able to follow the music.

She left the hall a couple of hours later, feeling

tired, her throat slightly scratchy from singing almost non-stop.

Her father stood outside the convention hall, clearly waiting for her.

"Dad?" she said. "What are you doing here?"

"Thought I'd see how rehearsals went," he replied, glancing behind her. Amanda turned her head slightly and realised they weren't alone. Another contestant was standing in the entryway.

"Come on," her father said. "I'll give you a ride home."

"Thanks, Dad," she replied.

It wasn't normal for her father to suddenly show up and offer her a ride home. Of course, Jim had done it a couple of times, but that was different.

As Amanda got in the car and buckled her seatbelt, she looked at her father.

"Okay, what's up?" she asked.

"I made a couple of calls and thought you should meet with a friend of mine. He invited us to dinner at his place."

She decided not to ask any more questions. Her father's policy had always been a 'don't ask, don't tell' one, especially when it came to her own life. She knew he'd tell her what was up when the time was right.

As he drove, he asked her about the audition. She hadn't had a chance to talk to him about what had happened that weekend.

"Jim told you about the floor manager," she said.

"Yes. I asked him to keep an eye on things, but I thought since this guy we're going to see is a friend of mine he might be more willing to talk to you." He stopped the car at a traffic light and glanced at her.

"How are things with you and Jim?"

"They're fine. Why?"

"You two seem to be getting along well."

"You mean, compared to when we first met? He's all right. He kind of grows on a person," she admitted grudgingly.

Her father laughed. "Yeah, they do that."

He had that kind of tone that had always irritated her as a teenager. Where he apparently knew something she didn't. She hoped he wasn't reading too much into her relationship with Jim.

"What are you trying to say, Dad?" she asked. "Don't go trying to matchmake. I'm perfectly capable of finding my own boyfriend. And Jim Andersen is definitely not boyfriend material."

"Sure, say that now." He continued chuckling. "You know, your mum and I hated each other at first."

"Do I really need to hear this?"

"I'm just saying that sometimes love and hate are two sides of the same coin."

"I don't hate him," she said. "I just … you know what, I'm not going to play this game. You keep your nose out of my love life."

He snorted. "Oh, well, excuse me for taking an interest in my daughter's happiness."

"This has nothing to do with happiness," she said. "Why don't you go out and get yourself a girlfriend? I mean, it's not like you're too old to date."

"And here I was thinking I should start looking at retirement homes," he said. "The way you go on."

She sighed. "Dad come on. I don't think that. Besides, it's been twelve years since Mum left."

As far as she knew, he hadn't really dated anyone

since the divorce. She knew he still had feelings for her mother, but Kim Steele hadn't made any effort to contact them, other than the occasional birthday card for Amanda. She hadn't even gone to the divorce hearing.

"I know, honey. And you're right. I've been holding a candle for your mum for too long."

He turned into a side street and slowed the car, obviously looking for the right house. It was getting dark, making it harder to see numbers on the letterboxes.

After a few moments, he stopped the car, parking it on the roadside before getting out. Amanda followed him up the path to the front door.

The owner must have seen the car as the door was opened just as they got there.

"Hey, Pete. Glad you could make it."

She studied the man who had greeted them. He was only a year or two older than her father, a good-looking man with thick, grey hair and a gleaming smile. She frowned. He looked a little familiar.

"So, this is Amanda, huh?" the man said. His accent had a slight twang to it which sounded to her almost the same as a boy she'd known in her first year of high school. The boy's family had moved from Australia a couple of years earlier.

He held out a hand. "Richard Butler," he said. "Well, I have to say, Pete, your daughter is prettier than you said she was." He waved his hand behind them. "Anyway, come on in. My wife's just putting the kid to bed for the night."

They followed the man into a large room which was clearly the living room. It was comfortably furnished with an overstuffed couch in chocolate brown suede fabric with matching armchairs. There were toys scattered in one corner.

He gestured for them to sit.

"Something to drink?" he asked.

"Beer for me. Honey?"

"Um, just orange juice, please," she said.

"Comin' right up," the man said. He went out through the double doors and came back in a minute or so later with drinks in hand.

Amanda glanced at her father before looking at the man.

"So, how do you know my dad, Mr Butler?"

"Oh, Richard. Please," he said in almost a booming voice. "Your dad was visiting on-set a couple of years ago."

"I was consulting on a storyline on the show," her father replied.

"Turns out your dad's a pretty mean cardsharp. We teamed up on some games."

"Yeah, he loves his poker," she returned wryly.

A woman with dark blonde hair joined them, sitting in one of the armchairs with a glass of wine.

"Pete, Amanda, this is my wife Zoe."

"Hello," the woman said. She didn't seem to know too much about them as she appeared wary.

"Anyway, your dad mentioned something about you doing Star Quest. I heard there was an accident at the auditions the other day."

She nodded. "How … I mean, why did you …"

"I'm a producer on my show," Richard told her. "I started off in theatre in Sydney, doing set design, then got into acting."

She frowned, remembering as a kid she'd watched a couple of Australian television soaps.

"Wait, you were in that show … what was it called?" She frowned, trying to remember what she'd seen him in.

"Which one?" he asked with a grin.

"The soap," she said. "In Aussie."

He nodded. "There are a few of them in Oz, but I know the one you mean. I left there and came out here about twelve years ago. Started in a comedy that hardly anyone saw and worked my way up into producing. It's how Zoe and I met," he added, smiling at his wife, who smiled back.

The conversation continued over dinner. Amanda glanced at her father, realising that he'd brought her here in the hope she could pick up a clue to what had happened in the audition.

"So, Rich, you mentioned something about problems with some of the equipment on your show," her father prompted as they were eating dessert. "Got any examples?"

"Like how a divider wall might fall on top of someone?" Richard asked with a wry grin. "Don't think I don't know why you really came tonight, Pete. Always a cop."

"I notice you haven't answered the question," Pete returned, narrowing his eyes at his friend.

The man looked at Amanda, his blue eyes twinkling.

"Your dad's a sly one," he said. "Okay, Pete, I'll give it to you straight. There's no way in hell one of those things could suddenly fall like that. For one thing, they're at least a couple metres high, maybe even higher. The bases are pretty sturdy. Unless …"

"Unless what?" Amanda asked.

"Unless something happened to cause it to overbalance somehow. Give it a good bump and over it goes." He looked at her father. "Is that what you think might have happened in this case, Pete?"

"Don't know, but we're sure going to look closely into it."

Chapter Twelve

Jim had arranged to meet with one of the producers at the television studio after clearing it with Central. It was technically their case, but he figured the more officers working on it, the sooner it could be cleared up. The studio itself was based in West Side, which also worked in his favour.

As he parked his car and headed into the front office, his phone rang.

"Andersen."

"Hey, Jim, it's Billy."

"Hey, mate, what's up?"

"Well, I've been looking into that autopsy you and your friend were asking about the other day. When you've got a minute or three, can you pop up to the hospital?"

"Yeah. I've got an appointment to go to now, but I should be free this afternoon."

"Great. I'll see you then," his friend said.

Jim ended the call with a slight frown. Billy was doing him a favour by looking into the death, but he wouldn't ask to see him so soon unless the autopsy performed by the pathologist in charge of the case had uncovered something unusual.

He entered the office and smiled at the receptionist.

"Detective Andersen," he said. "I'm here to see Myles."

The woman nodded. She was an attractive woman, around thirty-five, he would guess, with lovely dark tan skin characteristic of Pacific Islanders.

"If you wouldn't mind signing the visitor book," she said with a smile. "Then take a seat. I'm sure he won't be long."

"Of course. Thank you."

He signed his name in the book and sat down on the leather couch. As he waited, he saw cast photographs from a show that had screened on television for five seasons.

"Detective?"

He looked up at the man who had appeared before him, recognising him from the studio's website. He'd read the man's bio and knew Myles Horton had been in the industry for well over twenty years. He was a director in the production company.

He followed Myles through a set of double doors and along a short corridor to a door marked 'Editing'.

"So, one of your colleagues at Central Police said you needed to see any footage from the accident on Saturday." Myles looked a little puzzled. "To be honest, I'm not sure what you're looking for."

"We have reason to believe this was not an accident," Jim told him. "We've heard there have been other accidents at other audition sites."

The man shrugged as he sat down in one of the chairs before two computer monitors.

"We edit all the footage in here," he said.

"You keep copies of the raw footage?" Jim asked.

"Of course. It's standard procedure."

"Show me. Take it a few minutes before the accident occurred."

He watched as Myles opened the file and selected the timestamp. As he did so, he explained that there were several cameras within the convention hall. While most of the footage would eventually be discarded, they used different shots to add a little colour.

He added that the convention hall was often used for different events, including expos. The staff were experts at rearranging the layout to suit the event. For the auditions, they had set up various scaffolding so some footage could be shot from above.

Jim saw Amanda enter the main hall where the auditions were taking place and hand her form over to the floor manager. The man directed her through the doors into the staging area. He smirked to himself. He knew she'd been nervous the night before and it was plainly obvious in the footage. It wasn't the way she usually appeared, considering how obnoxiously confident she could be.

He kept watching, glancing at the timestamp. The minutes ticked off slowly. The floor manager was standing next to one of the heavy dividers. It was taller than him by at least half a metre, Jim decided. Then it happened. He couldn't tell exactly how it had happened, but the divider toppled over, right on top of the man, who was thrown backwards to the floor, knocking his head hard on the surface.

Myles looked at him. "You see? I've looked at this several times and I can't see how it happened. If you're thinking it was some kind of sabotage, I don't see how."

"Did you even look at the base of the stand?"

"Of course, we did."

"So, nothing was out of place?"

The man looked uncomfortable with his line of questioning.

"No."

I smell a cover-up, Jim thought. Myles had something to hide. The question was what.

"I need a copy of this. I'm going to get our forensics guys to take a look and see if there's something we missed."

The producer looked put-out.

"Do you have to?" he asked.

"Unless you would prefer me to go to court and get a warrant for it," Jim told him. It would take longer but if the man really was trying to cover up accidents on the production, taking the matter in front of a Justice of the Peace would ensure the information would leak out anyway.

He quickly reminded the man that it was already known there had been at least two accidents at the auditions – one in which someone had been seriously hurt and another where someone had died. He didn't mention what Amanda had already told him.

He quietly added that if people began to think the accidents were not actually accidents, it could spell disaster for the production company.

The man complied, albeit somewhat reluctantly, handing Jim a copy of the footage on a flash drive.

He left the studio and drove into town, calling his

boss on the way.

"What did you find out?"

"They're definitely trying to hide something," he said. "This producer, Myles, was really reluctant to hand over the footage."

"Hmm, yeah, that sounds fishy. You heading back in?"

"Not yet, boss. Billy called me and said he might have something for me."

"All right. Get back with that flash drive when you can."

"Will do, boss."

He met Billy in a quiet corner of the hospital café.

"So, what did you have for me?" Jim asked.

Billy handed him a sheet of paper. "You know I shouldn't really be doing this. It's not my case. But I thought it was unusual enough for you to see as soon as possible."

Jim scanned the sheet. It was the preliminary autopsy report. A more in-depth report would be sent later. As he read down the page, he spotted something which he realised was what had his friend so concerned.

He looked up and stared at the doctor-in-training.

"Fibres?" he asked. They'd found fibres in his nasal passage and his throat.

"Keep reading," Billy said.

Jim continued reading. The man had stopped breathing late that Saturday night. It wasn't the skull fracture which had caused him to do so. He'd suffocated.

"You're kidding me! How did someone manage to sneak into the hospital and do that without anyone knowing?"

"That's what we're hoping you guys can find out," his friend replied.

Jim reported back to the office, relating it to his boss. Pete whistled.

"Doesn't make the hospital look good, does it?" he asked.

"Nope. So, we're definitely looking at a homicide. What do you want me to tell Amanda? Do you think you should pull her off the case?"

"We don't have any reason to think that someone may know about her involvement," the detective sergeant told him. "Amanda's quite capable of looking out for herself so I suggest letting her be. Besides, being backstage, as it were, she might hear something useful."

He called in on Amanda after work to tell her what had happened.

"Are you serious?" she asked, her eyes widening in incredulity.

"As a heart attack," he replied.

She snorted. "Cute."

"I'm not trying to be cute," he told her. "Someone involved with this show wanted your guy dead."

"Paul," she said.

He frowned at her. "What?"

"His name was Paul. I found out today. The crew are having drinks on Friday as a memorial since they can't hold the funeral yet. And no, I'm not invited. None of the contestants are."

"Pity," he responded. "You might have heard something."

She nodded. "Yeah. I did try, but they refused. Said it wouldn't be right because I didn't actually know him." She bit her lip. "So, if he was smothered, it had to be a pillow or something."

He nodded. That was his thought as well. He'd talked to one of his colleagues at the central station and they were looking into it, with the co-operation of hospital security. They had told him that the room had been secured once they'd discovered Paul had died. How secure was another matter.

Amanda looked thoughtful.

"I wonder if the killer set up the accident hoping it would cover up the murder." She looked at him. "Do you think it's possible the other accidents were just accidents? Or what if whoever did this actually set up all the other accidents to make people think that what happened this time was just another accident? I mean, if Paul had died from the skull fracture …"

"We might not have upgraded it to a homicide," Jim finished for her.

He was getting used to the way her mind worked. In the few months they'd known each other, he'd begun to realise that Amanda didn't think like other people. She tended to go off on tangents or see things from a different perspective. Almost as if she was able to see the different paths of logic.

He'd noticed before that she had good instincts. They were far from perfect. As he'd once told her, it took time to hone those instincts and learn to use them to guide one's thinking, but she had the potential.

Whether she was on the right track was something they wouldn't be able to answer until they had all the details.

"Your dad's asked us to find out about the other accidents. One of our guys down south is already going to talk to the contestant who dropped out."

She nodded. "You said the producer was evasive when you talked to him?"

"Not so much evasive," he replied, "as reluctant to give me the footage. I mean, I don't know what the forensics guys are going to find. I mean, needle, haystack, you know the drill."

"So, the guy's name is Myles?" she asked. "I'll see what I can find out."

He'd already investigated whether the man had any kind of criminal record. Myles Horton was squeaky clean. Not even a parking ticket. That didn't mean, however, that he wasn't up to something. Jim was very interested to find out if there had been incidents on other productions the man might have worked on.

Jim had sent a query off to the local health and safety office to see if there were any records of workplace safety violations. He doubted he'd get a response quickly, but it was still worth looking into, he thought.

Just as he decided he should get going, Penny returned home. She came in the door, followed by Matt Donaldson. Jim had liked the guy when he'd been asked to work with Amanda on the high school case, but he was still annoyed on his friend's behalf over the way the man had not only dumped her, but had also left the party without making sure she got home all right.

Penny was giggling as if tipsy, pulling the school principal into the living room, draping herself all over him. Jim wasn't fooled by the woman's behaviour. She was shooting Amanda dark looks as if daring the younger woman to say something.

Amanda just rolled her eyes and ignored her

flatmate, walking Jim to the door.

"You gonna be okay?" he asked quietly, glancing toward the couch where Penny was almost engaging in a lewd act with the older man.

"Yeah, I'll be okay," Amanda told him. She leaned against the door jamb, arms folded.

"You really should think about what I said the other day. You don't need to put up with this."

"I know. I appreciate the concern, but I decided I'm not going to let her bother me. She's just being an immature b ... brat."

He grinned, knowing exactly what she was going to say.

"You know, you don't have to censor yourself," he said. "You are a grown-up."

"It's less about self-censorship and more about self-respect. And I have far too much of that to sink down to her level."

She really had grown up a lot in the past couple of months, he thought.

Chapter Thirteen

The building had seen better days. It was thirty years old but hadn't been as well-maintained as those that were its neighbours. The external door tended to stick, making it difficult for anyone trying to enter. The tiles installed on the floor in the lobby were cracked and brittle. It was clear they had been there for some time as the colour had faded from the sun.

Amanda pulled open the lobby door with difficulty. It was a windy day and the force of the wind pushing on the glass door added to the challenge. Groaning, she forced her way through before it could slam on her. She'd heard just recently of someone who had injured their hand badly when the wind had slammed a door, jamming the hand in the gap.

She stood in the lobby, catching her breath for a moment before turning to look at the elevator. She decided against using it, knowing it was prone to mechanical breakdown every month or so.

She opened the door to the stairwell and dodged someone coming down as she made her way upstairs. The man smiled at her, his gaze dropping down her body. She gazed steadily back at him, keeping her expression blank. He slowly got the message.

He tried to look as if it was just an innocent, friendly glance but she wasn't fooled. She knew him through her friend, Rena, who worked with him. He'd tried flirting with her the first time they'd met, but she had quickly shut him down.

"Keep walking, Ford," she said.

He looked surprised. "What?"

"Rena would kick your butt," she told him.

He snorted. "Yeah, she could try."

Amanda chose to ignore him, walking up to the second floor. She entered through the double doors and smiled at the older woman on reception.

"Hi, Kathy. How are you?"

Kathy smiled. She was a slim woman with curly, dark blonde hair that tended toward frizzy on wet days.

"I'm all right, Amanda," she said. "Are you here to see Rena?"

She nodded. "Yes, ma'am. How's your son, by the way? I heard he was not well a couple of weeks ago."

The older woman nodded, confirming that her son was doing much better. While the reception area was empty, she didn't like talking about her personal business, especially because her son had been admitted to the mental health unit. Amanda didn't know the full details, but she had heard the man had attempted suicide a few months earlier.

"How's your dad doing?" Kathy asked. "I suppose they're keeping him busy at the police station."

"You know him. Work, work, work."

The older woman smiled again her lips stretched as if she was trying not to show her teeth. She picked up the phone and called an extension.

"Amanda's here," she said into the receiver. She listened for a second or two then nodded, putting the receiver down. "She'll be right out."

Rena came out a minute or two later. Amanda smiled at her friend, admiring the colourful vest the other woman was wearing over the top of a cream blouse. The contrasting colours were perfect for her brown skin tone.

Rena Morris had been in her final year of high school when Amanda had been starting her first year. A school prefect, she had been assigned by the principal to help the new students adjust. Amanda had admired the older girl, who had been involved in a lot of school activities from the Kapa Haka group to community service.

What had been most remarkable about her was that she had come from a very poor background. Both her parents had been heavy drinkers and smokers and neither one had a job. Amanda suspected the father had also been involved in the local gang, but her friend had never confirmed it.

Rena had been taken from her parents by social services when she was ten and put into foster care. She had been lucky to have been placed with foster parents who cared enough to put her on the right path. Determined to succeed, the older girl had told Amanda she was going to be the dux of the school and wanted to be a reporter.

She did exactly what she had set out to do, resulting in several awards by the time she finished her last year. She had gone on to earn a degree in journalism.

After Amanda had completed her part in the investigation at Fraley High, she had discovered her old school friend was a reporter at the West Side Tribune. It was a small community newspaper, but at twenty-four, Rena was already the chief reporter.

They decided to go for lunch at a small café in the main street instead of going to the mall.

"I haven't seen you since your birthday," Rena said. "How's it going? How's the job?"

"Oh, the job's good," Amanda said, sitting back as their coffees were brought over. She waited until the server had gone back behind the counter before leaning forward. "Don't tell anyone, but I'm working at Star Quest."

Rena frowned, picking up her sandwich to bite into it. "Working? What about your job?"

"That's it," she said. "I'm working undercover. You know that story you did about an accident a few weeks ago? Well, there have been more. They asked us to check it out."

"Wow! I heard there was another one at the weekend. They said he died."

"Put away your reporter's notebook," Amanda teased. "I can't tell you everything, obviously, but yeah, the floor manager."

"It's not always about the story," Rena grumbled, pretending she was miffed at Amanda's teasing. "Is that why you wanted to have lunch?"

"Yes and no." She paused. "I heard about something and I thought you might be able to help me track this person down. Do you know the name, Rochelle Conley?"

Rena's eyes widened. She put down the remainder of her sandwich to stare at Amanda. "Do I? Hell, she's famous! What about her?"

"Well, I don't know exactly when, but she was starring in a production of *Jesus Christ, Superstar*. She had to drop out for some reason. I just thought I should check it out."

"I can look it up on the 'net, do a bit of research. You want me to track her down for you?"

Amanda nodded. "Yeah. I want to go see her, talk to her about what happened."

"All right. But you better keep me posted on what's going on. I'm gonna need the inside scoop if we're going to beat the Press." She sipped her coffee. "Oh, want to hear the latest? The editor of the Press called me and asked me if I was interested in jumping ship. Can you believe that?"

"Well, he'd be nuts if he didn't consider you. You're so talented."

"Yeah, but I'm happy where I am. Even if the boss drives me crazy. He can be such a jerk sometimes. He made one of the junior reporters cry the other day."

"Can't you report him? I mean, aren't there policies on bullying?"

"Yeah, there are, but unless the girl actually makes a complaint, there's not much I can do except try to run interference."

"Well, that sucks," Amanda replied.

"Tell me about it."

Rehearsals were again that afternoon and Amanda met her coach, Debbie, at the studio instead of the convention centre. As she entered the room, she heard the older woman on the phone.

"You didn't have a choice, you know that." There

was a pause. "No, I get that, but you've seen the numbers. We're between a rock and a hard place. If we don't co-operate and let them do their investigation, they'll shut us down. If they do find something, we might have to shut down anyway. It's a lose-lose situation. At least if we are seen to co-operate, we might salvage something from the whole mess."

Amanda stood there biting her lip, wondering if she should let the other woman know she was there. She had heard enough to pick up what sounded like a vital clue. Knowing Jim had already talked to one of the show's producers, it sounded to her like Debbie was involved in the company.

The conversation seemed like it was coming to an end. Amanda coughed politely. Debbie turned and looked at her before telling whoever she'd been talking to that she had to go.

Her expression quickly changed from one of annoyance to a smile of greeting.

"I forgot the time," she said. "Why don't we get started? Have you warmed up?"

"Not yet," Amanda told her.

Debbie took her through the warming-up exercises once more before sitting down at the piano. They were yet to choose the song she would sing at the first show.

The coach took her through the procedure. The first show would be a follow-on from the auditions where contestants would sing in front of the judges and in the final show, the audience at home could vote for their favourites. Amanda knew that already but didn't tell the other woman.

"So, this is like a popularity contest?" Amanda

asked as she sipped from a bottle of water.

"In some respects, I suppose people would look at it like that," the other woman replied.

"I was talking to someone the other day and he said something about one of those competitions in Australia. That there was a woman who was obviously very talented, but she didn't have the looks."

Debbie scowled. "Yeah, unfortunately, it comes down to what people perceive. You could be the most amazing singer or actress, but if you don't look a certain way, you have to fight harder to get people to take you seriously."

"Was that what it was like for you?" Amanda asked, noting the other woman appeared rather bitter.

"Afraid so. I wasn't stick thin like many of my so-called rivals. The industry is extremely harsh."

"It's no wonder most of them get into drugs or whatever," Amanda replied. "All that pressure."

She was suddenly very glad she was only doing this as an undercover assignment and not as a real competition. She'd seen enough in her last case the problems drugs could cause.

"Well, you won't have anything to worry about. You've got the looks and the talent," Debbie assured her. Then she made a sort of grimace. "Mind you, we shouldn't get too complacent. You still have some work to do before you'll be ready for the first show."

Amanda nodded. "Then let's do it," she said.

She returned to the office after the session to write up her report on her activities that week and catch up on some of the administrative work. Mr Moody paused in the doorway, his coat on, suggesting he was on his way out for the night.

"Don't stay too late," he warned her.

"I won't," she promised. "I just wanted to catch up on some work and maybe do a little digging."

He looked at her curiously. "Found something interesting?"

She told him about the phone conversation she'd overheard. He nodded.

"You're right. That does sound interesting. Check the companies register on their website and see if anything comes up on the production company."

She hadn't thought of that. Amanda accessed the website and looked up the listing for the company. Her boss hovered beside her.

"There. She's listed as a director," he said.

"Well, that's not suspicious at all," Amanda commented.

The elder partner of the firm looked steadily at her.

"Are you going to question her about her involvement?"

She shook her head. "Not yet. There was something else I wanted to check out about her first." She related what the singer and actress had told her on their first meeting and the lunch with her friend.

"If anyone can find Rochelle, Rena can," she told her boss.

"That's a good, solid lead if it pans out," he said. "But not everything does lead somewhere."

"I know, but you're the one who taught me to follow any potential lead. Even if it does turn out to be nothing."

He looked surprised, remarking on the fact that she had actually listened to him on the rare occasion that he did share some of his wisdom, both as a former cop and as a private investigator.

He left a short time later, again telling her not to stay too late. Amanda sat back, lost in thought. She initially had found Mr Moody to be a little too gruff, a little intimidating. Lately, he had been praising her initiative, even supportive. He was the one who had suggested she go undercover, although it was her other boss who had suggested she audition.

Bob Moody was a hard one to figure out, she thought.

As she packed up to leave, her phone rang. Amanda glanced at the screen, not recognising the number.

"Amanda Steele."

"Hey, Amanda, it's Tama."

She smiled. She had liked the man on sight and had enjoyed working with him, preparing for the audition.

"Hi, Tama. What's up?"

"I was wondering if you're free for dinner tonight. I know it's late …" It wasn't really since it was only six-thirty, but being almost June, it was already dark outside. "Unless you have plans?"

"No, no plans," she said. "I'd be happy to have dinner with you. I'm at the office. I was just about to leave to go catch the train home."

"Well, how about I pick you up in about fifteen minutes?"

"Great. Sounds good. I'll see you then."

Tama was outside waiting when Amanda left the office exactly fifteen minutes later. He drove downtown to a restaurant that was part of a hotel.

The maitre d'hotel greeted them courteously and

told them it would be a short wait. The restaurant was busy and almost every table was full. Amanda could see someone cleaning up a table in the middle of the dining room.

Once the table was cleared, they were escorted to it and the waiter pulled out her chair for her. He handed them each a folder.

"The wine list," he said. "If you would like some recommendations, we do have an excellent sauvignon from a Marlborough company."

Amanda's palate wasn't that sophisticated, but she had drunk enough wine to knew what she liked. Despite her preference for the sugary vodka/soda mix, she preferred dry wines to sweet ones.

Tama looked at her and she nodded. He returned his gaze to the waiter.

"We'll try the sauvignon, thanks."

The waiter left, returning a few minutes later with a bottle of the wine, pouring them each a glass. He pointed out the dinner menus and left them to decide.

"So, how are things going with the case?" Tama asked.

"Well, right now, I'm just following up some leads," she told him.

"You did great on the audition. The other judges were very impressed. Your boss was right. You are talented. Did you ever think about singing professionally?"

She shook her head. "I do like to sing, but no, a professional career isn't for me." She quickly changed the subject before he could quiz her on the coaching. "How are the rest of the crew doing with Paul's death?"

Tama sighed. "They're taking it pretty hard. Paul was a good friend to a lot of us and a hard worker. I've known him since my Young Talent days. I'm sorry you couldn't be at the service tomorrow."

"It would have been good to listen to some of the things people were saying about him, but I think it would have looked odd if I was there."

"Yeah. So, do you have any ideas? About the accident?"

"I would have thought the police would have updated you," she said. "They're treating it as a homicide. That's all I can tell you."

"I'm sorry," he said, sounding a little sheepish. "We're just anxious to get this over with. A lot of people are getting nervous."

She nodded. "Tama, I can't change that. These things don't get solved overnight. You need to give me some time to work out exactly what is happening."

He stopped asking her about the case once their dinners were served and moved on to ask her more personal questions. Like why she was working for a private investigator.

"I wanted to be a cop, actually," she said. "But I failed the entrance interview. I guess they thought I needed a little more life experience."

"That's a shame," he said, sympathetically.

"What about you? I mean, you were on track for a pretty good singing career after you finished Young Talent."

He nodded, looking thoughtful as he chewed his steak.

"The problem is, we're still pretty isolated as a country. If you don't get a name for yourself in either

Britain or America, your career kind of stalls. I tried for a couple of years in the UK, but it just didn't work out."

"I'm sorry," she said.

He shrugged. "Well, you know, sometimes opportunity doesn't knock for some people. And anyway, I like what I'm doing now. I know it all seems a bit crazy, but we do find some really unique talents through these shows."

Amanda had learnt a little about body language and tone and Tama didn't seem to be giving off any kind of signal indicating he was lying or covering up any bitterness.

Jim had told her to learn to trust her instincts and those instincts were telling her the former singer was being honest. He was clearly anxious about solving the problem with the accidents, but she couldn't hold that against him.

Chapter Fourteen

"Hey, Jim, I thought you'd want to see the report on that kid you wanted brought in for questioning."

Jim frowned as he looked up from his desk at Kirsten Taylor. She handed him a thin folder and he opened it to look at the front page. The photograph was from a couple of years ago when the kid had been arrested on drug charges.

He'd almost forgotten about the boys harassing women outside the local mall almost a week ago. Or the fact that Amanda had told him the same kid was harassing contestants lined up waiting to audition for the show.

Taylor had obviously tracked down the boy – Robert – and had brought him in for questioning over his behaviour and what he knew about the accident.

Robert had denied all knowledge of the accident, saying security had run him off. He'd claimed he was just chatting up the girls. Jim doubted that. From what Amanda had said, he had been trying to intimidate some of the contestants into leaving before they could even audition.

Jim had checked up on the youth's story of his sister being part of the auditions. The records they had on him indicated that he was an only child. Given his previous history of lying to authorities, Jim wondered if the boy was concocting the story just so he could hide some other purpose for being there. He might have been trying to steal items from those waiting in line.

The file didn't give him any of the answers he was looking for.

The forensics team hadn't been able to find anything on the video file he'd passed onto them either. Those who had done the scene examination had discovered that the welding on the base holding the wheels together had cracked. They'd concluded that stress on the metal had caused it to crack. How that stress had occurred was unknown at that stage, but they were continuing testing.

Some interesting information had turned up, however, when Amanda had told her father she had overheard a phone conversation when she'd gone to meet with her singing coach. From what she'd heard, it sounded like the woman and the producer he'd interviewed were connected.

Jim had asked someone to dig into the production company's accounts. He hadn't heard back from them about those accounts but knew it would take a couple of days to get the necessary information from the department assigned to take on that kind of task.

He decided to call in Myles Horton for questioning. The man looked a little nervous as he entered the interview room. Jim gazed at him coolly.

"Thanks for coming in, Mr Horton," he said.

The man was immediately on the defensive. "You guys didn't give me much choice," he responded.

So that was how it was going to be played, Jim thought. He gestured toward the hard plastic chair on one side of the table and opened the file. He showed the man photographs from the scene examination.

"You told me the other day that your crew didn't spot anything out of the ordinary that might have explained the fall. Are you still wanting to stick to that story?"

Myles studied the photograph. "That wasn't like that when I saw it," he said. "Your guys must have …"

"Are you accusing one of my officers of impropriety?" Jim replied. He stared at the producer, knowing the way to get any answers out of the man was to try to intimidate him into talking.

The man's cheeks slowly turned red. He clearly knew something. "Uh, no, of course not."

"Then let's start again, shall we? Did you or any of the crew spot anything unusual the day of the accident?"

There was a long pause where they continued to stare at each other before Myles nodded, going on to confirm that the crew had brought the fault to his attention, suggesting it could have caused the set divider to fall.

"Why did you lie to me when I questioned you about this earlier?" Jim asked.

"Look, you have to understand, I'm under a lot of pressure here. The first show is in two weeks and I …"

Jim raised his hand and glared at the man. He

didn't care about the man's stress or what pressure he was under. Another man was dead, and he needed to know what was going on.

"Just answer the question, Horton! Why?"

"Because I was afraid they would shut down the production," Myles blurted. "We've got a lot riding on this."

"Why? Is your company in trouble?"

The man looked down, one hand tracing the edges of the photograph.

"Yes," he said finally. "We hadn't had a decent production contract for months and if we lost this one, we might as well close up shop."

"I see." Jim looked at the other man steadily. "Myles, did you have anything to do with Paul Davidson's death?"

The man's eyes widened. "What? No! I mean, it was an accident. A tragic accident." He suddenly appeared uncertain. "Wasn't it?"

Jim shook his head. "Afraid not. We're treating it as a homicide."

"But … he was, it was just a head injury!"

Police training had taught him not to reveal too much to anyone who might be considered a suspect in a homicide. If he kept the information back, anyone who knew what really happened might trip themselves up by revealing how the man had died.

Jim was still treating Myles as culpable in the accidents, even if he wasn't a suspect in the actual murder. From the man's reaction, he decided it was unlikely the producer had been involved or had any knowledge of what had happened in the hospital, but he wasn't going to call it a certainty just yet.

"There are other factors, which we're not

releasing at this time."

The other man was clearly stunned. "Are you telling me I have a murderer on my crew?"

"We don't know. Right now, we don't have any suspects." He closed the folder. "Did Paul have any enemies that you know of?"

"No. Everyone liked him. Paul was a good guy. I can't believe it," he said. "Why would someone … I just …"

Jim figured a little sympathy couldn't hurt, at least to let the other man feel he was on his side.

"I'm sorry," he said. "I know news like this is never easy to hear." He walked the other man out. "Thanks for coming in."

He returned upstairs and knocked on his boss' door. Pete was on the phone but beckoned for him to enter. Jim closed the door and sat down, waiting for the other man to finish his call.

The detective-sergeant nodded at him and hung up after a few minutes.

"That was the DHB," he said. "They're investigating what happened in the hospital the night Davidson died."

"You think they'll find anything?" Jim asked.

He'd spoken to one of his colleagues in Central and they'd told him they had questioned the staff at the hospital. Davidson had been put in a private room but there had been no security in the ward, or on the floor. The guard who was supposed to have been on duty on that level had gone out for a smoke with a patient.

The hospital's security cameras hadn't picked up anything unusual either. Just patients and staff wandering the floors.

It was clear that whoever had killed the floor manager had planned it very carefully.

"I don't know what the health board's going to find if our guys couldn't pick up anything," he said.

Pete shrugged. "Yeah, I know. The team's going over the video with a fine-toothed comb."

"It looks like Amanda was right. Well, sort of, I guess."

His boss cocked an eyebrow. "Are you actually saying my daughter might be right about something?"

"Well, I don't know. I mean, she was thinking out loud, but she said a couple of things that might even be logical."

"Do tell."

"That whoever's behind this might have set up all the other accidents to cover up a murder."

His boss looked dubious. "That's a bit of a stretch. And rather a lot of effort to go to."

Jim shrugged. "Either that or the other accidents really were just accidents and they figured they could use that to cover up the murder."

"I s'pose we won't find that out until we figure out who did this and what their motive is. Anyway, how'd it go with the producer?"

"Honestly, the guy's a bit of a dick, but he acted shocked when I told him it was being treated as a homicide."

Pete frowned. "Surely the production company would have known about that by now, what with Central being all over the show."

"I guess that depends on what the guys chose to tell the crew."

It could happen, he thought. It was standard

procedure for police to be called in when there was a sudden death, even if it was ruled accidental, so they could investigate the circumstances and decide if charges needed to be laid.

He wasn't sure which line of enquiry to follow next. If the hospital hadn't been able to come up with anything, he had no idea how they were going to find the killer.

He decided to look over all his notes and see if anything jumped out at him. He spent the next hour reading and just trying to find something that seemed out of the ordinary, but soon gave up, thinking he needed to focus on something else for a while.

"Let me guess. You got bupkis."

Jim looked up and stared at Amanda.

"Bupkis?"

"Yeah, as in zero, zip, nada."

He stood up, closing the cover of the file before scowling at her.

"I don't need an English lesson," he told her.

She shrugged. "Actually, I thought I was being sympathetic. No need to be a dick about it."

"If anyone's being a dick …"

She laughed at him. "You can't call me a dick, Andersen. I'm female. My reproductive organs happen to be on the inside, not the outside."

He rolled his eyes. "My god, you really do love the sound of your own voice, don't you?"

She huffed. "What kind of comeback is that?"

Jim shook his head. What was it about this girl, no woman, that annoyed him so much? And here he thought they were beginning to build a friendship of a sort.

"There's just no beating you, is there?" he said. "You always have to have the last word."

"Hey, I'm not the one who got all defensive. I was <u>trying</u> to show some sympathy!"

He nudged her, forcing her to move aside so he could put the folder in the drawer behind her.

"Well, try harder," he told her, turning his back to her.

"Ugh. You know what? You're impossible! You have to be the most annoying person I've ever met!"

He turned his head to glare at her. "I'm annoying? Well, you drive me nuts! You walk in here like you own the goddamn place and then you act like you think you know better than me."

Amanda's eyes widened in indignation.

"I never ..."

"What's going on here?"

Jim looked guiltily at his boss. Pete was glaring at the two of them.

"I could hear you two arguing from the corridor. Somebody want to clue me in?"

"He started it," Amanda began, pointing at Jim, who had spoken simultaneously, telling his boss the blonde had been responsible.

Pete sighed. "I don't care who said what. If you two want to argue, or whatever, take it outside."

Jim stared at him for a second, wondering exactly what his boss meant by 'whatever'. There was no way in hell there would ever be anything except antagonism between him and the boss' daughter.

"And Amanda," Pete continued, "you know the boss doesn't like you just walking in whenever you feel like it."

"Chris Chapman let me in," she replied, her lower

lip jutting out in what looked to Jim like a pout.

Her father growled softly. "Don't think you can thrust out that lip at me, young lady. You're an adult now, not a child."

"Fine!" she said.

The older man nodded his head toward his small office. "Both of you. In there."

Jim huffed but followed Amanda into the detective sergeant's office. He turned toward the door, refusing to even acknowledge her, waiting as Pete closed the door.

The sergeant ran a hand through his greying blond hair.

"Look, I don't care what is going on between you two but save the arguments for outside the office. I mean it," he said, looking at his daughter. "Mark isn't exactly happy that you seem to think you can come and go as you please. Just because you've been basically allowed free rein since you were a kid, it doesn't mean he's going to overlook it."

Jim frowned at him. He remembered the station commander's reaction when he'd heard Amanda had been involved in the case at the school.

"Does he know Amanda's on this case?" he asked.

Pete shook his head. "No. And I want to keep it that way for as long as possible. Which means you need to keep out of trouble, Amanda."

"I can't exactly do my job and stay out of trouble, Dad."

"I get that. Which is why I want you to keep Jim updated of anything you find out."

"You're asking me to work with him again?" she said.

"Sounds to me like you're already doing that

anyway," her father told her. "Now it's official. And I don't want to hear any more grumbling from you. Is that understood?"

"Yes, Dad."

Pete looked at Jim. "Do I have to make it an order, Andersen?" he asked sternly.

"No, boss," he said. "That's not necessary."

"Good." He pulled over a chair from beside the desk. "You two sit and talk. I'll be in the bar. Come and join us when you both have managed to pull your heads out of your arses."

He left them alone. Amanda sat, folding her arms over her chest.

"I hate when he does that," she said with a sigh.

"What?"

"Pull rank."

"Well, he is my boss," he reminded her.

"I don't know what's worse. Him being my dad or your boss."

"Pretty much on par, I think," Jim told her. He sighed. Maybe he had acted a little on the defensive earlier. "I'm sorry. About before. I guess I was being a dick."

She shrugged. "Yeah."

"So, in the interests of sharing information, I called in Horton. One of the producers."

He related what he'd learnt in the interview. Amanda sighed.

"Well, he's right about the possibility of them shutting down production. I had a meeting with Sarah and Mr Knight this afternoon. Paul's death has really shaken them all up. There's talk of cancelling the show."

Jim frowned. It had earlier occurred to him to

wonder if there was an insurance policy on either the studio or the production being shut down. He'd mentioned it to Amanda, and she'd agreed to follow up on it.

Then again, if there was, why would Horton try to cover up an obvious attempt at sabotage? It didn't make sense.

Chapter Fifteen

Amanda pulled into the angled park and got out of the car, locking the door. She looked around, trying to get her bearings. Despite having lived in the city all her life, she was in an area she rarely visited.

She went to the meter and sent a text to pay for her parking. The city had upgraded the parking system some years ago and installed more modern machines which allowed people to pay through their phone accounts rather than by coin or card. Parking was expensive but she didn't expect to be there long.

According to the directions on her phone app, the coffee shop she was meant to be visiting was about one hundred metres from where she was standing. Amanda began walking in that direction, checking the storefronts. She spotted the paved walkway of the alley and turned down it to approach the shop.

A woman sitting at one of the outside tables smiled and waved at her.

"You must be Amanda," she said. "Rena described you perfectly."

"She's always been good with details," Amanda

returned with a smile. She put her bag down on the chair beside her before sitting down opposite the woman.

Rochelle Conley was a beautiful woman in her late fifties with long, glossy black hair and a lovely olive complexion.

"Uh, have you ordered?" Amanda asked her.

"I've only been here a couple of minutes myself," Rochelle responded. "I thought I would grab a table first. What would you like?"

"Oh no, let me. I asked for this meeting."

The older woman smiled. "Thank you. That's very kind of you. Their chai lattes are excellent here."

"Great," Amanda said. She picked up her bag. "I'll be back in a minute."

She went inside the shop and ordered two chai lattes at the counter. The cashier promised she would bring them out in a few minutes.

Amanda returned to the table.

"So, what can I do for you?" the former singer and actress asked.

"I wanted to ask you about dropping out of a show. I think it was *Superstar*?"

Rochelle gazed at her for a moment. Her expression was unreadable but Amanda wondered if the hesitation was to do with opening old wounds.

"May I ask why you're interested?" she asked quietly.

"I work for a private investigator. We were asked to investigate a series of accidents at Star Quest." She started to explain about the show, but Rochelle stopped her.

"I know about it," she said. "They asked me if I wanted to come on board as a coach or a consultant, but I said no." She visibly relaxed. "I heard about that poor man's death." She clearly hadn't known the man.

"I don't know if I can be much help to you but ask away. I do know a few people in the industry, although it's been a few years."

Amanda paused as the drinks were brought out. She waited until the cashier had returned inside before turning back to Rochelle.

"I'm actually working undercover at the show, as a contestant. One of the coaches there is a woman named Debbie Burns. She mentioned she understudied you and took over the role when you dropped out. She said it was for personal reasons."

Rochelle's expression darkened a little.

"And you thought there was more to it? You have good instincts, Amanda. Yes, there was more to it. Debbie and I had a, what I supposed you could call intense rivalry. We were always competing for the same roles. Not to cast aspersions on her character, but she could be rather ..." She paused as if searching for the right word, "... abrasive when she lost."

"So, why did you drop out of the show?"

"There was an accident on one of the sets. I'm not trying to place blame, but it looked like one of the set builders hadn't secured a platform properly and it gave way. I lost my balance and fell off the stage. Broke my ankle."

Amanda winced in sympathy. "I'm sorry."

She shrugged. "My ankle hasn't been right since and I've never really been able to take on any more physical roles."

She explained that she now taught singing

privately and made a fairly good income doing so. That much had already been confirmed by the research Rena had done on the singer. She hadn't been in any major shows since that accident. She didn't appear particularly worried about having missed out on them.

"Do you know who was working on the sets back then?" Amanda asked.

"No. I'm sorry. I don't remember everyone who was working there then. I'm not bitter, but I chose to put it behind me and move on. I wish I could be more help."

"It's all right. But ... where the accident was concerned ..." Amanda wondered how she could approach it diplomatically, given the older woman's feelings about it. "Do you think it might have been done deliberately?"

"I don't know. If you are thinking Debbie might have done something to set me up so she could take my place, well, back then, considering our rivalry, it's possible. I'm not saying she was vindictive, but she was rather immature back then. This was twenty years ago."

Amanda considered the question on the way back to the office. If Debbie was the type to cause an accident which would basically force her main competition to drop out of a show, she might also be the type of person to set up someone else in a supposed accident.

But, she thought, if Debbie was one of the directors of the production company, she stood to lose a lot more by the show not going ahead.

She remembered Jim had asked her to follow up on whether there was any insurance on the show or the contestants. She really needed to check that out, she thought.

Once she was back in the office, she called Tama. He didn't pick up, so she left a message for him to call her back.

Mr Knight was in his office. She knocked on his door. He looked up and smiled at her.

"Amanda. What's up?"

"I was hoping I could get your opinion on something."

She told him about the meeting with Rochelle. He listened as she related what she had learnt so far, leaning back in his chair with his elbows on the armrests and his hands laced together. He appeared completely at ease.

"Tell me something," he said. "What made you think there was more to the story Debbie told you?"

"I don't know. I mean, she was kind of matter-of-fact when she talked about it."

Her boss talked a little about body language and the ability to read it being useful when questioning someone about their activities. Amanda was familiar with the concept but hadn't learnt the nuances of body language herself.

The older man questioned her further.

"Did you notice anything about her demeanour? Did she perhaps seem tense?"

Amanda thought about it. The other woman had mentioned it casually. She hadn't even seemed too concerned. Then again, she had to have been an actress as well as a singer if she was performing in stage musicals. Had she been hiding the truth?

"She did say it was for personal reasons rather than an accident."

Her boss scratched at his upper lip.

"Hmm. The way Ms Conley spoke about the rivalry between them and the fact that your coach did mention something similar makes me wonder if she does know more than she's telling about what happened."

"But if I confront her about it, won't that blow my cover?"

"You'll have to use your own judgement on that. Considering Ms Burns' financial interest in the production, I would think she wouldn't want to do anything to jeopardise it."

"Unless there was a hefty insurance policy," Amanda said. "I called Tama about that, but he didn't pick up."

"Perhaps you should also speak to your friend Mr Andersen."

"He's not my friend," she said adamantly.

Jerry Knight grinned. "Frienemy, then, I think is what you kids are calling it these days. Regardless, he may be able to talk to Ms Burns about the past incident, if you are concerned about revealing yourself too soon."

"You're right. Thank you."

"Any time," he said with a smile. "I'm always here if you need a sounding board."

Amanda went to rehearsals that afternoon determined to watch her singing coach and see if there was any change in her behaviour. Since it had been determined that Paul's death was now a homicide, police detectives had been infrequent visitors to the convention centre, talking to the crew.

She figured since it had happened in the central city, Jim would be unlikely to be part of the main investigation and she hadn't seen him since the previous Friday.

With just over a week to go to the first show, all the contestants had to attend rehearsals. While they had to perform their solo acts, singers were also expected to join a group to see how well they could work in harmony with others.

Debbie had chosen a group with a variety of singing skills for Amanda to join. The girl she had met on audition day was one of them. Julie had appeared relieved to see a familiar face and her confidence had improved from that first day.

There was a man who was a year older than Amanda. He had a pleasant deep baritone. The final two of the group were two women who both acted like they thought they were the best out of the quintet. Both had glared daggers at Amanda from the wings when she performed her solo.

Amanda looked around for her coach, but Debbie was nowhere to be seen. Knowing she couldn't just leave the centre in the middle of rehearsals, not without blowing her cover at least, she decided she would just have to stick it out.

She saw the two women from her group talking with Julie, who appeared upset.

"What's going on?" she asked as she approached them.

"Nothing," Tracey said sharply. "Stay out of it."

They'd only been rehearsing together for a couple of days, but Amanda had already figured the older woman out.

Tracey was a brunette in her mid-thirties, although she tried to convince others she was a lot younger. She was attractive and a good singer but didn't seem to have that certain quality that would give her the edge over other performers. At least, according to Tama, Amanda thought, recalling an evening when the judge had gone over some of the contestants with her.

Tracey and the other woman in the group, Krystal, had been very critical of the youngest member, claiming she was dragging the rest of them down with her 'mediocre' talent.

Krystal, a 25-year-old redhead, glared at Amanda. "This is not your concern."

"Hmm, well, it looks to me like you're bullying Julie. And that is my concern."

Julie looked at her gratefully. While she lacked confidence, she was a sweetheart who tried not to speak badly about anyone. Amanda knew if she'd asked, the younger girl would have said they'd just been chatting, despite her expression suggesting otherwise.

"Why don't you just back off, bitch?" Tracey said. "This has nothing to do with you."

Amanda stood in front of the woman. "Listen, I don't know what your problem is, but if you think you can intimidate me, you've got another think coming. I'm telling you right now to lay off Julie. I don't care if you're jealous because she's a far better singer than you."

"You …" Tracey made to look like she was going to hit her, pulling her arm back, her hand forming a fist.

"I don't think you want to do that, miss," a deep voice said.

Amanda turned, hearing Jim's voice. She sent him a look as he approached, half in gratitude, half in warning not to give her away.

"Sorry," he said. "I was here talking to one of the producers and couldn't help overhearing."

Tracey glared at him. "Who are you?" she said.

Jim pulled out his identification. "I'd rethink the attitude, ma'am, unless you want to be taken in for attempted assault."

As far as Amanda knew, Jim was bluffing, but the threat was enough to make the other woman subside.

"Don't call me ma'am," she grumbled.

The stage manager called out to them.

"You four need to get ready to go on stage," he said. "And you ..." he added, looking at Jim.

"Sorry, I'm with West Side police. I'll get out of your way." As he turned to leave, he shot her a look. Amanda figured he needed to talk to her. While the others didn't seem to notice the look, she figured if they had, she could always explain it as knowing him through her father.

Rehearsal went about as well as she expected, which was not at all. Tracey and Krystal seemed to be smarting from the earlier confrontation and weren't willing to co-operate with any of them. Even Seth, a trained singer from the Waikato, grew frustrated.

One of the judges, who had been coaching another group, spoke to them.

"You people need to put aside your differences and work with each other if you want a good score in the competition."

"It's not my fault," Tracey grumbled. Krystal nodded in agreement with the other woman.

"I don't care," Deirdre said. Amanda remembered she was the actress from the UK. "We all have to work with people we don't like sometimes. The mark of a true professional is someone who can ignore those feelings and work with them anyway."

Tracey and the other woman scowled and walked away. Amanda looked at Julie and Seth, who both sighed and went to help themselves to a bottle of water each.

Amanda turned to Deirdre.

"It sounded like you were speaking from experience," she said.

The woman looked at her, then nodded.

"I was on a long-running tv series in the UK. Let's just say that I had a difference of opinion with a co-star. Next thing we know, it's in the gossip magazines as an all-out catfight." She shook her head. "Don't believe everything you read in the gossip columns."

"Oh, I don't read those magazines," Amanda assured her. "I've never been much of a magazine reader anyway."

The other woman smiled. "You seem to have your head screwed on right. I remember you from the auditions. Amanda, right?"

"Yes."

"You sang very well. Plus, you've got a great attitude. I think you'll go far in this competition. Unlike madam over there," she added, frowning in Tracey's direction. "I don't know why she's trying again."

"What do you mean?" Amanda asked, realising the other woman had just given her a vital clue.

"I was a judge on a similar show in the UK. I'm sure I saw her audition in the UK show about five years ago. I could be wrong, but I don't think so. The faces tend to blur, but you always remember the ones with the wrong attitude."

Hmm, Amanda thought. The actress turned away, but Amanda continued to watch Tracey and the other woman. The pair appeared to be whispering as if they were scheming something.

She bit her lip, wishing she could somehow get close to them so she could overhear what they were saying, but they seemed to realise they were being watched as they turned and walked off, leaving the backstage area.

With two members of the group now absent, they were unable to continue rehearsing and the other two opted to call it a day. Amanda decided to stick around, hoping she might be able to pick up on some more clues. She sat in the auditorium, watching other groups rehearse together on the stage.

Hearing the rustle of clothing, she glanced over her shoulder and saw Jim sitting in the row behind her, two seats away. He was clearly trying to be unobtrusive.

Fortunately, it was dark enough in the auditorium that she doubted anyone on stage would see them together.

He leaned forward. "They're good," he said, indicating the quartet on stage. They'd been rehearsing an acapella performance of Pharrell Williams' song: Happy. Amanda had to admit they were very good.

She didn't reply to him but turned her head slightly, indicating she was listening as he continued speaking. "I saw your solo act before. You are good, I'll give you that."

She fluttered her eyelashes and fanned her hand.

"Such compliments could go to my head," she replied.

He snorted. "By the way, forensics figured out what happened."

"And?"

"Somebody used some kind of corrosive on the wheels, so they'd give way. All it needed was a good shove to make it fall at the right time."

"So, you're saying the floor manager was definitely the intended target?" she asked.

"That's exactly what I'm saying."

Which meant someone had had it in for him.

"They must have thought the skull fracture would be enough to kill him," she mused aloud.

"And when it wasn't, they had to go to the hospital and finish the job."

"Any luck on getting anything from the hospital?" she asked.

"Not yet. They're still going through all the security cameras footage."

"It'll take weeks at this rate," she answered, sighing.

"Yeah, I know."

"I've been trying to find out if the show has an insurance policy if it gets cancelled, but Tama hasn't called me back." She remembered her conversation with her boss. "But get this. You know how I went to talk to Rochelle Conley?"

She'd told him about the conversation with her coach and her plan to talk to the former actress/singer.

"What about it?"

"She didn't leave the show for personal reasons. Debbie lied. Apparently, they had this big rivalry.

Anyway, Rochelle broke her ankle on set."

"Well, that's not suspicious at all. I think I need to have a talk with our friend Debbie."

Suddenly there was a loud crash on stage. Amanda started, half-rising from her seat to stare in stunned silence at the light which had fallen from the scaffolding above. One of the rehearsing singers was sitting on the stage, clearly in pain as he clutched his leg.

Another member of the group called out: "Somebody call an ambulance."

Amanda dashed up toward the stage, aware of Jim following behind her. He pushed past her to mount the steps, telling them he was with the police before advising he'd done some first aid training.

"What happened?" he asked.

"It just fell. I think he broke his leg."

Jim knelt and carefully examined the leg. The young man screamed at any attempt to move it.

"Yeah, that's definitely broken," Jim concluded. He turned to gaze at Amanda for a few moments.

She looked around and spotted Tracey standing in the wings. Krystal was with her, looking just as shocked as everyone else, but the other woman didn't seem to be showing any emotion at all.

Chapter Sixteen

Jim rapped with his knuckles on Chris Chapman's desk. The blond detective looked up.

"What's up?" he asked.

"Grab your gear," Jim replied, smirking a little at using the line from a tv crime show.

Chris grabbed his jacket and wallet as he stood up.

"What is it?" he said.

"Going to make a housecall."

The rookie detective followed him out to the parking area. Jim handed him the keys to the silver Holden Commodore. It was the same model as the uniformed branch used but didn't have any insignia. It was still equipped with everything the other cars had but being unmarked, detectives could remain incognito.

As his colleague waited for the gate to slide open to let them out, Jim looked at him.

"So, you're from Palmy?"

'Palmy' was what most people called Palmerston North, a small city about two hours north of

Wellington. While it was not the most exciting city in the country, it had what Jim felt was one of the best university campuses. Then again, he supposed he was biased, since it was where his stepmother taught.

The other man nodded. "Yup. Born and bred. Went to Massey."

"You didn't happen to take forensic psych by any chance?"

"Thought about it. Wait, Dr Andersen, is she related to you?"

"Yep. My mum. Well, step-mum, but she's always been Mum." He smirked. "She prefers not to use 'doctor'. Her philosophy is the only time an academic should be referred to as 'doctor' is when they have an MD, not a PhD."

"I guess." Chris drove out into the street. "So, where are we going?"

"Take the western motorway out to West Harbour," Jim told him. "I'll give you the address when we get off the motorway."

The other detective was quiet for a few moments as he navigated the streets and found his way to the highway which was the main artery in and out of the city.

"So, your parents live in Palmy?" Chris asked.

"Yes, they do. My dad retired as a cop and owns a small security company. What about yours?"

"Mum moved to Christchurch about five years ago. My grandparents live there. My dad's still in Palmy."

"Your parents divorced?"

"Yeah. Mum cheated. She keeps telling me she didn't mean it to happen, but ..."

"That's a sad excuse."

"Yeah, I know. I mean, I'm not mad at her or anything. Things between my parents were kind of bad for a while. Not like physically bad. They just stopped talking to each other I guess." He was quiet again for a minute or so. "Amanda told me her mum walked out when she was a kid."

"Yeah, that's what the boss told me."

"She misses her, sometimes. Not that she tells her dad."

"Well, why would she?" Jim replied. Pete had done his best to fill the void left by his ex-wife but even he admitted that he hadn't been the perfect parent. There had been times when he'd had to put work ahead of his daughter's needs, as much as it had hurt, but he'd done his best to help her understand why. He'd always tried to make it up to her.

A few minutes later, they left the motorway and Jim guided his colleague to a house on the main road, not far from the local shopping complex.

The house was modern, clearly having been built within the last five years. A white Mercedes was parked in the driveway.

Chris whistled as they got out of the car.

"Somebody must be pretty well-off," he said.

Jim doubted it. Horton had hinted at it in the interview, but Jim had dug deeper, discovering that the company was not only in trouble, but they were also looking at bankruptcy. They were depending on the income from the talent show to get them out of the hole they were in.

If his suspicions were correct, the house and car would also be casualties if the production were to be forced to shut down.

He knocked on the door and waited. About a minute later, a woman with hair dyed blue-grey opened the door.

"Yes?" she said with a husky voice.

She was wearing a heavy perfume, but it still could not disguise the smell of cigarettes on her. He did his best not to make a face.

Jim nudged Chapman and took out his identification.

"Ms Burns? We're detectives with West Side police. We'd like to ask you a few questions."

She looked hesitant but opened the door.

"Uh, my kids are home," she said, walking away without a glance.

"That's all right, Ms Burns. I'm sure they can occupy themselves while we chat."

She led them down a short hallway to an open-plan kitchen and dining area. Two youths in their mid-teens were sitting in a living room playing games on a console.

"Martin, Richard, could you boys please go and play that in your bedrooms. The police are here."

One of the boys got up. He was just shy of Jim's own height at almost 1.9 metres. He glared at them and asked them brusquely for their identification.

"Richard, that's enough," Debbie admonished him. "Please go to your room."

"What do you want with my mum?" he asked rudely.

"We just want to talk to her," Chris replied, even though Jim still hadn't told him what it was about.

"Do you have a gun?" Martin, obviously the younger of the two asked. He was shorter than his brother by at least twenty centimetres.

"We don't normally carry guns," Jim told him.

"But you have tasers, right?" Richard asked. "I think I read about that somewhere."

"We do, but we don't usually take them if we're just wanting to have a chat with someone," Chris told the older boy.

Jim didn't comment. He knew from experience that even a general chat could escalate into something else and he'd had to use a taser in that situation before.

"Boys, please, just go to your rooms," Debbie told them, looking exasperated. She turned to look at her visitors. "I'm sorry. Teenagers." She studied them for a moment. "Do either of you have children?"

"No, ma'am," Jim said, realising she was pleading for understanding. "But I do know what kids are like."

She nodded before guiding the boys out of the room and pushing them down the hallway. She returned a few moments later.

"Would you two like a coffee?" she asked.

"Coffee would be great. Thank you," Jim said if only to be polite.

The woman made the drinks and indicated for them to sit at the table.

"So, how can I help you … officers? Detectives?"

"Detective," Jim corrected her. He decided to get right into it. "I understand you're a director on Horton Productions."

She lifted her cup to her lips and took her time sipping her drink before replying.

"Yes, I am. Myles and I … we …"

"You're not just business partners, I take it."

"No," she said. "We live together."

"I see."

"Is this about the accidents on the show?" she asked. "Because I really don't know any more than Myles about them."

"Sure. Perhaps you'd like to tell me why Myles lied to me about Paul Davidson's accident?"

He knew from what Amanda had told him that Debbie had told someone they needed to co-operate with police, fearing if they didn't, the production could be shut down.

"I have to be honest with you, Detective. We need this show to keep the wolves from the door."

"So, you're in financial crisis?" he asked, hoping she would confirm what he already knew.

"We barely have enough to pay our crew right now." She sighed. "We know these shows can be a bit of a con, but the advertisers love them and if we have a successful run, it will lead to something else."

"I can understand that."

"These accidents can force us to shut down production. If that happens, we lose everything. Even this house," she said, confirming Jim's earlier suspicions. They had everything riding on it. She added that her partner was using his own funds to pay his employees.

Debbie leaned forward as if to speak confidentially. "The boys don't know how much trouble we're in. We haven't told them."

Chris nodded. "That's understandable." He looked at Jim with a frown, as if wondering why the line of questioning.

Jim had one more card to play.

"Ms Burns, would you care to tell me about your

history with a Rochelle Conley?"

Her face paled. "Uh … what?"

"I believe you had some kind of rivalry with her," he went on.

"We competed for a lot of the same roles. Yes. She was more experienced than I was. But … that was twenty years ago."

"I understand when she was forced to drop out of a production of *Jesus Christ, Superstar*, you took over the role. Why did she drop out?"

"Uh, you might have to ask her that," she said. "I believe it was for personal reasons."

"And not because she had an accident in which she broke her ankle?"

The woman stared at him with wide eyes. Her tone was cool when she spoke again.

"I don't like what you're implying, Detective. If you're suggesting I had something to do with what happened to Rochelle, or that I might have something to do with these accidents that keep happening on Star Quest, I would never …"

Jim raised his hand. "I'm sorry, Ms Burns," he said, convinced by her passionate outburst. "I had to ask." He paused. "Are you insured?"

She frowned at him. "Insured? You mean the company if the show has to shut down for any reason? No. We couldn't afford it." He didn't know much about insurance on such things but it was probably unethical.

When they left, Jim took the keys to drive back to the station. Chris turned to him.

"You just ambushed her," he accused.

"How do you think we find our suspects, Chris? Offer them tea and scones?"

"No, but …"

"I had to catch her off guard."

"Well, you did that all right. What was that all about, anyway? How did you know about Rochelle Conley breaking her ankle?"

"Just information from a source," he said, not knowing whether Amanda had told Chris about her role in this.

"Are you thinking there might be a connection between that accident and the ones happening now?"

"I don't know," Jim told him. "Right now, I'm just following any lead. No matter where it takes us."

Back at the station, they reported to Pete.

"Do you think she was being honest with you?" the boss asked.

"I do. Yes."

"I still think you ambushed her," Chapman interjected.

"Do you think I should have been more gentle with her? Given her time to come up with a lie?"

"Well …"

"Jim's right, Chris," Pete told him. "It doesn't make us popular but sometimes an ambush, as you put it, is the only way to catch them out in a lie. Having said that, from what I've heard, I think your assessment of the situation is correct. She was telling the truth about the incident with her rival."

Chapman frowned. "But she did lie when she said it was personal."

Jim knew it could sound confusing to the rookie detective. While he was obviously trained in all other aspects of police work, he didn't seem to have a good grasp on human behaviour. Jim figured he had the edge given that his mother was a psychologist and she'd taught him enough to help him work these things out.

He explained his reasoning to his colleague. Debbie had probably convinced herself over the years that her rival dropping out of the show had been personal. She had seemed shocked that they'd even thought for a second that she would have had anything to do with the accident that had ended Rochelle's stage career.

His boss asked him to write up the report on the interview before telling Chris to go through the reports from other centres where the local police had been checking into the accidents there.

He had just completed writing his own report when Dave Campion, a detective who was usually on a different shift, stopped by his desk.

"You got a visitor," he said.

Jim frowned up at the blond detective.

"Yeah? Who?" he asked. It was most likely not Amanda as Dave already knew her by sight.

"Some guy named Horton. He looks pissed off, by the way."

This had to be about the morning visit to his partner, Jim thought. There was nothing for it but to go out and face the man.

Myles was waiting just outside Kerry's office. Jim shot the redhead a look and she shrugged, mouthing an apology. His working relationship with Amanda's best friend had been difficult at first, especially after the night she had got drunk.

He still remembered the way Amanda had kissed him that night. While she had been very drunk and her breath had been rather sour, it had been enough to make him want more. As much as he'd wanted it though, he knew that drunk as she was, she wasn't of sound mind enough to know what she was doing.

He'd been more than convinced of that when she'd woken up the next morning stunned and completely mortified to find herself in his bed, dressed only in her underwear.

He hadn't been able to resist the temptation to make her think something had happened between them, but the worry and concern she'd caused both him and her father had soon had him yelling at her. Enough to send her running for the toilet.

He should have felt bad then for yelling at her, considering the state she was in, but he remembered watching her throwing up and realising it could have been a whole lot worse. That had made him mad all over again.

Kerry had been pissed off with him for days after hearing all the gory details from Amanda. It wasn't until after the case had been solved that he'd finally been able to clear the air with the commander's secretary and tell her exactly why he'd got so angry. The woman had promised not to say anything to Amanda.

The truth was, he did like the girl. Sure, she could be annoying, but she had what his father would call spunk. The term had taken on a different meaning since his father's day, but it still felt the best way to describe Amanda's gutsiness.

His mind still on the young blonde, he was taken aback when Myles Horton began screaming in his face.

"Who the fuck do you think you are?" he said. "How dare you accuse my partner ..."

Jim raised his hands. "I'd be very careful, Mr

Horton. Remember where you are."

"You had no right to go to my house and …" He quickly shut the other man down with a stern look.

"As a detective, I have to follow up on leads. I'm sorry you feel I was intruding, but I was only asking questions. I made no such accusations. I'm satisfied your partner had nothing to do with the accidents or Paul Davidson's death."

Horton seemed calmer when he spoke again.

"Why did you ask her about something that happened twenty years ago?" he said.

"As I said, I had to follow up on some leads. That's all you need to know."

"Who told you about …"

"That's none of your concern. The only thing you need to worry about is helping us find out who killed Mr Davidson and why. Are we clear?"

"Yes. I'm sorry, detective. It's just this whole thing … the stress is getting to all of us."

"I'm not surprised. Someone either working for your company or competing for a place on your show has committed murder. I'm sure many people working there will be wondering who's next."

"You really think it will happen again?" Horton asked.

"I hate to speculate. There's already been another accident."

"Yeah, I heard. Contestant broke his leg. But Debbie wasn't there when it happened. She was home. Sick."

That didn't really mean anything, Jim thought. He wasn't about to tell the man that, however, considering he'd basically just talked him down off a proverbial ledge.

He returned to his desk to go over the reports again. The hospital board still hadn't released any information on what had happened the night Davidson died. Pete had told him his counterpart at Central had argued with the boss of the hospital board trying to sort it out but hadn't had much luck.

They still had no leads on who was behind the accidents and whether they were connected to the murder. There didn't seem to be any motive for either and that was the stumbling block.

He wondered if Amanda's theory – that someone was using the accidents to cover up a murder – might have some traction after all.

There was only one thing to do, he thought. Go talk to the girl and see if they could figure out the puzzle together.

He dialled her cell phone number. It went straight to voicemail, so he left a message for her to call him when she was free. In the meantime, he thought he'd go over all his reports and see if he could find a common thread. It was almost the end of his shift when Amanda called back.

"What's up?" she said.

"I figured we should get together. Talk about the case."

"You mean, my case," she said. "What's wrong, Jim?" she added with what sounded to him like fake sympathy. "Stuck for leads?"

He groaned to himself. Why did she have to sound so smug? he thought. It almost sounded like she knew something he didn't.

"Look, I get that you don't like me, but really?"

"Who said I don't like you?" she replied. "I just like yanking your chain."

"You're a pain in the arse, you know that?"

"Yeah? Feeling's mutual. I'll be home by six-thirty. Bring food. I'm starving."

"Any preference?" he asked, ignoring the fact that she'd just ordered him to buy her dinner.

"Mmm, no, not really. I'm not fussy."

Jim left work half an hour later, stopping off at a local restaurant that sold spicy chicken dinners. He had no idea if Amanda liked spicy food. He'd once shared Chinese takeaway with her and that hadn't been too spicy.

He hesitated before ordering but decided to go for the medium heat option. Getting back at her for her snarky comments was one thing but making her eat something she might not be able to handle was another. It was not the best method of revenge, he thought.

Then again, she would probably think that she was getting to him if he tried that trick.

"Lame, Andersen," he told himself.

"Sir?" The teenage girl on the counter frowned at him. She was holding a large bag filled with the containers of food.

"Thanks," he said, taking the bag.

"Have a good night," she said before turning to help another customer.

He drove to Amanda's house. Her car wasn't parked in the driveway and he assumed she was still driving back from the central city. Traffic could be a nightmare, even at six-thirty at night.

Penny spied the bag when she answered his knock. "Ooh, did you bring me dinner? Aren't you kind?"

"This isn't for you," he said coolly. "Amanda's on

her way home."

The woman scowled, then shoved rudely past him to stand on the porch, lighting a cigarette.

"You really should give up," he said. "Most guys I know find smoking to be a really unattractive quality in a woman."

"Screw you. You're not the boss of me."

She deliberately let out a puff of smoke in his direction. The smoke drifted into the house. Amanda had told him the landlord had almost refused to rent them the house when he'd learnt that Penny was a smoker until she'd threatened to file a grievance with the Tenants' Union.

He had had little to do with Amanda's flatmate. By choice. The first time they'd met, he'd just come to speak with Amanda about the case she'd been working on and Penny had basically ignored him. The second time he'd met her, she had tried to flirt with him as soon as she figured out there was more to their relationship. He got the sense she was jealous of Amanda.

Jim put the food down on the table.

"You still going out with Matt Donaldson?" he asked the woman.

"Yes," she said sharply. "Why?"

He wondered if she was going to try her usual trick of batting her eyelashes at him and trying to attract his attention away from Amanda. She'd sidled up to him the night of Amanda's birthday and flirted, even though he'd clearly been there with a date.

"You know, there's something wrong with a guy who dumps a girl then turns around and goes out with her flatmate in less than a week."

"What's your point?" she asked, glaring at him.

"Nothing. I just think it's bad manners, is all. Then again, it is you, Penny. No one could ever accuse you of having good manners."

He saw the lights of Amanda's car as she drove up the driveway. Penny continued to glare at him hostilely as the blonde got out of her car.

"What's going on?" she asked.

"Nothing. I was just talking to your flatmate while I was waiting for you."

Amanda shrugged. "Okay. Whatever. What did you get?"

He showed her the bag and she sniffed appreciatively.

"Mmm, I love spicy chicken. Did you order extra hot?"

"No, but I think they put in some packets of hot sauce."

"Cool." She looked at Penny, who had finished her cigarette and stood in the doorway, still looking annoyed. "Go away, Penny. We've got business to discuss."

The brunette snorted and stomped away to her bedroom, returning a few moments later with a jacket in one hand and car keys in the other.

"I'm going to the movies," she said. "I know when I'm not wanted." She sniffed as if hurt by the rejection.

Cry me a river, Jim thought, wondering for probably the fifth time why Amanda still lived with this woman.

Chapter Seventeen

Amanda watched her flatmate leave before turning to Jim. "What was that all about?" she asked.

"Nothing," he replied.

"Yeah, right. That's why she was glaring daggers at you."

"I can't stand women who think they're God's gift. Like if they snap their fingers guys will come running."

It was funny that the first thing she thought of was a character from an old tv show who did precisely that; although the character was male, not female.

"I think you might be confused. It's usually men who think that way."

He shrugged. "Maybe they do, but I've known a few women like that."

"So, you're saying you're not one of those guys who finds that kind of self-confidence attractive?"

He shook his head. "Besides, that's not self-confidence, that's arrogance."

She nodded, watching as he unpacked the food.

The aroma of the spices reminded her of a restaurant her father had taken her to on her sixteenth birthday. She loved experimenting with different flavours and the restaurant was known for a range of dishes catering for people with varying tastes. It had been her first time at the restaurant and the first time her father had taken time off work specially to spend time with her.

They'd talked and laughed all evening and the waiter had brought out a dessert just for her, singing happy birthday. It had been embarrassing but at the same time, wonderful. It was the best birthday she could remember. Too many times, her father had been unable to spend her birthday with her because of his job. She understood that things happened at work, but it still hurt just the same.

She again sniffed the aroma and smirked to herself. Penny wasn't a fussy eater, but she didn't like spicy food.

"Good thing Penny left," she said. "She'd pitch a fit at this."

Jim looked at her, cocking an eyebrow. "She's not a fan of spicy food?"

"Not really. The first time I cooked dinner it was spicy, and she lost it. Basically, told me I was a horrible person." She shrugged. It wasn't as if Penny had told her of her aversion to the dishes.

"I still think you should move," he said. "I don't like the way she treats you."

She didn't much like the way Penny treated her either, but she had already started looking and there were no rentals available that she could afford. She'd also heard there was stiff competition for many of the properties listed and her chances of getting one that was suitable were slim.

"As much as I'd like to move," she said with a heavy sigh, "I don't get paid that much. Rents aren't cheap."

"Yeah, I know," he agreed. "I mean, don't get me wrong. I like Craig and Susan but now that they're married, I kind of feel like a fifth wheel. Or third wheel." He frowned. "Whatever."

They fell into a comfortable silence while they ate the food. Once they had eaten everything, Amanda disposed of the rubbish and went to the fridge to get them something to drink, only to find one bottle of Sprite that had less than a cup left in it. Penny, she thought. Of all the inconsiderate …

At least there was ice. She grabbed a couple of glasses and filled them with ice and filtered water. Jim looked at her.

"No Sprite?"

She shook her head. "No. Guess Penny drank it all."

"Oh, well, water's healthy at least."

She sipped the water and sat down beside him.

"So …"

"So, I went to see Debbie Burns. Talked to her about the accident twenty years ago."

"What did she say?"

"She felt she was being accused of causing the accident."

"Did she?" Amanda asked.

"I don't think she did," he told her. He related what had happened during the conversation with the woman and a later talk with her partner.

It seemed like it really had been an accident, but Amanda wasn't convinced. It was almost too much of a coincidence that the one person who had been the victim had been one of the stars of the show.

When she expressed her concern to Jim, he nodded in understanding. "I get where you're coming from, Amanda, but I don't think Debbie had anything to do with it. Yes, they were competing for the same roles back then, but it would be extremely petty."

"I guess so," she said. "Just out of curiosity, if someone did deliberately cause Rochelle's accident …"

"It would be considered a crime. Yes."

He went on to explain that it would be treated as an attempt to cause grievous bodily harm, and depending on the actual charge, could be sentenced to a maximum of fourteen years.

"Having said that, however, because this happened twenty years ago, it might be too late to file charges."

Well, so much for that, she thought.

"Do you think there might be a connection to this case?" Jim asked.

"I don't know. I guess I'm just wondering aloud. I did find out something interesting the other day, though. You know one of the judges was on a similar show in the UK about five years ago. She swears that one of the contestants had been on the UK show."

"Which one?" he asked.

"Tracey. Get this. After that light fell and the guy broke his leg, I saw her standing watching from the wings."

"Now, that is interesting," he said. "Can you confirm Tracey was on the UK show?"

"I've been looking on YouTube to see if I can find

her, but I haven't had much luck so far."

"Your better option would be to contact the producers of that show and get a list of contestants for around that time. See if they can send you any footage as well."

She doubted they would even give her the time of day, let alone any footage from the show.

"It's probably better coming from you. Or my dad, I guess."

He nodded. "Yeah. I'll talk to your dad. So ... Tracey, which one was she?"

"The brunette. She was the one I was arguing with the other day. You told her off."

He frowned. "Right. Yeah, she certainly looks like trouble. I might talk to Myles Horton and see if I can get her bio. If she's prepared to commit assault in front of witnesses, she might have a history."

Jim set his empty glass on the table.

"That's a good lead, Amanda. We might just solve this thing yet."

She nodded and grabbed her bag to rummage for her wallet. The detective put out a hand.

"Nah, I got this one. You can get the next one."

"Thanks," she said. "I will."

She got up to see him to the door. He paused in the doorway, looking down at her.

"Think about what I said about moving. Even if you have to share another place with someone. You deserve better than this."

She looked at him askance. Usually, they were bickering, but it seemed like he was genuinely concerned about her.

"I'll think about it," she replied quietly. "I promise."

He gazed at her for a long moment before turning and stepping off the porch to go to his car.

Penny was in a foul mood when she returned home. Amanda had decided to have an early night and was reading in her room when her flatmate slammed the front door. Less than a minute later, she came stomping down the hallway and flung open the door to Amanda's bedroom, hard enough for the door to crash against the wall.

"Your boyfriend is an arsehole!" she exclaimed.

Amanda frowned at her. "What boyfriend?"

"What boyfriend? The one who basically kicked me out of my own home! That one!"

"First, Jim is not my boyfriend, and second, I told you we had business to discuss."

"And you couldn't have done it elsewhere? You could have at least shared some of your dinner!"

"It was spicy chicken, which you hate, need I remind you."

Penny just scoffed. "You have no consideration for me at all, do you? Who cares about Penny? She can go off and do whatever!" she added, waving her hand.

Amanda got out of bed, knowing it put her at an extreme disadvantage with this kind of confrontation. If her flatmate was going to pick a fight with her, then she was going to make sure the other woman couldn't intimidate her.

"I should show consideration?" she asked, standing practically nose-to-nose with the woman. Penny was slightly shorter than her but her high heels put them on almost the same level.

"That's hilarious!" she continued. "How many times have I had someone here only for you to stick your nose in where it's not wanted? And every time a guy has shown the least bit of interest in me, you have to flash your boobs and make out like I'm invisible."

"Well, if you weren't such a frigid little …"

"Don't you dare say it!" Amanda shot back. "You know, I only moved in with you because your brother thought he was doing us both a favour. I didn't realise I was moving in with a complete narcissist!"

Penny stared at her. "What the hell did you call me?"

"I'd explain it, but you're too caught up in your own self-importance to understand it."

"That's it! I want you out of here!"

Amanda continued to glare at her.

"Well, good luck kicking me out since my name's on the tenancy too."

"We'll see about that," Penny responded. She turned and walked out, slamming the door closed.

Great, Amanda thought.

Rehearsals the next day hadn't gone any better than they had a few days earlier. By the time they were over, it was past dinner time. Amanda didn't want to deal with another argument with her flatmate and called her father.

"Hi, Daddy," she said when he picked up.

"Hi, honey. I was going to call you. I sent off a request to the producers in the UK. We will hopefully get an answer back tomorrow. Are you at home?"

"No. I'm just … Actually, can I come and stay with you for a couple of days?"

"What's wrong?"

"Penny and I had a big fight. I need to move out."

"Of course, you can stay, sweetie. You don't need to ask."

He was watching the late news broadcast when she arrived.

"There's some leftover roast beef if you're hungry," he called, not bothering to look up from the television screen.

"Thanks, Dad," she said, going to the kitchen. She decided to make herself a sandwich with the roast meat. Once done, she joined him in the living room, sitting on the couch.

He waited until the ad break to turn to her.

"So, what happened with Penny?"

She told him everything that had happened the night before and what Jim had been telling her.

"I can't afford to live on my own," she said. "The rents would take more than half my wages."

"Well, let me ask around at work. See if I can find someone who's looking for a flatmate. I know it's not the ideal solution, honey, but you're right. You can't afford rent on your own, but you can't keep living with Penny. She strikes me as a very selfish young woman. I'm surprised you stood it for this long."

"The thing is, when she's not acting that way, she can be a good friend."

"Honey, with friends like that, who needs enemies?" He patted her knee. "Let's face it. You've been miserable in that house."

He was right, but then he usually was about most things.

"So, how was rehearsal?" he asked when the next ad break was on.

"It was okay. Tracey was being difficult, as usual. I've been keeping an eye on her, just in case I'm wrong about that accident the other day."

"But you don't think so?" he asked.

She shook her head. "There's just something about the way she was acting that got me thinking she might have had something to do with it. Or at least knows something about what happened."

"Well, be careful, honey. If she is behind the accident, she could be responsible for the others as well."

That was the thing that was bothering her. If Tracey was the one causing the accidents, had she caused Paul's as well? Amanda could handle her own in most things, but she remembered what had happened last time she had gone up against someone prepared to commit murder to get what they wanted.

It felt like a vital piece of the puzzle was missing, but she had no clue what it was.

Chapter Eighteen

"Amanda's staying at my place for a couple of days," Pete announced as Jim entered his boss' office.

"Really?" he asked. "How did that happen?"

"Apparently she and Penny had a huge fight. She won't give me all the details but ..."

"It probably had something to do with what I said to the woman. I'm telling you, boss, she's a grade-A b ..."

"Don't say it," Pete said, holding up a hand. "I know what you mean. I never liked her, but it was Amanda's choice to rent a flat with her."

"I thought you kicked her out?"

The fair-haired man raised an eyebrow. "Is that what my daughter told you?"

Jim nodded. "Her exact words."

Pete chuckled. "I suppose from her perspective it would look that way. I encouraged her to find a place of her own. If that's kicking her out, then so be it."

Jim sat down in the chair in front of his boss' desk. "I don't know. Maybe it's being sexist but ..." Or maybe he was just a cynic, he thought. Given what he'd seen the few years he'd been a cop, he felt Amanda had been too young at barely nineteen to strike out on her own. It was different for him, but then, he'd joined the army at eighteen.

"You think she should have lived with me a bit longer? Jim, my daughter's been taking care of herself since her mother left. If I had suggested she wasn't ready to live on her own, I would have been accused of mollycoddling, or being over-protective." He sat back, folding his hands. "Despite what you might think, Amanda's extremely capable."

Jim smiled but didn't comment. His boss would probably deny it, but he was sure the older man had had a lot to do with why his daughter was so self-reliant. A lot of people these days, regardless of their gender, weren't quite so capable. Then there were people like Penny who thought they were doing others a favour by letting them live with them, only to take advantage of that fact by making them do all the work.

He wanted to have a few words with that woman.

"Whatever you're thinking, don't do it. The whole situation is messy as it is, and with the first show coming up, I don't want Amanda distracted. You hear me?"

"Sure, boss. What about the first show?"

"She's told you her theory about Tracey?"

He nodded. He was yet to do some checking into the woman.

"If she is behind these accidents, she may set her sights on Amanda," Pete said.

"Which would be bad. Amanda's going to have to watch her back."

"Oh, you're right about that." Pete began

rummaging for something on his desk, shifting various papers around. The desk was always messy. It was a wonder the man could find anything. "Here," he said.

Jim frowned as he took the card his boss handed him. He glanced at it.

"This is a ticket for the show on Saturday," he said.

"Well spotted, Andersen. I want you there in case anything happens. Keep an eye on this Tracey."

"Speaking of whom, I really need to go and do that research on her. I never got around to doing that yesterday."

"Why not?"

"We had another assault in the Lyndale Mall. I haven't written the report up yet, but we do have a witness who thinks she can identify some of the kids involved."

Pete frowned. "They were kids?"

He shrugged. "Either that or young adults – early twenties at the oldest, I'd say. If the reports are right, these are the same kids who have been doing the rounds in the central city."

"They're getting cocky," the senior sergeant observed.

The attacks had stopped for a few weeks but suddenly seemed like they had started up again. Jim had been co-ordinating with Central on the case, as well as the murder of the talent show floor manager.

"Unless this is a different group," he suggested.

"Hard to say. Go see if you can find any background on Tracey Brooks. I haven't got around to checking my emails yet, so I don't know if there's anything from the UK."

Nodding, Jim got up and left the office, still holding onto the ticket he'd been given. The last thing he wanted was to have to sit through some show, but since Pete had asked him to back up Amanda and keep an eye on things, he knew he had to.

Kirsten Taylor was sitting in his chair when he got to his desk.

"What's up?" he asked.

"That attack yesterday. I've been talking to the witness and you wouldn't believe who she identified."

"Who?" he asked.

"Remember that kid you said was hassling women at the mall and at that audition?"

He stared at her. "You're kidding." He remembered from the file that Robert Hutton had priors for drug offences, but nothing suggesting violence in his history.

"Curiouser and curiouser," he mused aloud.

Could there be a link to Robert and his gang, and the talent show or was that a coincidence?

He smirked. Both his father and Pete Steele had a fondness for a television show where the main character would often say there was no such thing as coincidence. Both Eric and his boss considered it almost gospel.

"So, what are you working on now?" Kirsten asked.

"There's this woman on the show. A source of mine thinks she might be responsible for some of the accidents."

"How does that work exactly? I mean, if these accidents were at other auditions in other centres –

it's not like she would have been travelling around the country, is it?"

That was true, Jim thought. It didn't make sense. Unless she had an accomplice. Still, it was an awful lot of trouble to go to if she was trying to eliminate some of the competition.

Then again, he thought, people were known to do some horrible things to get what they wanted.

He gestured for the senior constable to get out of his chair and began searching the file he already had on some of the show's contestants.

Kirsten grabbed another chair and sat beside him.

"If these accidents are happening in other centres, surely we'd be looking at a crew member rather than a contestant."

"We're also looking for motive," Jim told her.

"Well, how about I look at the crew files and see if I can't find some kind of connection," she suggested.

He nodded. "Yeah. Thanks." He was sure Central had already been questioning the crew after the accident, but it couldn't hurt to have a different pair of eyes looking into it. Especially if they were looking for a connection to the woman Amanda had identified.

His search on Tracey Brooks did turn up something interesting. She had a charge as a juvenile for shoplifting. While that wasn't so bad, what was more interesting was the fact she had assaulted a mall security guard trying to get away then had mouthed off to the judge in court.

It had been noted in the file that the then-15-year-old had an attitude problem. It looked like her attitude hadn't improved in twenty years. While she hadn't been charged with anything since then, about ten years ago, she had tried to get out of a speeding ticket by first flirting with the attending officer and then becoming belligerent when her original strategy didn't work. She had quickly subsided when the officer had warned her not to cross the line. There was a report on what had happened in the file.

An email alert popped up and Jim checked it. Pete had forwarded a video file from the producers of the UK show. He'd also copied his daughter in the email.

Jim began playing the video. It was raw footage from a show dated five years earlier. He'd seen a few episodes of it, since his sister, Lydia, was a big fan. She had come to stay with him a couple of days when he had still been living in Wellington and had wanted to watch the show. His flatmates had decided to go out for the evening, but the 13-year-old had kept him practically hostage. Since it meant he got to spend some time with his baby sister, he didn't mind all that much.

She had kept up a steady stream of chatter throughout the show, telling him which judge was always critical, which judge seemed friendly and whether she thought the contestants deserved the comments.

In the video he was watching, he recognised Tracey as the dark-haired woman walked out on stage to stand in front of four judges. He also recognised one of them as someone his sister had told him could be quite caustic in his remark.

Tracey stood centre stage, practically glaring at the two women and two men as if daring them to kick her out. She was not even trying to make a good impression. She hadn't even dressed well, wearing ripped jeans almost too tight to be decent. The shirt she wore looked just as bad, showing far too much cleavage. She was well-endowed in the chest and it looked like she couldn't care less.

Her act began well enough. She was trying to do a cover version of a Blondie song. The lyrics had a lot of attitude but while she could carry a tune, she just couldn't pull off the attitude the song needed.

She was stopped before she'd even got halfway through. One of the judges, a balding man in his forties, spoke first.

"Do you have any other material to show us or is that it?"

"What d'you mean, is that it?" she asked, glaring at the man.

The second judge, whom Jim recognised from the local show, looked at her colleague and spoke up.

"Look, it's not that you're not technically good, but the material … it's really not the best song for you."

"You what? Why don't you come up here and sing you stupid tart?" Tracey asked. "It's not fuckin' easy to come up here and do this, you know."

"That isn't the point, young lady," the third judge, a man aged about fifty told her. "We know how difficult it is. The point is if you can't take constructive criticism …"

He wasn't given the opportunity to finish as Tracey began shouting at him, even threatening. She was quickly surrounded by security who hauled her off.

"Well, she's charming, isn't she?" Kirsten observed.

"They're right, though. Just because someone can sing, if they can't take constructive criticism, they won't survive as an artist. I can't sing to save my life but even I could tell it was the wrong song for her."

"Yeah. Me, too."

Chris Chapman came in, dumping a notebook on his desk. Jim looked at him.

"Hey, Chapman, did you finish that report on the Star Quest accidents?"

The other man nodded. "Yeah. Why?"

"We're just trying to figure out who might be causing them," Kirsten replied. "What did you find out?"

The younger detective shrugged. "Not much, really. They weren't investigated until we got involved. All I did find out was that all four were caused by some kind of mechanical fault."

Jim looked at Kirsten. She nodded and returned to her list of crew members who had worked at all five auditions. Chapman walked off to sit at his desk.

They were clearly looking for someone who had some technical expertise. Either a grip or someone employed in a similar capacity, he thought, sharing his thoughts aloud with his colleague.

It was still a question of whether they had been employed locally for the auditions in other centres or if they were part of the permanent crew with the production company.

Given those parameters, Kirsten was able to eliminate all but about a half dozen people.

He suggested they check out the background of each crew member and quickly fired off an email to Horton's assistant for her to send back their resumés. Meanwhile, Kirsten began cross-checking each one against any criminal records.

The work took most of the rest of the day. Pete

came out of his office just before the end of the shift.

"How's it going, guys?" he said.

"We've pretty much narrowed down a list of six crewmembers," Kirsten told him, handing him a list.

"This is good," the boss replied. He sighed. "Just quietly, I've been getting a bit of flak from both the company and the boss on why it's taken so long to find an answer."

Jim raised an eyebrow. "Two days ago, we didn't even have this, boss," he said. "I mean, what are they expecting? None of the accidents prior to Paul Davidson were even investigated because they didn't think there was anything there to investigate."

At least, not where the police were concerned, he thought, since the local health and safety office had been assigned to investigate it. Despite there being four accidents before the day Amanda had auditioned, they hadn't seen anything out of the ordinary.

That meant they had to be looking for someone who had enough skill to make it look like mechanical failure instead of sabotage.

He looked at Kirsten. "Thanks for your help. I don't think there's much more we can do until we look at their employment records."

"No problem," the woman said with a smile. "Going for a drink?"

"Yeah. I should see if Gaby's free tonight," he said. He hadn't seen his girlfriend for a few days and figured he owed her some time.

When he made it to the police bar, he found the Geek Squad officer sitting at one of the tables with Amanda. He frowned at the two women, who appeared to be quite chummy.

"I thought you'd be rehearsing," he said. "Since the first show's tomorrow."

"I've been doing that all day," the blonde replied, her voice a little hoarse. "As you can tell from the state of my voice."

"Oh. Yeah, it's important to rest it," he replied. He kissed Gaby on the cheek and turned away to place his order at the bar. When he returned to the table with a bottle of beer, the two women had resumed their conversation.

"Are you sure you don't mind?" Amanda was asking.

"Hey, I'm looking for a flatmate, you're looking for a flat. It's perfect."

Jim frowned at them. "What's this?"

Amanda smiled. "Gaby's flatmate is leaving. She's got a new job down south."

He pulled her aside. "Is that a good idea? I mean, she is my girlfriend."

"So? She knows we're friends. Frienemies," she amended, rolling her eyes.

He sighed. "Fine." As much as he liked going out with the dark-haired woman, he wondered if things might get complicated should they break up and he was still working with Amanda. Knowing Pete's daughter, she would be constantly coming to him for advice.

"Well, if it's that much of a problem ..." Amanda huffed.

"I didn't say anything!"

"You didn't have to. Your face speaks volumes!"

"That's ridiculous!"

"Look, you're the one who told me to move away from Penny. Now you're worried because your girlfriend invited me to move in with her!"

"Well, I … I didn't think you two got along so well." Then again, they had been friendly the night of Amanda's birthday.

"Actually," Gaby interjected, "we've been getting to know each other quite well the last couple of weeks. Anyway, I know what you're worried about. You think it would cause complications if you and I should stop going out but you're still coming around to talk to Amanda." She shrugged. "I think we're mature enough to work things out. Well, I am. I don't know about you."

The jibe stung a little. He stayed silent, figuring the less he said about it, the better. He was just glad Amanda was moving out of her flat.

"So, uh, we think we might have started to narrow down who's responsible for the accidents on the show," he said.

Gaby scowled. "Could you avoid shop talk for one evening? Besides, can't you see Amanda's shattered?"

He looked at the other woman and realised his girlfriend was right. Amanda had dark circles under her eyes and appeared pale. She explained that she had been rehearsing since seven that morning and it had already been a long day.

It appeared she hadn't had a chance to view the video her father had sent her.

"We do need to talk …" he began, but a look from the blonde shut him down.

"Can we please talk about this tomorrow?" she said, still sounding hoarse. "My head's just buzzing from everything today."

"Well, what time do you have to be at the

convention centre tomorrow?" he asked.

"About two, I guess."

He nodded, telling her he would come to see her at her father's house around lunchtime, deciding that would give her plenty of time to see the footage.

Chapter Nineteen

Amanda spent most of the morning reading through the information the UK producers had sent and watching the raw footage. The woman who had told her about Tracey was right. She had the wrong attitude and would never advance to the next level if she couldn't take constructive criticism. She clearly thought just being able to sing was enough.

"Amanda?"

She looked up and smiled at her father. "What's up, Dad?"

"I bought a hot chicken for lunch. Didn't you say Jim was coming over?"

"Yeah, he wanted to talk. I guess about the video and the competition tonight."

She closed the lid of her laptop and went to join her father in the kitchen. He had bought fresh rolls and ingredients for a salad, so she began helping him make it.

"Everything else okay?" he asked as they worked.

"I guess. Did Jim tell you Gaby Rutledge offered me a room?"

"Yeah, he did. That's great, honey. Are you going to take it?"

"I think so. She's a nice person."

Amanda had spent a little time with Jim's girlfriend the Friday before. When the other woman had realised Jim had to work that weekend, she had invited Amanda to go to the movies with her after she finished rehearsals.

"Jim was a little worried last night. I mean, they are dating. I guess he's worried that they might break up and it would make things awkward if I need to work with him again."

"It's just as awkward with them both being cops," he said. "There's a reason some offices have a policy against inter-office dating."

"Sure, but you can't help who you're attracted to."

"That's true," he conceded. "I mean, I don't have a problem with it myself. If two of my officers decided to date, who am I to stand in the way? They're mature adults. They know the risks if things don't work out."

Amanda nodded. It had been different for her parents. They had met when her father had been a young constable, testifying in his first trial. Her mother had been working as a Paralegal for a barrister who often represented the police in High Court trials. Kim had helped her boss with some of the research for the trial, which had necessitated interviewing Pete.

They'd begun dating after the case was over. Herr boss had had her transferred to another department in the firm when he'd become concerned there might be a conflict of interest in any future cases.

Kim had decided to give up work when she

became pregnant, but she'd also begun drinking heavily not long after Amanda was born.

Amanda glanced out the kitchen window and saw Jim parking his car in the street. She went out to greet him, opening the door as he was walking up the path.

"Hi," she said. "We're just making lunch."

"Great," he replied.

They discussed the video while they ate.

"Sure seems like she has a real axe to grind," Pete mused.

Jim nodded. "We both know some people will do anything to get what they want."

"Even kill," Amanda agreed.

As much as she felt she could look after herself, having had a couple of run-ins with the older woman, and knowing she was now a suspect in both the accidents and the murder, Amanda wasn't sure she relished the idea of being in the show. Tracey had already implied that she saw her younger rival as one of the ones to beat.

She had already informed the clients of her suspicions about the accident a few days earlier, and they had both expressed their concerns about Tracey's behaviour.

Amanda was determined to finish what she had started, however. She wasn't about to let the woman intimidate her or the thought of what the older woman might do stop her from solving the case.

"Just be careful," her father told her. "I don't want you becoming a casualty."

"I'll keep an eye on things tonight, boss," Jim promised.

Amanda's face fell. She looked at the detective.

"You're coming to the show?" she asked.

"Your dad gave me a ticket. Not to watch the show but to make sure nothing happens to you."

She looked at her father. It was bad enough that she was going to have to perform in front of an audience of about two hundred people, but did she have to do it in front of the man she so often clashed swords with?

"What's wrong, Princess?" Jim said with a smirk, obviously having correctly interpreted her expression. "Performance anxiety?"

She scrunched her nose and glared at him. "If anyone has to worry about performance anxiety, it's you."

He snorted. "You better not be implying what I think you're implying, kid, because I happen to be very good at it."

"Oh, listen to that ego. Besides, that's not what Gaby told me."

"You two talk about me?" he asked, his eyes widening in incredulity.

She put on a mischievous smirk. They hadn't really talked about Jim at all, but he didn't need to know that.

"Really?" he said.

She looked at her father, who was grinning like a loon. He winked at her. She turned once more to Jim who appeared to be almost sweating. She decided to let him off the hook.

"No, not really," she said. His relief was palpable. "I just love making you squirm."

He narrowed his eyes at her. "You, Amanda Louise Steele, are trouble."

She gasped and glared at her father. "You told

him my middle name was Louise?" she accused. She'd always hated the name. Pete had insisted he'd chosen it for its history in royalty, but her mother had been equally insistent that it had come from a famous 19th-century author.

Either way, as far as Amanda was concerned, it was ridiculously old-fashioned.

"He didn't need to," Jim replied smugly. She glared at him and he shrugged. "Well, I am a detective."

She threw a bread roll at him and he caught it, taking a huge bite out of it, smirking at her.

By the time the show was due to start, she was so nervous she had butterflies in her stomach. She sat backstage, her backside numb from having sat so long on one of the hard plastic chairs the crew had set out for contestants. She slowly drank water in a disposable cup and meditated, hoping it would get rid of the anxiety.

Someone sat down beside her, but she was so focused on the meditation that she didn't know who it was until they spoke.

"Just keep breathing nice and slow," the woman said. "Just like I taught you."

She turned her head to look at Debbie. The other woman smiled at her.

"You look like you're about to throw up."

"Ugh, don't say that. I might just do it."

"Relax, hun, you'll be fine. It's not like you actually need to win this thing."

Amanda paused in the middle of lifting her cup of water to her lips and stared at the older woman.

"Uh, what?"

"It's all right," Debbie said kindly. "I talked to

Sarah. She told me."

Amanda swallowed hard. "Um, no one was supposed to know about that," she said.

"Well, it wasn't that hard to figure out when I got a visit from the West Side police. Friends of yours?"

"They work with my dad," she admitted.

"I can understand why you might have thought I had something to do with what happened to Rochelle." Debbie sighed. "I was an arrogant little bitch in those days." She grinned. "I can admit it. I really thought I was better than her. I wasn't."

"So, when you said she dropped out for personal reasons ..."

"I had a long talk with Myles about that. I kept telling myself it happened that way so I didn't have to face the thought that I might somehow have caused her accident myself."

Amanda frowned at her. "What do you mean?"

"I know it sounds crazy, but sometimes you want something so badly that you find yourself wanting something bad to happen." She chewed her lower lip. "Rochelle and I had a huge fight one day at rehearsals. I was really angry, telling her I thought she wasn't suited for the role and that I was better. Then I said I wished something would happen so she would have to drop out."

She was silent for a few moments.

"I was there when it happened. One minute she was up on that stage, singing her heart out, the next she was on the floor, almost screaming in agony. It all happened so fast. The platform she was on just gave way."

"I'm sorry," Amanda told her. "I ..."

The older woman shook her head. "Don't

apologise. You were doing your job." She seemed lost in thought for a few moments, gazing across the room. "We can't afford any more accidents," she said quietly. "I think you know the company's in a lot of trouble. Financially. These accidents, and poor Paul's death … If this show doesn't go ahead, the company will have to be wound up. This was our last chance."

"I'm so sorry," Amanda said. "If it helps, I think I might know who's behind the accidents. She probably has an accomplice though. Someone on the crew."

"Who?"

"I don't know who the crew member is, but I'm pretty sure Tracey Brooks is at least planning it."

Debbie looked concerned. "Why doesn't that surprise me?" she said. "I'm sorry I put you in the group with her, but I figured you wouldn't stand for her bullshit. I'd watch your back. I overheard Tracey talking about you earlier. I didn't catch all of it, but it sounded to me like she was going to make sure you didn't make it into the next round."

"Yeah, don't worry. My dad asked a colleague to look out for me." She rolled her eyes.

The other woman smirked. "This wouldn't be the cute guy with the dark hair, would it?"

"He's not that cute!" Amanda replied.

Debbie laughed. "You know what Shakespeare said, don't you? It's okay to admit you like the guy."

Amanda huffed. "He's all right. In small doses."

The other woman patted her arm. "That's kind of the way I felt when I met Myles. We were friends first. Drove each other crazy for a couple of years before we even admitted there was something there."

"Oh, hell no. There is no way in hell I would ever

consider Jim Andersen potential boyfriend material. He's obnoxious."

Debbie winked and got up. "You keep telling yourself that, sweetie. Anyway, break a leg." She grimaced. "I mean, not literally. It's ..."

"I know," Amanda replied, familiar with the saying. "Thanks."

She continued to sit quietly. A camera crew was conducting interviews with some of the contestants, watched over by the producer, Sarah. The other woman looked up and caught her gaze. She nodded, giving a brief smile.

Finally, Amanda's name was called, and she followed the production assistant through the maze of chairs and out a set of double doors to the backstage of the auditorium.

She was stopped by the presenter, who nodded and smiled at her. Amanda recognised her as an actress on a television programme Penny often watched. She was pretty, with cocoa skin and long, wavy dark hair.

"The one before you is just finishing up," she said. "She'll have to wait for the judges to give their comments and then I'll go out and announce you." The woman peered at her. "You okay?"

"Just nervous," Amanda told her.

"Don't worry. You'll be fine."

Amanda didn't answer, quickly looking around. She hadn't seen Tracey at all that day, and they were supposed to perform as a group later in the three-hour show. Of course, much of it would be edited before being screened on television. That was if the show was eventually picked up by the network.

There was no telling whether Tracey was going to

follow through on her threats, or what that would entail. Given that all the accidents had been caused by mechanical failure, she was sure the woman would have had to plan something well in advance.

Then again, it would be leaving an awful lot to chance. Unless Tracey or her accomplice was an expert in that area. Somehow, the other woman didn't strike her as particularly skilled in such things.

Amanda realised that her friend Julie was the contestant on the stage. She listened as the judges began to comment, telling her she was technically skilled but still not as powerful emotionally as she could be. The younger woman took the criticism quietly, without fuss, thanking the judges as they all agreed to send her through to the next round.

Julie left the stage looking flushed and breathless. The presenter smiled at her.

"You did great," she said.

The young woman sighed. "I messed up on the first verse though, and they didn't think I put enough emotion to it." As the presenter left to go out on stage, Julie spotted Amanda.

"Hi," she said, the greeting not as enthusiastic as it normally was.

"Hey, that wasn't too bad," Amanda told her. "It's only the first show. It just takes a little practice, that's all."

"I guess." Julie looked her over. Amanda had chosen to wear a short dress in a wine colour. The dress was sleeveless, with spaghetti straps, but was still fairly modest. "You look amazing. That colour looks so good on you."

"Thanks. I'm so nervous," she said, her hand trembling as she smoothed the skirt. While she wasn't as nervous as she made herself out to be, she thought it would help make the other girl feel a little better about her own performance.

"Don't be," Julie assured her. "You're going to do great."

The assistant handed her a microphone and gently pushed her toward the stage. Amanda walked out slowly, doing her best to ignore the audience. She remembered something her teacher had told her when the school choir had performed in a competition.

"Just imagine them all in their underwear," she'd said.

The last person she wanted to imagine in his underwear was Jim Andersen. She couldn't help but think of the night she'd got drunk and waking up the next morning in Jim's bed. She had been too busy nursing a hangover to notice at the time, but he had been wearing only boxer shorts.

As she recalled that morning, she could recall his muscular body, the skin lightly tanned with just a sprinkling of chest hair.

Stop it, she told herself, looking up to face the audience. Thankfully, due to the stage lights, she couldn't really see in the darkness of the theatre. She could only just make out the judges' table, which was lit by a spotlight. Both Deirdre and Tama smiled at her.

"Hello, Amanda," Tama said. "You're looking a little nervous, but don't be. Just pretend you're singing into your hairbrush."

Amanda found herself snickering at the thought. She had confessed doing so to Tama the night they'd had dinner and he'd assured her it was something a lot of little girls did.

She'd chosen a song she knew had once been performed by the other female judge. It had won her accolades and, in many respects, launched her career. The title was rather apt, considering Amanda needed a lot of luck tonight.

She silently praised Debbie for her coaching. Despite her concerns about what had happened twenty years ago, the coach had taught her well.

She listened for the introductory bars and began the first verse. Just as she began to get into the chorus, she heard an ominous crackling sound. Suddenly the speaker just above her exploded in a flash of sparks and began to fall. She quickly jumped out of the way as it crashed to the floor.

Pandemonium erupted. Sally, the presenter, rushed out, along with a production assistant. All four judges got up from the table and ran onto the stage. Deirdre got to her first.

"Amanda, are you all right?" Her face was pale with shock.

"Shit, that was close." Amanda wasn't sure who had said it but didn't disagree.

She wasn't surprised when Jim came up to the stage. He quickly identified himself to the judges and the crew members.

"Are you okay?" he asked, his concern genuine.

"Yeah. I managed to get out of the way before anything got on me."

He remarked quietly it was a good thing she was already alert to the possibility of something happening. Luckily no one else heard him saying it.

There was no way the rest of the show could go ahead that evening. The audience members were quickly informed and told their tickets would be honoured for the next time.

Amanda was led out backstage to a small room where a production assistant with first aid training checked her over to make sure she hadn't been hurt in the near-miss. Jim stayed with her, hovering over her with a worried look.

"I'm fine," she said.

"You're shaking," Jim observed.

"Well, so would you if you just about got hit by an exploding speaker."

"I should go check in with Horton," Jim said. "I'm sure he's got his guys going over that speaker with a fine-toothed comb." He went to the door before turning to look at her. "I don't know about leaving you alone though."

"Why?"

"Because I'm afraid you're going to do something stupid."

"Like what?" she asked.

He rolled his eyes and left the room. Amanda sighed. Maybe she hadn't exactly considered the consequences of her actions in the past, but she wasn't that stupid.

The production assistant was called away, leaving Amanda alone. She sighed again, looking around the room, wondering what she was supposed to do next.

She'd been left with a cup of water and sipped it slowly, drumming her fingers on the table next to her.

The door opened behind her. She didn't bother turning around, figuring it was either the assistant or Jim returning.

"I heard you were hurt."

Amanda turned around and confronted Tracey as she closed the door with a snap.

"Heard? Or hoped?" she asked.

The other woman paused, her eyes widening for a moment. She quickly tried to cover up her surprise by frowning at her. "What do you mean?"

"Do you take me for an idiot, Tracey?"

"Are you trying to accuse me of something?"

"Oh, I'm not trying to do anything. I know it was you. What's wrong? Couldn't stand the competition?" The other woman scowled.

"You're dreaming. As if you thought you ever stood a chance in this thing anyway."

"Oh, I know I don't stand a chance. The point is, you're still labouring under the delusion that you think you do. How many times are you going to keep trying before you get the message that you're just not that good enough?"

"You bitch! You have no idea what it's like to want something that badly."

She was wrong about that, Amanda thought, but that didn't matter.

"What? That you'll do anything to get it? Even murder?"

Tracey gasped. "What? What are you … I didn't … you think I killed that man?"

Amanda studied her. Tracey's reaction was one of shock. It appeared she had had nothing to do with the floor manager's death. Then again, there would be every reason to think she was faking the reaction.

"Well, did you?" she asked. "Then again, I don't think you've got the guts to do something like that. Maybe if he was a rival."

Tracey's expression was ugly.

"Those judges know I'm the one to beat. They're jealous. They're all jealous. That's why they have to keep pushing me down."

"No, you're not the one to beat, Tracey. The fact is, you're just not cut out for this business."

"And you are?"

"No," she said, shaking her head. "But I was never in it for the prize money. Who are you working with, Tracey? Who set up the accidents?"

"I did it all by myself," Tracey replied proudly, clearly deciding there was nothing to lose by confessing.

Amanda shook her head. "No. There's no way you're smart enough to figure out how to make a speaker explode, or how to cause a spotlight to fall. Besides, some of the accidents happened at other auditions. And I don't see you travelling up and down the country just to set something up."

"Well, you just think you're so clever, don't you?" the other woman snarled.

Tracey's arm came up as if she was about to strike. Amanda saw just in time that she was holding a hammer that had obviously been left in the room.

"I should smash your skull in, you bitch!"

Amanda raised her arm, blocking the blow before grabbing the other woman's wrist, forcing it down. Tracey screamed in what sounded more like anger than pain, trying once again to lift the hammer.

She was forced to drop it when Amanda smacked her wrist against the edge of the table. Tracey grabbed a handful of hair with her other hand and pulled hard. Amanda felt some of the hair give way painfully at the root. Her eyes stung with tears.

She was shoved back into the table, her lower

back taking most of the impact. She lashed out blindly, her fist colliding with something and suddenly she was free.

Amanda quickly moved so she wasn't cornered. The older woman screamed again, one hand on the side of her head as she crouched, picking up the hammer. Amanda raised her hand, attempting to block the intended blow.

"I'll take that, thanks."

She was never more relieved to hear Jim's voice.

Chapter Twenty

Jim wasn't sure about leaving Amanda alone, but he had to check in with either the producers or with his colleagues from Central, who had no doubt been called in. He returned to the empty theatre. Horton was sounding stressed as he talked to one of the technicians.

"How could this happen?" he was demanding.

His partner was watching from the sidelines, looking worried. She glanced up at Jim and nodded as he stepped forward.

"I think that's going to be something for our forensics team to figure out," Jim interjected before the technician could reply.

The other man turned to look at him. His expression mirrored his partner's. They were both clearly worried about the show and how the incident would affect their chances getting it screened on the television network.

"Are you sure that's necessary?" Horton asked. He began complaining that any investigation by forensics would just delay proceedings and cost them more money. Debbie spoke softly to him, clearly trying to calm him down.

Leila Said, a constable whose family had left Iran when she was just a baby, spoke up.

"Yes sir, it is necessary. We need to find out exactly what was done so we can track down the person who did this." She glanced at Jim and offered a small smile.

He pulled the constable from the Central station aside.

"There's a woman, brunette, about thirty-five. I'm pretty sure she knows something about who set up these accidents."

"If you're meaning Tracey, I saw her just a minute ago," Debbie told him.

She added that it looked like the woman was heading in the same direction Amanda had gone. He stared at her. The singing coach's eyes widened.

"You don't think …" she began.

Jim left Leila and her colleagues to handle the removal of the evidence and raced back to the room. As he ran along the corridor, he heard Amanda cry out in pain. He burst through the door in time to see Tracey raise a hammer, clearly about to strike.

"I'll take that, thanks," he said, grabbing her wrist.

He glanced at Amanda as he forced the woman to drop the tool.

"You all right?" he asked.

Her relief was palpable. "I'm fine. Now."

"She was about to attack me …" Tracey began.

"Save it for the judge, Ms Brooks," he said. "You're under arrest."

"No, you don't understand," she protested as he

took out his handcuffs and forced her hands behind her back.

Leila and another constable from Central, Steve Hammond, appeared in the doorway. Jim turned, nodding his head toward the hammer.

"Bag that," he told Steve. He made his prisoner sit on a chair and asked Leila to complete the arrest procedure and watch over the woman while he turned back to Amanda.

He checked her over. It looked like some hairs had been pulled out by the root as her scalp was bleeding a little. He gently touched the area and she winced.

"Sorry," he said.

"How bad is it?"

"Bad enough. Where else were you hit?"

"My back's going to have one hell of a bruise tomorrow."

He held up three fingers, figuring he should check for concussion anyway. "How many fingers am I holding up?"

"I don't have a concussion," she told him. "I just got scalped is all."

"Do you need to see someone?" Jim asked, thinking she should probably get her injuries looked at. Amanda shook her head.

"I'm okay. I mean, I'm not great, but I'll survive."

He gently told her to stay put while he sorted out the details with his colleagues. Tracey was going to be taken to the central station to be booked. He decided the best option was to call Amanda's father and tell him what had happened so she could go home and recover.

It turned out to be unnecessary. Tama had already called Pete and informed him. The detective senior sergeant arrived while Jim was talking to one of the production assistants, making sure all the staff knew not to touch anything until forensics had been over the two crime scenes.

"Where is she?" Pete demanded when he appeared, sounding upset,

Jim looked at the older man, figuring he was worried about his daughter.

"Boss?" Pete turned to him and gave a sort of grimace.

"They called me and told me Amanda had been hurt."

"One of the assistants was checking her over," Jim told him. "She's fine. She got in a fight with our suspect. She'll probably be bruised for a few days, but she insists she doesn't need medical attention."

Pete nodded. He was led away by Tama, presumably to find his daughter and take her home. While Jim still had to talk to Amanda and get her statement on everything that had happened, he figured he could leave it until the morning.

Leila returned from Central an hour or so later and informed him Tracey had been booked and would be available to be interviewed the next morning.

By the time Jim left the convention centre, it was already well past one in the morning.

He was up early the following morning and left the house without getting coffee. Pete had obviously been expecting him as the door opened as soon as he pulled up in the driveway of his boss' house.

"Amanda's in the kitchen," the detective sergeant told him. "She's got one hell of a headache."

He followed the older man into the kitchen. Sure

enough, the blonde was leaning over the counter-top, looking extremely pale. She was holding what appeared to be an icepack against her head.

"How are you feeling?" he asked quietly.

"Lousy," she answered. "I can barely move this morning. Dad had to put some stuff on my back. For the bruising."

"Ouch," he said in sympathy. "Are you up to giving me a statement?"

"I guess so," she replied, not looking very enthusiastic about the subject.

"Sorry. It needs to be done," he said.

"I know."

He watched as she slowly straightened up before limping across the floor to the table. Her father slipped past her to pick up the coffee pot.

"Coffee, Jim?" he said.

"Thanks, boss." He sat down at the table, taking out his notebook. "So, what happened after I left you?"

"I was just sitting there when Tracey came in. We talked, then she grabbed the hammer and attacked."

"What did you say to her?"

"I think I told her I already knew she was behind the accidents. I might have implied she had something to do with Paul's death as well."

"And?"

"She tried to make out she was acting alone."

Jim listened as Amanda slowly related what had happened. It sounded a little as if his friend could possibly have provoked the other woman, but he realised she'd been trying to trip Tracey up. No matter what, it shouldn't have provoked the other woman into trying to kill her.

He finished up the interview by making Amanda promise to see a doctor if things didn't improve.

He drove to Central police station an hour later and spoke to the officer in the Watchhouse. Andy Jones had trained with him at Police College.

"I'm here to interview Tracey Brooks," he said.

"I heard Pete Steele's daughter was caught up in that mess," Andy said.

"Yeah."

The other man leaned on the desk. He was a little shorter than Jim and already had grey hairs despite being a year or so younger.

"So, is she cute?"

"Andy, come on."

"I'm just asking, mate. Is she?"

"I'm going to plead the fifth on that one," Jim replied, hoping his friend would just drop the matter.

"Which means she is cute," Andy commented. "You wouldn't be saying that if she wasn't."

"I'm not even going to go there since she is the boss' daughter."

He knew what his colleagues thought. Especially after the last time he and Amanda had had to work together. They were not fully aware of the circumstances, so of course, they would gossip about the frequency of the young woman's visits to the station.

That didn't mean he was going to answer his friend's questions either.

Andy laughed, pressing the button to allow Jim access to the inner sanctum. The senior constable led him down the corridor to the interview rooms, keys to the cells jangling in his hand.

"I'll be right back," he said.

Jim sat in the interview room, making sure the recording equipment was working properly. He opened his notebook on the table, waiting for Andy to bring the prisoner in.

About a minute later the door opened and Tracey Brooks was brought in. She was looking more than a little worse for wear. The make-up she had worn for the show the night before had run, leaving her with dark circles around her eyes and marks on her cheeks.

"Sit down, Ms Brooks," he told her.

"I don't want to."

"Sit. Down!" he repeated firmly, making it clear he wasn't about to take any nonsense from her.

She sat reluctantly. He kept his gaze on her.

"You want to tell me why you were about to attack Amanda Steele with a hammer?"

"Self-defence," she said. "She attacked me first."

"Self-defence?" he repeated. "That's what you're going to go with? Seems to me like Amanda was the one acting in self-defence since she had no weapon to speak of."

"You don't understand. She ..."

"Are you aware of the serious nature of the charges we intend to bring against you, Ms Brooks? You not only intended to cause Miss Steele grievous bodily harm, but it also looked to me like you were about to kill her. That's attempted murder."

The woman's eyes widened at the last charge. She tried to deny it.

"No. See ..."

Jim didn't let her finish, telling her that she was also the main suspect in the accidents which had plagued the show.

"It's very clear you were not working alone. Who is your accomplice?"

She shook her head, refusing to answer. He held her gaze, hoping to intimidate her into giving up the information. When she still refused, he assured her they would eventually find out. Even that failed to impress upon her the seriousness of what she was facing.

"Did you have anything to do with the accident that led to the death of Paul Davidson?" he asked, finally.

Tracey began to cry – heaving sobs that would have fooled a less experienced police officer. Jim knew she was just doing it for effect.

"I just wanted to win," she lamented. "I swear, I didn't do anything to that man."

He nodded. Davidson had been a floor manager. Considering she had intended to force contestants to drop out of the running, she had no reason to target a crew member. Unless she was lying, he thought.

Head hung in defeat. Tracey slowly began to talk. It was clear she was still trying to protect her accomplice as she was careful not to mention them at all, but her story poured out. She was desperate to become a singer. She had entered two other competitions before. Five years ago in the UK and two years earlier in Australia.

Determined to get through this time, she had decided the only way she was going to win was by forcing other contestants to drop out. She had heard of an incident where the star of a show had been forced to quit because of an accident and had figured the same scheme would work.

It had, he thought, until Sarah Kennedy had decided to hire Amanda's firm.

Tracey had targeted Amanda, thinking she was going to be the one person in her way. When the speaker had fallen, she had hoped it would have fallen on Amanda, but for her quick reflexes.

Frustrated, Tracey had gone to confront the blonde. Her personal hatred of Amanda and her fear of her scheme being discovered had led to her picking up whatever was handy.

"I wasn't intending to kill her," Tracey cried. "She was just in my way. I couldn't …"

"You attacked her with a hammer," he said. "You really expect me to believe you weren't intending to kill her?"

She fell silent. Jim thought Amanda had been incredibly lucky she had at least learnt some self-defence skills or otherwise they'd be looking at another homicide.

He again asked her about Paul Davidson, but she told him she had auditioned on an earlier occasion. She hadn't been anywhere near the Convention Centre that day.

It still didn't mean she had nothing to do with it, he thought. Her accomplice could have done it. They wouldn't really know until they managed to find him. Or her. He sighed.

"We're pretty much back to square one," he told Amanda later when he returned to her father's home. "You haven't seen anything that might give us a hint as to who we're looking for?"

She shook her head. She still looked a little worse for wear. There were scratches on her face and a nasty bruise on her hand which he guessed had been caused by the punch.

"I wish I could help," she said with a sigh.

Her father put a cup of coffee down in front of Jim. "Seems to me the only way you're going to find who killed Davidson is to figure out your motive first."

Jim looked at him. "I know, boss."

Half the problem was they had been looking at it from the wrong angle, thinking it had been connected to all the other accidents. Tracey had been adamant she had had nothing to do with it. He wasn't totally convinced of that, but didn't have enough evidence either way.

Amanda was frowning, pushing her coffee mug around and around in a circle.

"Maybe this is a dumb question, but the company's in trouble, right?"

He nodded, sipping his own coffee. "Yes."

"Well, how did it get in trouble?"

He considered that for a moment. While they'd been looking into the production company's finances, they hadn't really looked too deeply into why things were so bad. The assumption had been that it was just because of the economy.

What if it wasn't? he thought.

"That isn't a dumb question at all," he told her, again thinking that she was beginning to develop great instincts. After all, she was the one who had considered the possibility that the murder had been a separate matter from the accidents she'd been sent to investigate.

He knew there no point trying to push Amanda for more. She had done her job. It was now up to him to figure out the rest.

Pete got up to answer his phone in the living room. He returned a few moments later.

"That was Kirsten," he said. "She might have something."

"Great. Thanks, boss," Jim replied. He placed a gentle hand on Amanda's arm. "Get some rest."

She nodded. "Thanks, by the way. I don't think I said that last night."

He smiled. "No thanks necessary. I'm just glad I was able to get there in time."

He drove to the station and entered the bullpen. Kirsten was sitting at her desk, gazing at her computer.

"What's up?" he said.

"Myles Horton had his assistant send over these," she said, turning the monitor around so he could read. They were the resumés they had asked for.

"Did you find something?" he asked.

"You tell me," his colleague replied. "Didn't you say something about an accident on a theatre production set twenty years ago?"

He nodded, reminding her he had taken Chris Chapman with him to interview Debbie Burns. He again read through the resumés.

"Well, I'll be," he said.

One of the crewmembers on the list they had managed to narrow down as a suspect in the staged accidents had worked on a theatre production of *Jesus Christ, Superstar* twenty years earlier. Jim quickly cross-checked the dates with everything Amanda had told him.

Knowing he needed a little more solid proof, he dialled a number.

"Hello?"

"It's Detective Andersen. I need to know something about that accident twenty years ago."

Debbie sounded a little puzzled. "What does this have to do with what happened last night?"

He told her what he'd discovered.

"Yes, I remember working with him. And the reason I remember so well is because he's my ex-husband." She went on to explain that they had begun dating during that production. "Why?"

"I can't divulge that right now. But I think you and Myles need to come in."

"What do you mean, 'come in'? Are we suspected of something?"

"No. But we still have a homicide to solve and I think the two of you might be able to help with that."

"Oh. Of course. Will tomorrow morning be suitable?"

"That will be fine."

"How is Amanda? I was worried about her last night. She looked a little banged up."

"A few bruises, but she's fine. Her dad's looking after her."

"That's good. She's a sweet kid."

"Sweet?" He cocked an eyebrow, even though the woman couldn't see it over the phone. "Are we talking about the same Amanda?"

Debbie laughed. "You know, she apparently feels the same way about you. Guess she's not the only one in denial."

"Oh, hell no. Pigs would fly first," he replied, before saying goodbye.

Something was still niggling at the back of his mind. He decided to go over the notes he'd made in his interview with Tracey. She'd told him she'd got the idea from an accident on a show several years ago.

"I wonder," he murmured.

Kirsten looked at him. "You got something?"

"Not sure." He picked up his phone and dialled the number for Leila Said.

"Constable Said."

"Leila, it's Jim. I need you to go talk to Tracey again. Is she still in the cells?"

"Yes."

"Has she been appointed counsel yet?"

There was a brief pause as his colleague looked up the information.

"Tess McCloskey has been assigned."

He heard the sigh from the constable. "Great," he said. He had had a few run-ins with the solicitor since the case with the high school drug rapes. The woman was, as some of his colleagues liked to say, a barracuda-in-heels.

Despite the fact they'd got what amounted to a confession out of Tracey, the solicitor was likely to refuse to allow any further questioning without her presence. Nevertheless, Jim was still determined to try.

"If you can get past the blockade, ask Tracey if the incident she mentioned involved Rochelle Conley. If she's as much into show business as she says she is, she'll know the name."

"Will do."

He hung up a short while later. Kirsten once again looked up.

"What was that all about?" she asked.

He told her everything that had happened the night before and what he'd learnt from Tracey. The woman nodded.

"People will do some terrible things just to get their way. I remember when I was first studying to be a detective, there was this case where a couple was murdered and it turned out the wife's father did it simply because he didn't like her husband and had never approved of the marriage. Some people thought there was some kind of incestuous relationship going on, but that was never proven. They had a little boy, too."

"Evil comes in all shapes and sizes," Jim agreed. "I don't think Tracey's evil, per se, but I do think she's not all that bright. I wonder what the connection is between her and Debbie's ex," he mused.

"I don't know but I intend to find out," Kirsten replied.

Chapter Twenty-One

Amanda was at work reasonably early the next morning. Her bosses had asked her to be in before nine so they could debrief on the weekend's events.

She was making coffee when Bob Moody walked in. He winced when he saw the bruises.

"That looks nasty," he said. Amanda knew her father had already told her bosses what had happened. "How are you feeling?"

She shrugged. "Honestly? I wish I could say I've had worse scrapes when I was a kid, but ... what is it with women when they fight? I mean, they seem to go straight for the hair."

He smiled in sympathy. "I can't really say for sure since I'm not a woman, but I suppose in a way it's to do with vanity."

"Not to mention it really hurts!" Amanda put in. He smiled.

"Very true. Anyway, the thing about vanity probably dates back to when long, thick hair was considered to be a measure of a woman's beauty. I may not be the most forward-thinking of men when it comes to equality, but I do know a little something about this." He made a face. "Although, if you ask my ex-wife, she'd call me a fuddy-duddy."

Amanda laughed softly. "You're not a fuddy-duddy. I think you're right. I mean, I wear my hair long because I like the way it looks." She sighed. "After this, though, I may have to get it cut short. At least until it grows back."

"It might be a good idea," he replied as he poured himself a cup of coffee in his Superman mug.

"Don't you normally have tea?" she asked curiously, having practically memorised her boss' habits.

"So I decided to have coffee for once," he responded with a grin. "Sue me." They sat at the table. "Actually, I had a check-up at the doctor's the other day and was told I had to stop drinking and smoking. And no coffee. The smoking, yeah, I'll concede, but a man's gotta have a vice."

"Ooh, you rebel, you," she teased. He laughed.

She continued to banter back and forth with her boss, enjoying the fact that they had got to a point in the working relationship where he was not as closed-off as he had been when she'd first started working there. She supposed it helped that she'd turned to him for advice on the case as well.

Mr Knight came in, grabbing the coffee pot. He poured his own drink, turning to look at them.

"I guess I don't need to ask how you're feeling," he said. "That looks like it hurts."

"Yeah, it still smarts a bit," Amanda agreed. She bit her lip. As much as she had wanted to be a cop, this was twice now she had been hurt on the job. She knew that would be a risk in the police, but they still had defence training. "Is it always like this on the job?"

"As a police officer?" Bob asked. "Yes. And no."

Jerry nodded. "I remember there was this kid. Fresh on the job. Probably been out of police college a month. He'd attended a suspected assault in a supermarket car park. Suspect was trying to make a getaway in the victim's car and the kid was in the way. Guy ran him down. Broke his leg in about three places, if I remember right."

Amanda winced. "Ouch! Was he okay?"

"He was on ACC for a couple of months, but as soon as he was able, he was back out there. One hell of a brave kid."

She nodded. Given the circumstances, it was no surprise he'd have to use the entitlement offered by the government entity while he recovered from his injuries.

Bob looked up at the clock. "Right. Amanda, would you mind making some more coffee?" He frowned. "I think we'll need enough for five more people."

"Five?" she asked.

He nodded. "Your friend, Detective Andersen is coming." He told her Debbie Burns and her partner along with Sarah and Tama were also coming in for the meeting.

She frowned. Her father hadn't said anything that morning before he'd left for work and Jim hadn't mentioned it when he'd come by for a follow-up the day before.

She quickly set things up, putting out cups in the boardroom before going out to greet the visitors. Jim arrived first, accompanied by Debbie and Myles

Horton. The older woman hugged her.

"I'm so glad you're all right," she said. "I was really worried."

"I'm okay. It was pretty sore, but not as much now," she added when the woman looked over the injury to her scalp.

"I hope you're going to throw the book at Tracey Brooks," Myles commented, looking just as concerned.

"That's up to the judge to decide," Jim told him. "But she is facing some pretty serious charges." He looked at Amanda. "Boardroom?"

She nodded. "There's coffee already brewed." She was about to lead them to the room when Sarah and Tama came in. She greeted them, nodding at their concern, leading everyone to the boardroom.

Once everyone was settled around the long table, her boss pulled out the folder.

"Thank you for coming, everyone," Bob said. "We thought it best to hold the meeting here to discuss what happened on Saturday. Amanda, why don't you bring us up to speed?"

She nodded, explaining how she had suspected Tracey of being responsible for the accidents and ending with the confrontation backstage.

"I admit I might have provoked her a little," she said.

"Nothing you did or said justified her attack," Jim told her. "On that note, I should tell you that Tracey is appearing in court this morning charged with intent to cause grievous bodily harm. She has admitted to her part in this whole mess. While she has refused to give up the name of her accomplice, we believe we have identified a possible suspect."

"My ex-husband," Debbie said, nodding. "He does have the technical know-how," she added. "I just didn't think he would do something like that."

"Tracey mentioned she got the idea from an accident on a show a few years ago. Given your ex-husband's work history, it's not a huge stretch to guess that Rochelle Conley's accident was the one she was talking about. Unfortunately, her lawyer wouldn't allow my colleague at Central to question her further on this." Jim took in a deep breath. "We're looking for your ex but so far we haven't had much luck locating him."

"Given that you now have someone in custody, I think this is where our part in the investigation ends," Jerry put in.

"Actually, we think Amanda should stay for a little bit longer," Myles interjected.

Sarah nodded in agreement. "While it would be understandable for a contestant to drop out, having come so close to being hurt, as far as we're aware, no one else knows her role in this. I don't see a problem with her continuing in the competition."

Tama added his thoughts. "Amanda is a good singer. She could actually go all the way. Or almost. I think it would help the other contestants as well. There are already murmurs of others dropping out. Out of fear, I imagine."

"I've already talked to the network this morning and they're still willing to let us go ahead," Myles told them. "If we can keep the contestants we have."

"It's not so much the network as the sponsors," Sarah reminded her boss.

"And our marketing department is still working on that."

Amanda listened to the debate quietly. She knew Myles was depending on selling the show to the network and the advertising companies sponsoring it.

She guessed Sarah felt he was more concerned with making money than the safety of the contestants but with the company needing that money, it was understandable. It was also one of the reasons the producer had taken the initiative and hired private investigators to uncover the truth about the accidents.

"You're forgetting one thing, Myles," Debbie spoke up quietly. "You haven't asked Amanda how she feels about all this." She looked at Amanda. "What do you think, sweetie? Do you want to continue?"

There was still the matter of the murder. As much as it wasn't her job to solve that, she was determined to uncover the truth about that.

"I want to continue." She grimaced. While Tracey hadn't managed to take a huge chunk of her hair, it had been enough to make it look a little odd. "I need to do something about my hair, though."

"I know somebody," Debbie assured her. "We'll fix it. Don't worry."

She smiled at the older woman. As much as she had been wary of the singing coach initially, she found herself liking her.

"There is one other thing that is bothering me," she said. "How did the company get in so much trouble that this show is make or break?"

Myles looked down at the table surface. "Uh, that's my fault."

"No, it isn't," Debbie told him. "It's mine. My ex-husband's actually. Up until about a year ago, he was a director in the company. He made some bad investments and used company funds."

"You lost everything?" Bob asked.

"Almost. Unfortunately, the funds invested were from unsecured loans. We never should have let him get away with it," Debbie added. She hesitated, her eyes dancing back and forth. "But we believed him when he said the gamble was worth it."

"Does he have a history of gambling in high-risk ventures?" Jim asked.

"It's one of the things that broke up my marriage," Debbie told him. "He used to gamble a lot but when he came on board as a director, he told me he had changed. He wasn't doing that anymore. I guess I was a fool for believing him."

Amanda sent the woman a look of sympathy. She wondered if there was much more to the story. Something Debbie had said just didn't ring true.

"All right," Jerry said. "I think we're agreed that Amanda can continue in her role." He looked at her. "But we want you to be very careful, young lady. You've already been hurt. Don't take any more chances."

She nodded. "Yes, sir."

Jim stayed behind while the others left.

"You sure you're okay to do this?" he asked.

"Why? Don't you trust me?"

He gazed at her evenly. "You really want me to go there?" he replied. "I mean it, Amanda. If you're not one hundred per cent sure you can handle this, you can drop out."

"You worried about me?" she replied, smirking.

"Stop it. We are not doing this. Your dad is

worried about you and frankly, so am I."

She chewed her lower lip as she studied his expression. As much as she enjoyed the occasional banter between them, she knew he was deadly serious. The confrontation the other night with the woman now in police custody had been more unnerving than she wanted to admit.

"Okay," she said. "You're right. I'm sorry."

He looked a little taken aback at her apology but didn't say anything.

"I want to do this," she continued. "I mean, it's not just the fact that it will help the other contestants if they see I'm determined to go on. Someone out there is a killer."

He nodded. "But you have to promise me that the minute things start looking dodgy you will get us to sort it. No heroics, you understand me?"

"Yes. I understand."

When she arrived at rehearsals later that afternoon, she received some odd looks from those contestants who hadn't heard what had happened. Since they had so many, the first round of eliminations had to be done over the course of several nights instead of just one.

Julie spotted her and ran over. "Oh my god!" she said. "Are you okay? I heard about what happened. Did she really …"

Amanda nodded. "Yeah. But she's in police custody."

Krystal Jenkins came over. "I knew she didn't like you, but I never thought …"

"Did you even know what she was doing?" Amanda asked.

"No. I swear I didn't," the 25-year-old replied,

adding that Tracey had not taken her into her confidence. They'd stood around gossiping about the accidents, but the younger woman had never thought for a second that the other contestant had been behind them.

"What's going to happen to her?" she asked.

"I don't know," Amanda said. She hadn't heard anything from Jim about the woman's appearance in the District Court that morning, but it was more likely that he hadn't heard anything either.

Debbie approached them.

"Girls, why don't you go work on your scales," she said. "Amanda? Can you spare a moment?"

"Sure," she said.

She stepped aside with the coach. "Is everything okay?" she asked.

Debbie spoke in a low voice. "Myles has hired extra security."

Amanda frowned. Where was he getting the money to do that, she wondered. The other woman explained that Myles was using some of his own money. While it wasn't a fortune, it was enough to keep things going until the company could get paid.

"You know, he didn't start out wanting to do shows like this," Debbie told her. "Before I met him, he had dreams of producing wildlife documentaries. Like David Attenborough." She looked troubled. "I think if things go badly, he might decide to just leave."

"What about you?" Amanda asked.

"I can't just up and leave. Not with the boys still in school." She sighed. "This has been really hard on all of us, you know?" Amanda nodded in sympathy.

"After that show where Rochelle got hurt, I took a

good long look at myself and realised that wishing ill on someone wasn't worth the fifteen minutes of fame."

"Do you think it's possible your ex might have caused Rochelle's accident as well?"

Debbie bit her lip. "I've been thinking about that. I've done nothing but think about it since your friend told me he was a suspect. He was learning to be an electrical engineer when I knew him. He has the know-how."

Amanda nodded. Given that knowledge, the man could very easily have caused the speaker to explode.

"There's something I wanted to ask you," she said. "This morning I got the impression you were holding back something about those investments. What was it?"

Debbie sighed. "I knew you'd catch that. You're right. It's one of the reasons we forced him to resign as a company director. He used that money without telling us. I'm sorry. I just didn't want to admit how much of a fool I was. He begged me to give him a chance and I have to admit I felt sorry for him."

"Is he still gambling?" Amanda asked.

"I don't know," the other woman admitted. "We told him he needed to stop. I even told him he couldn't continue to work for the company unless he cleaned up his act, but I can't exactly watch him."

"No, you're right," she said. "Thanks for telling me."

"Anyway, I also wanted to tell you I set something up with a friend of mine for your hair. I mean, it's not that bad, really, but if you're set on cutting it, he'll do a great job. He helps women who are going through chemotherapy."

Amanda smiled and nodded. Tracey had only managed to get a little bit and there was a patch about half the size of a ten-cent piece, but it was enough to make her feel a little self-conscious.

"Thanks," she said. "Anyway, I should get back to rehearsals."

She heard enough through the rest of the afternoon to guess that Myles' hunch that it would help boost morale if she continued was the right one. A couple of the contestants who had been in the waiting area that night had told her they had considered dropping out after hearing what had happened to her, but seeing she had returned, they had changed their minds.

Chapter Twenty-Two

The detectives gathered in Pete's office early Tuesday morning. The senior detective studied each one of them in turn.

"All right. What do we have?" He looked pointedly at Jim.

"Tracey Brooks appeared in court yesterday and she was granted bail. Under strict conditions that she approach no one from Star Quest. Especially not your daughter, boss."

"Good. Any luck on finding Grant Burns?"

"Not yet. Central sent some guys around to his apartment yesterday but there was no one home. Neighbours said they hadn't seen him for a few days, although they said he mostly kept to himself."

"What's his profile?"

Kirsten Taylor spoke up. "Grant Burns. 55. Loner. He and his ex-wife have been divorced for over ten years. She has full custody of their sons. We spoke to the building manager and he'd only been living in the apartment for about two months. Prior to that, it looks like he's been moving every few months."

Jim nodded in agreement. From what they'd managed to glean so far, Burns had got behind in rent payments and it looked like he had moved out before he could be evicted. How he'd been able to get a place managed by a property management company was a mystery. Most such companies required references.

"We've asked the company for any references he might have provided them," he said.

Jim suspected the man had asked a friend to provide the reference, falsifying information that he was a reliable tenant. It was his hope that the friend might know the man's current whereabouts.

"Anything else?" Pete asked.

"The man has a history of offences dating back twenty years," Kirsten told the others. "Mostly DWIs. He did get one for disturbing the peace after he was trespassed from the casino in Hamilton a few years ago. Report said he was demanding his money back and saying the machines were rigged."

"Why doesn't that surprise me?" Jim murmured.

The woman nodded and smiled. "Here's something else you might find interesting. Remember that kid Robert? The one you were looking at for the attack at the Lyndale Mall?"

"What about him?" he asked.

"He's related to Burns. They're cousins."

He stared at her. It was too much of a coincidence.

"It could be a coincidence," Dave put in.

"There's no such thing as coincidence," Pete replied.

Jim sniggered, thinking once again of the character from the television crime show.

"Let's bring our friend Robert back in for an

interview," Pete said. "Kirsten, why don't you handle that?" He instructed Chris Chapman to take a constable from the uniformed branch to pick up the teenager.

Jim knew what Pete was doing. Since Robert had been seen harassing women, he would be aggravated by the fact he was being questioned by a woman. Kirsten was tough and wouldn't take that kind of nonsense. His boss' strategy appeared to be trying to force the kid to blurt out something without thinking.

Pete's phone rang and he picked it up.

"Steele." He listened for a few seconds. "All right. Thanks, Kerry. Tell her Jim will be right out."

Jim looked at his boss. The older man nodded.

"Amanda's out front. She apparently has something important to tell you."

That was odd, he thought. Amanda usually managed to talk her way into the bullpen without any trouble. He wondered if the young woman was being cautious. Since most of the detectives now knew of her involvement in the case, there didn't seem to be much point in her trying to keep that a secret.

The detectives filed out of the office and he went to open the main door out into the upstairs reception. He stopped in the doorway, staring in shock at the woman in front of him. She had short hair, almost in a pixie cut. Coupled with her slim body, curvy hips and long legs, she reminded him of a young Audrey Hepburn. If the actress had been blonde.

She was talking to his girlfriend and Kerry, the commander's secretary.

The woman turned as the door shut behind him.

He realised it was Amanda.

"Wow!" he said. "You cut your hair."

She self-consciously touched the short strands.

"Uh, yeah," she said.

The cut had been skilfully done, the short layers covering the area where she'd been injured. While Jim had liked her with long hair, the short cut gave her a sort of elegance, emphasising her elfin features.

Now that he thought about it, she and Gaby shared many of the same facial characteristics.

"I think it looks great," Gaby was saying. "Don't you, Jim?" she added pointedly.

"Sure," he said, adding that he hadn't seen the problem with her injury. It wasn't as if it had been that much, he decided. Surely she could have styled her hair so it could be hidden?

"Of course, not," Kerry said in response to his comment. "You're a guy."

"What does that mean?" he asked.

"Think about it," Gaby replied, giving him a glare.

Amanda looked at the other women and shook her head. She grasped his elbow.

"Um, I need to talk to you," she said, pushing him back in the direction of the door.

He lifted his lanyard and swiped his access key over the reader. The door beeped and he opened it, ushering her through. His fellow detectives looked up and stared at Amanda as he led her to one of the interview rooms.

"Are you okay?" he asked, noting she was quieter than normal as she sat down.

"Yeah. I'm just …" She touched her hair. "I guess I'm a little self-conscious about the cut."

The worst part, she explained, was that after the

haircut she had gone back to the flat she shared with Penny to pick up some of her belongings and the other woman had been there. Amanda's make-up hadn't covered her pallor or the bruises on her face and her ex-flatmate had been rather nasty about it.

Jim snorted in disgust at the older woman's attitude. You'd think she'd show some concern that her 'friend' had been hurt, but no, he thought. It was yet another check mark against the former flatmate in his opinion.

He quickly assured her that he liked the new style and that Penny had been completely in the wrong. Amanda nodded and smiled, appearing a little happier about it.

"It's a little shorter than I wanted to go, but Debbie's friend thought it would be better this way." She added that the hairdresser had told her the cut not only helped cover up the small patch, but it would grow out more evenly.

He shrugged. "I guess. It does suit you though. I'm not too much of a guy that I can't see that."

"I just … I feel like an idiot that it got that far. I mean, I should have been able to defend myself."

"Well, if it helps, I can teach you a few self-defence moves so you'd know what to do next time. If there's a next time," he added. "When I was training in the army, we used to have these boxing matches. I hated getting socked in the jaw, but I was never very good at blocking." He went on to explain that one of the sergeants had helped him get over that by teaching him to block. He rarely won a match but at least he'd stopped getting hit in the jaw. "Usually the worst place to hit a guy is below the belt," he told her.

"Yeah, I can understand why," she said. "Anyway, I was talking to Debbie last night and she admitted that her ex took the money without telling them." She explained that she'd had a hunch and had asked Debbie about it that evening at rehearsals.

He'd already sensed that the other woman hadn't been telling them everything about her ex-husband's behaviour at the meeting the day before.

"I figured that was what had happened. She doesn't exactly have the greatest poker face."

Amanda looked a little concerned. "You're not going to hold that against her, are you?"

It was plainly obvious she liked the older woman and was worried she'd get into trouble for omitting that little tidbit of information.

"No, she won't get in trouble," he told her. "It seemed to me she was feeling conned by her ex and I can understand how that can make her feel a bit embarrassed."

She nodded. "I guess sometimes we just put our trust in the wrong person, but that doesn't make us bad, does it?"

"No, you're right. It doesn't. I appreciate you coming by to tell me though."

"Well, I figured it was important." She pulled her phone out of her bag and pressed the button on the side. "Anyway, I should go. More rehearsals."

She stood up to leave. He got up to accompany her to the door.

"Good luck with that," he said.

Pete was at Jim's desk as Amanda passed. She sent her father a small smile before leaving the bullpen. He looked a little taken aback at the short style but smiled in reply.

Jim watched her leave before turning to his boss. The detective senior sergeant looked a little worried.

"That's quite a different look," he said.

"I take it you didn't see it before you left this morning," Jim asked his boss.

"She got in late last night and was still asleep when I left." He shot Jim a look. "I don't normally feel the need to check up on my daughter every minute of every day. She's a grown woman." He made a face. "As much as it kills me to admit it. Means I'm getting old."

Jim suppressed a smirk. "I know, boss."

The older man frowned. "You know, it's funny. Normally I find the bickering between you two rather aggravating but strangely enough, I miss it. What's going on between you two?"

"Nothing, oddly enough. You're right. She wasn't her usual sunny self today. I think it has something to do with Penny." He told his boss about Amanda meeting her former flatmate and the things the woman had said to her. Pete scowled.

"I'd like to give that young woman a piece of my mind," he said.

Jim smiled. "Heh, get in line, boss. At least she's moving in with Gaby."

While he still had a few reservations about it, he realised Gaby was probably the best person for Amanda to share a place with. They were both very similar in nature, but not so similar that it would cause clashes now and then. Having been raised by a cop, Amanda would understand the constant shift changes and the odd hours.

Chris Chapman stopped by his desk later that day to tell him that Robert Hutton was in the interview room with Kirsten.

"You want to watch?" he asked.

"No," Jim responded. "I think Taylor will have it all under control."

He continued to look through all the information they'd gathered on the case. Burns' financial records, which they'd obtained from the bank via a warrant, showed he was not very good at managing money. He'd been overdrawn on more than one occasion and his credit card was at maximum.

As he read, he came across something very interesting. Burns had made several cash withdrawals over the counter, of five thousand dollars. They'd been made at weekly intervals.

It seemed odd that the bank would allow such transactions without red-flagging them. The account also showed odd amounts of deposits – some as little as a few hundred to several thousand.

Jim printed out the last few transactions. The final cash withdrawal had been within days of Paul Davidson's death.

He got up and went to his boss' office, knocking on the door frame. Pete looked up.

"I think I've got something, boss," he said.

The older man raised an eyebrow. "Oh?" He gestured for the detective to enter the room.

Before Jim could show him the sheet, Kirsten came in behind him.

"Oops, sorry." It looked like she hadn't expected the boss to already have someone in with him.

Jim looked at her. "No, it's okay. What did our young friend have to say?"

"Well, he claimed he didn't know anything about what Burns was up to, only that he was supposed to meet his cousin there."

"What about what he told Amanda? That he was there to cheer on his non-existent sister?" Jim asked.

"Yeah, he knows he was caught out on the lie," Kirsten replied, "but he's still not giving up the real reason he was there."

Jim wondered if the youth had been told to provide some sort of distraction for security so the older man could set things in motion. From what forensics had told him, it would have been a matter of minutes before the corrosive ate through the cheap weld holding the metal pieces together.

Kirsten left the office to write up her report on the interview. Pete looked at him.

"So, what have you found out?"

He handed over the bank records. His boss looked them over thoroughly.

"Hmm, the only time I've ever seen transactions like that, it was someone being blackmailed."

"Is it possible Davidson knew something and was demanding money?" Jim mused aloud.

"We won't know for sure until we find Burns," Pete replied. "Have you checked with the city casino?"

"Yeah. He's apparently been banned from that one too." He sighed. "You know, Amanda told me Debbie admitted he stole the money from the company. Why would she try to protect him like that?"

"I don't think it's a matter of protecting him," Pete replied. "I think it's more a matter of her not wanting to admit that the man she loved and trusted enough to marry is nothing but a criminal."

Jim frowned. "I really don't get that. I mean, they

were divorced. Why would she even trust him?"

"Not all marriages end acrimoniously. It sounds to me like his gambling addiction was the problem. God knows I know what that's like."

Jim studied his boss as the older man sat back, clearly thinking about his ex-wife. While he didn't talk about Amanda's mother much, it was apparent that he still had feelings for her.

"Gambling addiction is like every other addiction," Pete explained. "It's a disease. It's broken up quite a few marriages, I'll wager."

"Yeah, I don't think I'll take you up on the bet," Jim replied with a grin. "I guess Debbie felt kind of responsible for him, hence the second chance."

"If Kim had suddenly turned up again, I'd probably have given her another chance. If only for Amanda." He sighed. "Although, after she left her in the car to go play the machines, I would have to think long and hard about it."

Jim nodded. If he had been in his boss' shoes, he probably could have forgiven the woman's actions if a child hadn't been involved. His boss went on.

"Sometimes I wonder if perhaps she would have been better off being raised by her grandparents. They offered after Kim left. I guess they thought I would never be able to devote as much time to her."

He added that since they were his ex-wife's parents, they might have felt the need to take their daughter's side in the whole issue, which might have led to a whole set of problems. He'd felt that Amanda's grandparents had implied they weren't happy about his job, mostly because of the odd hours he had to keep.

Her grandfather had since passed away, but her

grandmother had moved to a small town about four hours' drive from the city.

"I don't know. I think she turned out all right," he assured the older man. "I mean, yeah, she can act a bit spoiled from time to time, but she's a good kid."

His boss cocked an eyebrow but said nothing.

Chapter Twenty-Three

Rehearsals continued for the rest of the week, preparing for the show on Saturday. Amanda wasn't as nervous this time around as Friday approached. All the contestants now knew what had happened and had been surprisingly supportive.

While it was obvious the producers knew her real reason for being there, they appeared grateful that she wanted to continue. It certainly helped to boost morale for those who had considered dropping out altogether, fearing they would be the next victim of an accident.

Amanda finished her rehearsals early on Friday. Tama had told her she was going to be the second performer up on the show the next evening and he wanted to make sure she got as much rest as she could.

She decided to go to the police bar for an hour or so. She had barely seen her father during the week and wanted to spend a little time with him.

The officers in the bar stared at her when she entered the room with her father. She touched a hand to her head self-consciously. Amanda had never considered herself a shy person but all the attention since she'd got her hair cut had been a little disconcerting.

She was a little annoyed when Stu Dawson wolf-whistled at her. Fortunately, Jim, who had been sitting in a group next to the other man's group, shot him a glare that quickly silenced him.

"What do you want to drink, honey?" her father said.

"Um, just a coke please, Dad."

Kerry and Gaby waved her over to their table and she moved to join her friends.

The dark-haired woman smiled at her.

"So, my flatmate's moving out next weekend. You're still interested in the room, right?"

Amanda nodded. "Yeah. I'm looking forward to it." She'd already given her notice to her landlord. He apparently had already known of the argument between her and Penny. To her surprise, the news hadn't come from her former flatmate, but from Jim.

The man's friendliness toward her had her questioning their relationship. As much as she liked yanking his chain and the occasional banter between them, the thought that he would go into bat for her, not only with her flatmate but with her landlord as well, was surprising and not at all unwelcome. Actually, she thought, it was kind of sweet.

Not that she was planning on dating the man, she decided. She rather liked the mock-adversarial relationship. She had to admit that he could give as good as he got, which was part of the fun.

Speaking of whom, she thought as he approached the table. He smiled at her.

"Hey. How are rehearsals going?"

"All right," she said. "You're not coming tomorrow night, are you?"

He smirked at her. "Why? You afraid you'll slip up and embarrass yourself?"

"Ha! As if I could. You on the other hand, would send them screaming for the exits."

"Good thing I'm not the one performing tomorrow," he replied. "What are you planning on singing, anyway? I'd think something from Disney would be more your speed."

"Like what?" Kerry asked, eyeing him with a narrow gaze.

"I don't know. How about *When You Wish Upon a Star*? That seems simple enough."

"Are you implying I'm incapable of singing something complicated?" Amanda asked, narrowing her eyes at him. His smirk told her he was suggesting she wasn't mature enough for anything except a song from a movie that had been aimed primarily at children. "Besides, at least I can sing," she reminded him. "You're only good enough for one of those Disney sing-a-longs. As long as everyone else covers their ears so they can hear themselves over the caterwauling."

He shot her a glare. She grinned mockingly at him, then subsided.

"If you must know, I decided to sing *Wild Horses*."

Gaby looked at her. "Ooh, is that the Rolling Stones version? I love that song."

Amanda nodded. Her father handed her a glass of Coca-Cola. He grinned at her.

"The 'Stones, huh? I can just see you up on the stage impersonating Jagger." He thrust his hips and pursed his lips in what she guessed was his attempt at imitating the group's lead singer. She glared at him.

"Oh yeah, thanks for the vote of confidence, Daddy!" she returned. He raised his hands in mock surrender. "Anyway, Debbie thinks it suits my vocal range." She turned back to Jim. "At least I didn't attempt to sing something from the Eagles on my first try."

Jim glared. "You had to remind me of that, didn't you?"

Gaby laughed at her boyfriend. "Well, you picked it. I didn't tell you to sing *Hotel California*."

"At least I sang. You just sat there and mocked," he replied.

She grinned back at him. "Because I know when something's not my game."

"You made me go up there!" he told her in protest.

Amanda mocked him with a pout. "Aww, poor baby!"

Jim made what sounded like a growl in the back of his throat and stalked off. The girls laughed at his retreating form.

Gaby grinned at her. "Living with you is going to be so much fun," she said.

Amanda decided to leave after an hour so she could get a good night's sleep. She wasn't surprised when she got up the next morning to find her father and Jim discussing the case over coffee.

"I thought this was your weekend off," she told him as her father stepped out to go grab the paper from the letterbox.

"You stalking me, Princess?" he teased.

"Memorising my roster now?"

"You wish."

"Sorry, kid, you're not going to get rid of me that easy. I wanted to talk to you anyway."

"You still haven't found Debbie's ex?"

He shook his head. "If the guy's smart, he'll stay well away from the show, but …"

"You don't want to take any chances."

"Do you always finish people's sentences?" he asked, sounding irritated.

She rolled her eyes, moving to the counter to pour herself a cup of coffee. She could see her father still out by the letterbox talking to one of the neighbours who had been out walking her dog. The pair appeared to be quite animated in their conversation. He was waving his hands rather wildly.

She frowned, wondering if there was something going on between her father and the neighbour. She hadn't had much to do with the people in the little cul-de-sac since she'd gone out flatting before he'd bought the place. Not that she begrudged him seeing anyone else. It had been twelve years since her mother had left. As much as he still cared about Kim, it was time he moved on.

She turned back to Jim.

"So, what's what anyway? With the case, I mean."

"I would have thought your dad would have kept you up-to-date."

"He doesn't discuss much with me if it's not relevant to what I'm doing."

She listened as Jim told her he'd found some irregularities in Grant Burns' bank accounts. Her eyes widened at the transactions totalling thousands of dollars.

"We're still trying to figure it all out."

"If he has a gambling problem, how would he make so much money? It's not like he would have got a huge salary from working for the company after he was expelled as a director."

"No, you're right. And we are looking into that angle."

She frowned. "What are you thinking?"

"Since his cousin Robert seems to be involved somehow, and the kid has a record involving drugs …"

"Is he dealing, maybe?"

"Could be." He seemed to be rather evasive on the subject.

"What are you not telling me?" she said.

"We looked into some real estate records and it looks like he has a rural property. What they call a lifestyle block."

"How could he afford that?" she asked. "I mean if he can't even pay his rent …"

Jim nodded. "I contacted a guy your dad knows. Busted him a few times for drugs. He's actually the guy who helped me identify that rapist a couple of months ago. From the school?" he added when she looked at him with confusion.

"Do you mean DJ?" she asked, shuddering inwardly at the thought of what had nearly happened to her. Her memory was rather hazy from that day, but it terrified her to think of how close she had come to being killed.

It was bad enough that DJ had got her drunk a few nights earlier – so drunk that she had been almost paralytic. She still didn't remember everything she had done that night, but she knew she had been extremely lucky DJ had only decided to get her drunk so he could get information out of her.

"Yeah. Anyway, Al still knows a few people in the drug scene. I told him what I suspected, and he said he'd sniff things out and get back to me. Meanwhile, we're waiting on a warrant to search the property."

"Why so long?" she asked.

He shrugged. "These things take time. Unfortunately. We have to show probable cause."

He rolled his eyes in annoyance. Amanda could understand the attitude. The legal system was not the best and despite what was often portrayed on television cop shows, such cases weren't solved within a fifty-minute episode.

"We just want you to be careful tonight. If Burns shows up …"

"He might cause trouble. Thanks. I'll keep an eye out."

"Don't get complacent, Amanda. If I'm right, the guy's committed murder."

"I know what I'm doing, Jim."

"Right," he said, gesturing toward her head. "You know so well you almost got a hammer in your skull last week. I'm not kidding. This guy is dangerous."

"I heard you the first time," she told him.

By the time she had to leave for the show, the nerves had returned. Enough for her to want to bolt.

"Tell me again why I agreed to do this," she said to Debbie, who was sitting beside her in the waiting area.

"You know why," the older woman said. "Just breathe and focus on the song. You've got this."

"I don't know why I'm so nervous. I'm not usually like this."

"If you weren't nervous, I'd be worried," the coach replied. "Trust me, it's normal."

"Was this what it was like for you the first time you performed?"

"Not just the first time," Debbie assured her. "The first night I went on as Mary in *Superstar* … God, I just about collapsed. Grant was the one who helped me keep it together. You know, he told me then he had a little crush on me." She sighed. "He was such a good-looking guy. I thought he was so sweet. By the time I realised he wasn't as good as he made himself out to be, we were married, and Marty was a baby. We'd been having financial problems and then someone told me he'd seen Grant playing the pokie machines in the casino."

Amanda listened as Debbie told her how she'd confronted her husband and tried to get him to address his gambling problem. It had eventually resulted in a huge fight in which he'd hit her. The worst part had been that it had happened in front of their two sons.

"So, I walked out. Went to Paul's place and filed for divorce."

Amanda frowned. "Paul? As in Davidson? The man who …"

"…died," Debbie finished. "He was the one who told me about Grant's gambling." Amanda gasped and the other woman gazed at her. "What are you thinking?"

"I don't know. I've got a hunch. Do you know if Jim's here? He said something this morning about keeping an eye on things."

"I did see some officers in the auditorium, but …" She looked up. "Honey, you can't do anything now.

The show's about to start."

Damn, she thought, realising she was out of time as the production assistant came to tell her to wait backstage.

Sally smiled at her as she approached. "Good luck, honey," she said kindly.

The presenter had admitted she had felt badly at what had happened, saying it could have been her. Amanda didn't blame her for thinking that way, even though she knew the truth about the 'accident'.

Sally went onstage, returning about a minute later. The assistant sent Amanda out.

She stood in the middle, half-blinded by the stage lights, trying to ignore the intense heat both above and below her. She noticed two cameramen on each side of the stage and a third below ready to record the reactions of the judges.

"Hi, Amanda," Deirdre greeted her. "How are you feeling?"

"I'm okay. A little nervous."

"Well, we can understand that. Coming back here after what happened took a lot of courage," the soap actress returned.

None of them voiced their concerns that it might happen again. As far as Amanda knew, security had been informed and ordered to keep a lookout for Debbie's ex-husband.

She stood quietly, listening for the first bars of the song, then took a breath.

"Childhood living, is easy to do ..."

Just as in the song she'd chosen for the audition, she called up memories of her mother, interpreting the lyrics to bring out the emotions of those first few years after Kim had left.

The final echoes of the song drifted away, and the audience erupted in applause. Amanda stood centre stage, waiting for the comments.

Steve Cooksley, a judge who had had a modicum of success as a singer a decade before Amanda was born, was the first to speak.

"I've heard that song performed a few times, but nothing with such a depth of emotion as you sang tonight. Well done."

She nodded her thanks, her hand trembling as she held the microphone in one hand.

Deirdre added her own compliment. "You were wonderful. You controlled your nerves and gave us a very powerful rendition. Thank you."

Tama and the fourth judge were equally complimentary. Each of them voted to send her to the next round.

Amanda left the stage, intending to head toward the waiting area before going to look for Jim. As she stepped backstage, she saw someone who looked like Grant Burns walking along the corridor.

She ran to catch up with him, not sure what she was going to say. Whatever it was, she hoped she could stop whatever he was planning.

She paused as he looked around before opening a door marked Staff Only. There was a narrow rectangular windowpane just above the door handle. Amanda waited until he had disappeared through the door before approaching it.

Grant Burns stood in front of someone sitting on a couch. She couldn't hear what was being said but he was clearly upset, gesticulating wildly.

She looked around, wondering where the security guard was. She quickly made her way back down the corridor and found the production assistant who had just led another contestant backstage.

"I need you to go find one of the police officers in the auditorium," she said.

The woman stared at her. "What?"

"Don't ask questions. Just go! Tell them to come to the staff break room. Hurry!"

She pushed the woman in the direction of the auditorium and went back to the break room. Burns was still there, his body language suggesting he was getting angry. He had raised his hand as if he was about to hit someone.

Amanda knew she couldn't wait for the officer to be found. She opened the door and pushed it open as quietly as she could.

"Look, you don't get it ..." he was practically shouting.

"Oh, I get it," the woman, whom Amanda now realised was his ex-wife. "It wasn't enough that you stole from us. You killed Paul!"

"Myles stole you from me!"

"Myles and I got together long after we divorced," Debbie told him. She flicked a glance toward Amanda but didn't greet her. She appeared pale, almost frightened. It became very quickly obvious why. Grant had a gun in his right hand.

"But you met him while we were still married," the man argued.

Amanda remembered the other woman telling her that she and Myles had been friends long before they'd begun dating, but clearly, Grant wasn't going to see reason.

Debbie said something in response which Amanda didn't catch. She was too busy trying to think of a way to de-escalate the situation before he hurt his ex.

"No, he stole you from me. He destroyed our marriage!"

"You did! With your gambling!"

"No," he said, shaking his head. "No, no, no. That's not what happened!"

Amanda swallowed. The man seemed to be totally unhinged. She had to put a stop to this before he killed someone.

"Grant," she said, stepping forward. "This isn't the way to deal with this. Put the gun down before someone gets hurt."

He turned, his eyes wide. It was obvious he had been so caught up in the argument that he had never realised she was there.

"You!"

"Yes, me," she said. "Put the gun down and we can talk about this."

His face screwed up in anger. "This is all your doing! Tracey told me …"

"What? What did she tell you, Grant? I'm not the one who started all this. The police know you were behind the accidents."

She eyed the gun in his hand. He fidgeted, his fingers curling around the grip. He looked from her to Debbie, his expression suggesting he was trying to decide what to do.

Amanda was about to tell him once again to put the gun down when the door crashed into the wall.

"Police! Drop the gun, Burns!"

Chapter Twenty-Four

Jim might have been teasing Amanda earlier, but he had decided to go to the show, just in case she got herself into trouble again. Two of his colleagues from Central were also in the auditorium, standing in the back so they could watch proceedings unobtrusively and keep an eye out for the suspect.

Half a dozen security guards had been placed around the centre as well. Jim recognised one of them as a former cop who had resigned after he'd almost been killed by a suspect they'd been pursuing.

Constable Leila Said smiled at him as he stood next to her.

"Everything all right, Jim?" she asked.

"It's fine. I thought I'd just keep an eye on Pete's daughter."

The constable nodded with a knowing expression.

"Of course."

"There is nothing going on between me and Amanda," he replied vehemently.

"Oh, I believe you," she returned with a grin at

her partner.

Jim rolled his eyes and turned to the stage. The presenter had announced the first contestant, a young man not much older than Amanda from the Waikato.

He was good, Jim thought as he listened. Probably good enough to make it all the way to the finals. From the judges' comments, it appeared they thought so as well.

Seth left the stage and the presenter returned.

"Our next contestant is a local girl. When you last saw her, she was almost hurt in an accident on stage, but she bravely chose to return tonight. Ladies and gentlemen, Amanda Steele."

Jim watched as the woman walked off and his friend walked on. She had chosen to wear a knee-length sleeveless dress. It was modest, not so tight that it revealed too much of her slender form, but not so loose that it looked like a sack on her. The short hairstyle accentuated her long neck, again giving her a look of grace and elegance.

He didn't listen to the judges as they greeted her, watching as she became accustomed to the lighting. It was obvious she was nervous, but the judges were understanding.

She stood poised as the first bars of the song began to play before lifting the microphone to sing the lines. The entire auditorium watched in rapt silence at the young woman who belted out the lines with passion and emotion, almost as if she felt every word she was singing.

That, he thought, was the difference between Amanda and the woman now in custody. She was a talented singer, not only because she was technically good, but she could draw on emotions which gave the song a meaning that was special only to her.

Tracey had probably never understood that. Her belligerence when the judges had tried to point that out to her probably hadn't helped her case.

"She's good, isn't she?" Leila remarked.

He nodded. "She is. I think she could go all the way in this competition if she really wanted to." He wasn't sure if Leila knew the real circumstances of Amanda's entry in the show but wasn't about to blow her cover.

The song came to an end and Amanda stood on the stage, clearly trying to get her breath back. The two cameramen moved closer, filming her reaction at every comment from the judges. Jim wasn't close enough in the two-hundred seat auditorium to see but guessed from her body language she was happy with what was being said.

He debated whether to head backstage, thankful no further incident had occurred to interrupt proceedings. He hoped with Tracey's arrest, her accomplice had probably been scared off attempting anything else.

Leila was whispering something to her partner. Jim glanced at her then realised a woman was walking up along the aisle by the wall, heading toward them. As she approached, he realised it was one of the production assistants.

She spoke to Leila and her partner. The two constables turned to Jim with puzzled expressions.

"What is it?" he whispered.

"She just said to come and get one of you and tell you to go to the break room. I don't know why."

"Who did?" Jim asked.

"The girl who was attacked last week," the assistant replied, obviously not knowing why. Amanda must be in trouble, he thought. There was no way she would have sent the assistant if something wasn't up.

He gestured toward the exit door and led her out so they wouldn't distract anyone in the audience. Leila and the other constable followed them.

"I want you to get security," he told the assistant.

"But ..."

"Listen to me! Just get two of the security guards and send them to the break room. Don't argue!"

He didn't want to cause a disruption in the auditorium so decided to circle around and use the main door to the centre. The two younger officers followed him through the waiting area. Contestants stared at them as they passed, turning to whisper to each other.

Jim had memorised enough of the layout of the convention centre to know where the room was located. He ran along the corridor, skidding slightly on the slick tiles before stopping just short of the break room.

Through the narrow window, he could see Amanda standing in front of a man holding a gun. Burns, he thought. Debbie Burns was sitting on a couch, looking terrified, her gaze shifting from Amanda to her ex-husband.

He looked at his colleagues. Neither one of them appeared to be holding a taser. Not that he really wanted to use one unless it was absolutely necessary.

"Back me up," he said softly.

They both nodded. Jim flung open the door hard enough so it crashed against the wall, startling all three people in the room.

"Police! Drop the gun, Burns!" he ordered.

The man stared at him, clearly weighing up his chances against three police officers. Just as Jim started to enter the room, he heard heavy footsteps. He glanced behind him and saw two burly security guards running along the corridor.

He turned back in time to see Amanda dart forward and grab Burns by the wrist, trying to wrestle the gun away from the man.

Dumb move, Jim thought, watching uneasily as the suspect's gun hand began to wave wildly. Fortunately for Amanda, her slight gamble had paid off. Burns hadn't had a solid grip on the weapon and the gun fell to the floor with a loud clunking sound.

The two constables and the security guards managed to wrestle the man to the floor.

"Mr Burns, you are under arrest," Leila told him before reciting his rights.

Jim turned to Amanda but before he could admonish her, Debbie got up. She was clearly shaky, and her smile was watery as she looked at the blonde.

"You just can't stay out of trouble, can you?" she said, sounding like a mother scolding her child.

Amanda just grinned and shrugged.

Jim stood aside to allow his colleagues to take the arrested man out, along with the gun. He turned to Debbie, allowing her to sit down on the couch. Amanda sat next to her while he grabbed a chair and sat beside the table, notebook open to take notes.

"Okay, what happened?"

She slowly related events. She had left the waiting area and had just sat down with a coffee when her ex-husband had burst into the room, shouting at her. She'd already been warned not to confront him directly with what he was suspected of doing but that hadn't mattered. He'd told her that everything he'd done, it had been because of her.

"He tried to claim that Myles broke up our marriage. It's not true."

Amanda looked at her reassuringly. "We know," she said softly.

The woman continued, telling Jim how Paul Davidson had been a close family friend. He'd grown concerned about Grant's gambling habit and had reached out to Debbie. She had confronted her husband and told him he needed to stop what he was doing, or their marriage was over.

Burns had stopped for a while but one trip to a racetrack several months later had started the cycle all over again. Paul had once again warned Debbie and she had chosen to walk away from her marriage.

Amanda turned to Jim, a question in her eyes. He shook his head. Whatever it was could wait until they could be alone. The other woman had already been through enough.

Security or the production assistant had obviously already called Myles as he came in, looking concerned for his partner.

"Are you all right?" he asked, hugging her.

She nodded. "I'm fine. Thanks to Amanda and Detective Andersen."

The man turned to Jim. "Thank you, Detective. And you, Amanda. If you hadn't been here, I …"

Jim wanted to tell the man he was just doing his job but knew it meant more than that to the couple.

"Do you need us?" Myles asked.

"Not tonight. But Central will need Debbie to make a statement. Will you be able to go in tomorrow?"

The singing coach nodded. "I will."

He watched them leave before turning back to Amanda.

"What are you thinking?"

"That her ex killed Paul out of revenge for breaking up their marriage."

He shook his head. "I don't think so, not if he was blaming Myles for breaking up the marriage. No, I'm thinking there was some kind of blackmail involved. We haven't gone through Paul Davidson's accounts with a fine-toothed comb, but …"

Amanda frowned. "If he was blackmailing Grant Burns, why would the withdrawals be in cash?"

He frowned, thinking about the question. "Hmm, good point."

"Maybe it wasn't Paul doing the blackmailing. Has anyone asked Tracey?"

"Unfortunately, her lawyer has already told her not to say anything further to police until it goes to trial."

"Well, we know there's a connection. When he saw me, he mentioned Tracey. I don't know what she told him, but he was onto me."

The only thing he could do, he thought, was question Burns thoroughly before someone like Tess McCloskey could get to him.

When he called into Central the next morning, however, he was told he wasn't going to be the one interviewing the suspect. He called his boss and told him.

"Well, technically it is Central's case," Pete told

him. "But I'll talk to Jack Nixon and see if we can at least observe."

"Thanks, boss."

A few minutes later, John 'Jack' Nixon came out into the foyer where Jim was waiting. He gestured for Jim to follow him.

"How is Pete these days?" Jack asked, saying he and the detective senior sergeant had worked together in the early years of their careers. "Haven't seen him since Amanda was about ten."

"He's good. You know, she just turned twenty."

"So, you've met her then? Even back then, she'd waltz on into the station like she owned the place. Always was kind of precocious."

"You mean a brat?" Jim said.

The man laughed. "Yeah, that too. I hear she's working for Bob Moody and his business partner. All I can say is good luck keeping her in line. She was always a stubborn one. Never liked being told what to do."

"Still doesn't," he replied.

"So, tell me about Burns," the senior detective asked.

Jim had already copied the Central station in on his reports but related everything he knew up to that point. Jack led him to an office where he could watch the interview through the monitor.

Burns was looking the worse for wear, his face unshaven and his eyes bloodshot.

"Tell me about Tracey Brooks," the interviewing officer asked.

"I don't know … who that is," the suspect replied.

"We have two witnesses who heard you mention her name. You've already dug yourself into a deep hole, Burns. I suggest you stop digging and start talking."

The man glared and folded his arms. "I'm not talking to anybody. I want my lawyer."

"We've already been to your flat, Burns. We traced the corrosive material you used to cause the accident which put Paul Davidson in the hospital."

"I didn't kill him," the man said. "He was my friend."

"Right. You were such good friends with him, you were paying him five thousand a week."

Jim glanced at the senior detective. Jack nodded.

"We found evidence that said Davidson was receiving the money."

"What was he doing? Spending up large?"

"No. He was betting with it. High stakes poker. Football games. Geek Squad got into his computer. Not exactly illegal but not exactly kosher either."

Burns was busy explaining the money, telling the interviewer he had been giving Davidson the cash because he needed it.

"Right," Jim said softly. "And I'm a monkey's uncle."

The story slowly poured out. The reason Davidson had known about Burns' gambling was that they had often gone out together.

"What about Tracey Brooks?" the interviewer persisted. "How did she get involved in this?"

"I didn't … she came to me. Said she knew I sabotaged somebody years ago. She wanted to win the contest and wanted me to make sure enough contestants dropped out so it would look like the show was jinxed or something."

"Is that really why you sabotaged the

equipment?"

He shook his head. "No."

"Then why do it?"

He lifted his head and looked directly at the camera.

"For Debbie."

"Your ex-wife?"

"I wanted her back. I told her I was clean. I wasn't doing that stuff anymore."

"What stuff?"

"She said I needed to earn her trust. I told her I'd stopped gambling. They wouldn't let me in the casino. She said she'd give me another chance. Brought me in as a director in the company. But she still wouldn't leave him. So, I took the money. I thought if I invested it, then made a ton of it back, she'd come back to me. Instead, she chose to stay with him."

Jim listened, almost riveted. Grant went on to explain that he'd known by causing the accidents that the show could be threatened with being shut down. The money he'd taken had left the company in financial trouble. Shutting down production would force the company into receivership. Debbie would have to leave Myles then, he reasoned.

Jim related everything he'd heard at the staff meeting the next morning.

"We still don't know where he was getting the money to pay Davidson," he said.

"We can't prove it's blackmail either," Pete said.

Kirsten frowned at them. "Do we have enough evidence to convict him of murder?"

"That's the problem," Jim said. "It's still mostly circumstantial. The corrosive was traced to him, but forensics concluded that it would still take a reasonably hard shove for the divider to go over."

"I questioned Hutton again and he still refuses to admit what he was really doing at the auditions that day," Kirsten replied.

"Amanda has a hunch he was there to cause trouble and distract security," Pete told them.

Jim nodded. He'd considered that possibility himself.

"The thing is, apart from the fact they're related, we've really got nothing to prove they were scheming something together."

His phone rang. He glanced apologetically at his boss and looked at the screen, recognising the phone number.

"I should take this," he said. He got up and left the office. "Al?"

"Yeah, thought you'd like to know that guy you were askin' about. He deals."

Well, that was interesting information.

"What's he dealing?"

"P," Al replied. Otherwise known as methamphetamine. Or what most of the officers he worked with said was the scourge of the city.

Further news was to come later that day when they managed to execute the search warrant on Burns' property. There were enough chemicals and pharmaceuticals stored on the property to manufacture thousands of dollars' worth of P. It was clear this was the source of Burns' income and explained how he could afford to withdraw thousands of dollars each week.

It still didn't prove he'd had something to do with Davidson's death, only with his accident.

Jim sighed in frustration, tapping his pen on the desk pad.

"You sound frustrated."

He looked up and smiled wearily at Gaby. "Hey. Yeah, I guess I am. We're trying to prove murder, but we just don't have enough to pin it on the guy."

"Is this the same thing Amanda's been working on?" she asked, sitting down in the chair opposite him.

"Yeah. The hospital sent over CCTV footage but … I don't know. Maybe we're looking in the wrong place."

"Or maybe you just don't know what to look for. This guy … he's something of a techno-wiz, right?"

"Yes. Why?"

"He'd know about the cameras in the hospital. If he was going there to commit a murder, he would most likely do something to cover his face."

Except something like that would attract too much attention if it was too obvious, he reasoned. He said as much to his girlfriend.

"What if it was something that wasn't obvious? Like, heavy clothing. A hoody, or a scarf," she suggested.

He frowned. Something like that would be overlooked by security. Still, he thought, wouldn't they have noticed someone trying to avoid their face being identified?

He brought up the footage and together they began looking through it but still felt like they were looking for a needle in a haystack.

"This is pointless!" he practically exploded after half an hour of searching through all the camera footage for the time in question. They'd even tried a window of about half an hour.

"Chill, James," she said. He frowned, wondering why the use of his name, rather than the shorter version seemed to grate. "Maybe you need to look at this from a different angle."

"What other angle is there?" he asked, his frustration clear.

She chewed her lip. "You're assuming that whoever did it was a visitor to the hospital. What if they weren't?"

He stared at her. "Are you suggesting what I think you're suggesting? But Burns isn't employed by the hospital."

"I know you want this guy to be guilty, but what if it wasn't him at all?" she said.

His eyes widened as he mulled over her words. As impossible as it sounded, he realised she might be right. What if they were looking at the wrong person?

Chapter Twenty-Five

Rehearsals had run late. Debbie had offered Amanda a ride home, knowing she hadn't driven her car into the city that day, and she had gratefully accepted.

"What is with the traffic?" the older woman grumbled as she tried to get into the next lane on the motorway. It was usual peak hour traffic but somehow it seemed heavier than normal. They were barely moving.

"Beats me," Amanda replied from the passenger seat. She was reading the music for the song she'd been rehearsing, trying to hear the notes in her head.

"You doing okay, hun?" Debbie asked.

"I'm fine. Just trying to focus on getting through the next round. If I get there, that is."

"I don't know why you wouldn't. Only one of the judges know why you're really there, right?"

"I guess so. I don't think Tama's said anything to the others." She glanced up and touched her friend's arm. "Watch out," she added as the car in front braked suddenly, almost causing them to hit the same car from behind. Nose-to-tail accidents were a frequent occurrence on the motorway at peak times.

"So, um, how are you feeling anyway?" she asked the other woman.

"I'm fine," Debbie replied, echoing her earlier words.

"Are you? Because from my perspective, that was no picnic the other night."

"No, but he's in custody now. Unless you know something I don't? I mean, let's face it. You do have a few friends in the police."

She shrugged. "I've been a constant visitor at the West Side station since I was little. They're used to me popping up." She stretched, putting the song sheet in her bag. "I mean, I guess I do kind of have an inside track, but my dad doesn't tell me everything."

"What about Jim?" Debbie asked.

Suddenly it felt like they'd collided with something. Amanda took the brunt of the impact, hearing the crunch and squeal of metal giving way. Her body felt like the time she had been accidentally tackled in a touch rugby game during a physical education class. The person who had tackled her had been almost twice her weight.

The wind had been knocked out of her and she'd felt like she couldn't breathe. For a moment, it had seemed like she couldn't move, then pain exploded through her nerve-endings. She hadn't broken anything but had had plenty of bruises the next day.

She heard Debbie scream beside her as the airbags inflated but she was too preoccupied with the sudden pain in her left side.

She looked around and realised a smaller car was the cause of the crash. They'd been hit side-on, forcing the car she was in against the barrier dividing the westbound lanes from the eastbound ones.

The airbags in the other car were covering half the windscreen, blocking her from seeing the other driver.

Despite the pain in her shoulder and the sudden pounding migraine, Amanda quickly took stock of the situation. The other car was badly damaged, the side panels badly dented.

"Amanda, are you all right?"

Debbie's words were slightly muffled through the ringing in her ears. Amanda looked at her friend, who had twisted in her seat to look at her.

"Can you open your door?"

She couldn't identify the voice but guessed it was a man. Someone had obviously stopped to help them.

She weakly pushed against the door with her right hand, but it wouldn't budge. When she tried again with both hands, she almost screamed with the excruciating pain shooting down her left arm.

The man tried opening the door from his side to no avail. He gestured for her to try sliding across the seats so she could get out the other side. She realised Debbie had already been pulled out and was being helped by someone else.

She did her best to manoeuvre herself across and let the man help her out. He half-carried her to the side of the motorway, sitting her down.

"The ambulance is on its way," he said.

"I saw what happened," a young Maori man told them, introducing himself. "Lucky youse were in the truck or you'd be dead. She was like gunning for you or something."

Amanda frowned at him, trying to make sense of

what he was saying.

"What do you mean?" she asked.

She did her best to follow as he told her what he'd seen. The smaller car, which she learnt was a Suzuki Swift, had been behind them one lane over when suddenly the driver had sped up and swerved to head straight for the passenger side of Debbie's SUV. The side of the Suzuki had crumpled against the bigger vehicle.

It sounded like there was no way the other driver had just lost control. Yet Amanda couldn't imagine that it had been deliberate. It just didn't seem possible that anyone would risk hurting themselves to do it.

"Who ..." she began.

The man, whose name she'd already forgotten, just shrugged.

"Dunno." He looked up. Emergency services had arrived while he'd been talking and were working on getting her out of the car. It was obvious she was in bad shape.

Ambulance officers took over, quickly assessing Amanda and helping her into the ambulance where she could sit on the stretcher. Debbie tried to protest when they told her she needed to go to the hospital as well to be checked over.

Once in the hospital's emergency department, Amanda was forced to wait on the narrow bed in one of the cubicles. The curtains had been pulled to give her some privacy but other than a nurse coming to take her obs, it felt like she was left alone for a very long time.

Suddenly the curtain was pulled aside, and her father came in.

"Amanda?"

She stared at her father. He looked pale and almost sick.

"My God, honey. When they told me ... I thought you'd been killed!"

"I'm here," she said, not wanting to lie to her father and pretend she was fine when she wasn't. Her arm was hurting like hell and she was sure she had a nasty cut above her eye. She'd touched the area with her right hand, and it had come away sticky with blood.

Debbie came in with her partner. She was clearly shaken up but didn't appear injured. She told Amanda she had already been discharged. She was obviously still very worried, however, not even trying to crack a joke like she had the night her ex had confronted her.

"Have you seen the doctor yet?" she asked after Amanda had introduced her father.

Amanda shook her head. Pete sighed.

"It's par for the course," he said. "You should go home. Get some rest. I don't think there's anything you can do to speed up proceedings."

She nodded. "At least you're here to look after your girl," she said. She looked at Amanda. "I'm so sorry you got involved in this mess. You got hurt because of m ..."

"Don't say it," Amanda told her quietly. "This is not your fault."

It was another long wait after the couple left. Amanda lost track of time, staring up at the high ceiling, trying to count the number of marks she saw above her while she listened to the sounds of activity buzzing within the department itself.

The curtain fluttered and soft footsteps were heard on the linoleum floor. A hand slipped through the gap and pushed the plastic material aside.

"Well now, what do we have here?"

Pete stood up. "My daughter was in a car accident," he said unnecessarily.

"I see. Where is the pain located?"

Amanda answered all his questions, trying not to cry out as he examined her arm.

"I do see a lot of bruising, but … we'll get you down to x-ray and make sure nothing's broken or dislocated. You could have torn some tendons. Anyway, I'll order that x-ray."

"Is that it?" her father exploded. "I've been sitting here for three hours and she was here at least an hour before that. Are you …"

"Dad, don't," she said. "You can tell they're busy."

The doctor looked at him. "Mr Steele …"

"It's Detective Senior Sergeant," Pete replied.

"Dad, stop!" she said, reminded of the time she had come off her bicycle when she was about nine. She'd ended up in emergency with a broken arm and needing stitches. Her father had tried to throw his weight around then.

The doctor's stare was unwavering. He was a little shorter than her father but clearly no shrinking violet.

"As your daughter has pointed out, sir, it has been very busy in the E.D. tonight. Your position does not entitle you or your daughter to special treatment." He smiled suddenly. "I can understand it from your perspective, Mr Steele. I have a daughter Amanda's age, too. God help us if anything like this ever happened to her."

"You're right. I'm sorry."

The man nodded. "I'll go see about that x-ray."

Things seemed to quiet down after she'd been taken to x-ray. Her father had disappeared to make a phone call, getting an update on the accident. He returned in time for the doctor to come in with results.

"Well, I have to say you've been very fortunate, Amanda. Your arm isn't broken, just very badly bruised. You'll need to keep it immobile for a couple of days. You will find you'll be bruised all down your left side for a while. If you were at all religious, I would say a prayer of thanks to whatever guardian angel you had watching over you, because it could have been a lot worse."

"Do I have to stay here?" Amanda asked.

"Not if you don't want to. Fortunately, there is no sign of concussion, but I do suggest someone keep an eye on you overnight."

"Don't worry," her father assured the man. "She's staying at my place, so I'll be there to watch her." His tone was oddly cool, a sure sign he was trying to control anger. The doctor sent him a confused look but nodded before turning away.

Once they were in the car, she turned to her father. His hands were practically squeezing the steering wheel.

"Okay, what are you not telling me?" she asked.

"The woman who hit you. It was Tracey Brooks."

Amanda was quiet the rest of the way home, letting herself process the information. Tracey had tried to kill her. Not once, but twice. This was clearly about more than a competition, or about her undercover role. From the sound of things, she had waited for the opportune moment, probably following them all the way from the centre. If Amanda had walked to the city centre to catch the train home, she had no doubt Tracey would have attempted something else. The woman had a score to settle.

She noticed her father quietly stewing in his own anger and guessed he was trying to get it under control. She could understand why he was so upset but it changed nothing. If she had been a cop, the circumstances might have been different, but she would still be in as much danger.

She waited until they were inside the house before bringing up the subject.

"Dad, I get you're upset, but ..."

"Upset? That doesn't even begin to describe how I'm feeling," he replied. "I'm not sure you should be ..."

"What?" she asked quietly, not wanting to stir the pot too much. "Not continue in this job? Quit? Is that what you're saying? Dad, if I was a cop, I'd be facing the same thing. Maybe worse. You can't wrap me in cotton wool, Daddy. I'm a grown woman."

There was a knock on the door, and she went to answer it, surprised to find herself wrapped in a sudden hug from Jim. He was careful to not put too much pressure on her arm, which was supported by a sling.

"Amanda, my God!"

She stepped back and stared at Jim. "What did you do that for?" she asked, taken aback by the hug.

"I'm sorry, I was just ... worried."

She sighed. "Yeah, you and my dad. Come on in."

Her father had already opened a bottle of ginger beer. He still looked extremely upset as he sipped from the bottle. His gaze was concerned.

"Amanda, I don't think you understand …"

"Dad, I do understand," she said. "Do you think I didn't worry about you when you were out there? Being a cop is a risky job, but it's a risk you have to take. I've never asked you not to be a cop."

Jim spoke up. "Boss, I get it. I do. The fact is, that's twice Amanda's got hurt on this job, but as much as we can teach her to defend herself, sometimes there are things you can't prevent. Besides, she could just be crossing the street and get hurt in a random event."

"But these things aren't random," Pete argued. "This woman deliberately targeted my daughter …"

"I get that, boss. I really do. Sure, there are more risks than most in this job, but you can't make her exist in a bubble either."

Her father nodded. "I suppose you're right."

Jim nodded in reply before looking at Amanda. "Anyway, I just came from talking to a couple of witnesses. They both said pretty much the same thing. The car was following but it looked like she saw a gap in the traffic and decided to ram you side-on. Luckily for you, the SUV is a bit bigger and tougher than a Suzuki Swift. The main point of impact was just below where you were sitting."

"It sure didn't feel like it," Amanda replied, wincing as she tried to flex her arm. Her hip was just as bruised but luckily nothing had been broken there either.

"I think what might have also saved you was the fact that she probably wasn't able to get up much speed. With the motorway so packed, she only hit you at about forty ks."

"Somehow that doesn't make me feel any better," she said.

Jim smiled and reached over to squeeze her uninjured arm.

"Well, if it helps, Tracey came out worse off. She'll be in the hospital overnight and then will have to appear in front of the judge tomorrow. I doubt she'll get bail this time around."

"You know something?" her father asked.

"Yes, sir. We figured it out. Tracey's the one who killed Paul Davidson."

Amanda stared at him. "What?"

Chapter Twenty-Six

Jim had been berating himself the moment he'd heard that Tracey had rammed the car Amanda had been in, blaming himself for his stupidity. The answer had been staring him in the face the whole time and he had almost missed it.

When he'd seen her in the camera footage the night of Paul Davidson's death, he'd realised the truth. Tracey Brooks had smothered the man, and no one had even thought anything of it because she'd been dressed in nurses' scrubs.

"Wait a minute," Pete said. "Are you kidding me?"

"We never even considered the possibility," he told his boss. "But I went back into her employment records and she was a nurse. Until she almost killed a patient two years ago." She had administered a near-fatal dose of a narcotic. They'd caught it in time to save the patient, but the damage was done.

"I called the woman who was her supervisor and she told me they'd investigated but could never prove it wasn't an accident."

"They wouldn't have tolerated such a mistake," the senior sergeant replied.

"No, and they didn't. They fired her. She took them to the Employment Relations Tribunal for unfair dismissal, but the judge ruled in their favour. Apparently, she was often rude and belligerent with both patients and staff and refused to take orders from the doctors claiming she knew better."

"Why doesn't that surprise me?" Amanda murmured.

He nodded and smiled. "Yeah, she does strike me as that kind of person."

"How did she get the scrubs?" his boss asked.

"Well, it seems she still had at least one friend on staff. Leila from Central went to talk to her and was told that they thought she was playing a joke on someone. The friend thought it was a bit odd, but Tracey convinced her it was harmless."

From what Leila had related from the interview, the friend had been shocked and horrified when word got around the hospital that a homicide had been committed in one of the wards but had never even connected the incident to Tracey's odd request, not knowing the connection.

Jim had sent officers to bring Tracey in so he could question her about the night in the hospital, but she hadn't been at the address in her court documents. It was then he'd heard about the accident.

"Essentially, Tracey lied in her interview when she implied she had nothing to do with what happened to Paul Davidson."

"I checked her alibi. She did go to an earlier audition, so it wasn't necessary for her to be at the Convention Centre the day of Amanda's audition."

Amanda frowned. "So why would Grant Burns have caused Paul's accident if he had nothing to do with the murder?"

"He's still an accessory. Tracey committed the murder, but they were definitely working together," Jim told her. He'd also confirmed the motive for the killing.

He'd asked the boss at Central if he could talk to Burns and was finally allowed to interview him. He'd confronted the man with what he knew and told him he was still going down for the murder, hoping it would force the man to start talking.

Burns had tried to avoid the subject but eventually, he'd confessed that Tracey had forced him to create the accidents, telling him she knew what he'd done twenty years earlier. Then Paul had threatened to turn him into the police for his drug manufacturing unless he gave him a share of the profits. Tracey was the one who had convinced him to cause that accident, suggesting if he did it right Paul would not be able to tell anyone the truth and no one would be any the wiser because it would just look like another in a series of accidents.

"Where does that kid come into this?" Amanda asked.

Robert Hutton was not just Grant Burns' cousin; he was also his dealer. Their suspicions were right. The teen had been at the audition that day to distract security.

Amanda shook her head in disbelief. "What a mess," she commented.

"Yeah, tell me about it. If Burns hadn't set up that first accident to impress Debbie, none of this would have happened."

"I don't know," she said with a sigh. "I think Tracey would have done something like this with or without him. It's like that fable."

He frowned. "What fable?"

"You know. The one about the scorpion and the frog?"

He shook his head in confusion, still not sure what she was getting at. Pete nodded.

"Scorpion wants to cross a river so asks a frog to take him on his back. Halfway across, the scorpion stings the frog. 'Why'? asks the frog. 'Now we're both gonna drown.' Scorpion replies: 'Because it's my nature'."

Jim stared at his boss. "Good story, boss." He sighed. "And on that note, I should get out of here. It's late."

"Thanks for coming by, Jim," Pete said.

Amanda saw him to the door. He studied her for a moment, taking in her arm in the sling. She was moving all right for now, but he could see she was beginning to stiffen up a little from the bruising on her left side.

"I'm sorry," he said.

"For what?"

"For not realising it was Tracey sooner. If I had, I might have been able to stop her before she nearly killed you."

"This is not your fault," Amanda told him. "Like I said."

"It's her nature. I get it. I'm still not happy about it."

"And as I told my dad, you can't wrap me in cotton wool, okay? It wouldn't matter if I was a cop or whether I was a guy rather than a girl. It's a risky occupation."

He nodded. She was right. "I still promised you I'd teach you some self-defence moves," he said.

"I'll take you up on that. Once I'm fully mobile again, anyway," she added with a rueful glance at the sling.

He gazed at her for a long moment. It felt like things had changed between them, but he couldn't really pinpoint what exactly had changed.

"So, um, the next show is on Saturday night," she said.

"You're going to stay, then?"

"Well, until I get eliminated, I guess. I'll leave a ticket for you. Would be nice to have a friend there to cheer me on."

"So, we're friends now? Not frienemies?" he asked, reminding her of her earlier assessment of their relationship.

She smirked. "Well, you grow on a person. Like mould."

He screwed up his nose in mock disgust. "Eww. Like that's a picture I want in my brain."

"Well, you know, it has its uses. I mean, penicillin, Fleming."

He looked askance at her. "You're a very strange girl sometimes, Amanda Steele."

Amanda laughed. "You know I just love yanking your chain," she said. He snorted.

"One day, Princess. One day I'll get the jump on you."

"Ha! It'll be a cold day in hell before you ever get the best of me, Andersen."

He sent her a long look. "We'll see about that."

She snickered. "Say goodnight, Gracie."

"Goodnight Gracie," he replied before turning and walking away.